Danny

Susan Vance

Danny

This is a work of fiction.
All characters and incidents are a product
of the author's imagination.
Any relationship to persons living or dead
is purely coincidental.

ISBN-978-0615836393

Cover design by
Kari Johansen

Printed history
First edition published in June 2013

Dedication

Always, to my Beloved, Jim. You are the calm I seek.
Thank you for standing by me through endless
hours of writing. I would marry you all over again.

To my children and entire family.

To my many great friends.

Acknowledgments

I want to thank my dear friend, Charlie.
If not for you, I would not have written this sequel.
Thank you for over forty years of friendship.
Thank you for always believing in me.

Kari Johansen
I love the new cover. Thank you for
all you do for me.

To the amazing editors
that worked so hard on the re-writes.
April Brooks, I love you. Your care and creative
thoughts that went into the editing.
How can I thank you enough?

Tricia Smith, you did it again.
Line by line you helped
pull this book together. It flows,
thanks to your efforts. Great job!

Dee Louchart, your proofreading always
amazes me. The way you can find a missing
comma boggles my mind. Many thanks.

Prologue

The organ was playing and the guests were all seated. The groom was at the altar and the wedding procession began. Half walking and half jumping, a very excited nine year old little boy walked up the aisle toward, an obviously nervous groom. Danny was grinning from ear to ear as he carefully steadied the ring pillow in his hands. Five year old Julie Ann began throwing her rose petals as she playfully paraded up the aisle. Trailing behind, but just as enthusiastic, were Rachael and Amanda. At the end of the procession was the bride herself. Jillian never looked more radiant.

It had been a long hard road for the happy couple and this was a day most thought would never happen. Everyone, that is, except Father Michael who proudly announced he knew it would happen, eventually. Jillian would always just shake her head, but in her heart, somehow she had always hoped he was right.

Chapter One

"I can't believe we are really married. Hawaii here we come." Jillian exclaimed breathlessly, "I am finally Mrs. Tom Bentley."

Tom smiled and raised a brow. "I never doubted it for a minute, my love."

Jillian put her hands on her hips and, curiously, gazed at him; standing just out of reach. Her long blonde hair was piled up with ivory ribbons falling on either side along with some Baby's Breath intertwined in her hair. Her rounded hips and slender waist complimented her ivory gown. Her blue eyes were large and bright, but it was her smile that was most beautiful on this day.

"Well, maybe just a little, but I held out for happiness." He admitted sheepishly.

Jillian smiled and stepped in a little closer. "There was a time that I had given up all hope, but here we are together."

Tom chuckled. "Did you see Morgan's daughter, Amanda, picking up the rose pedals as fast as Rachael and Julie Ann could toss them out? I almost started laughing. Everyone that saw her was smiling, too. She almost stole the show."

"I wasn't able to see her. I hope the photographer got a few shots of that."

"Maybe it will be in the video," he said as he squeezed her hand.

Realizing it was time to cut the cake, Jillian said, "Let's find Father Michael. I want him to be with us when we cut the cake. I only wish my mother could have been here to see us get married." Sadly, Mary, her mother passed away months earlier.

"I wish she could have been here, too. But we both know she would have been happy for us."

A brief wave of sadness passed over Jillian. "I know. I just miss her so much."

"Come on," Tom said seeing the sadness on her face. "I see Father Michael standing over there with your brother, Morgan."

As the newly married couple walked toward Morgan, Jillian couldn't help but notice what a lovely family her brother had. His wife, Melissa, looked as radiant as Jillian felt. The children were sweet, well behaved and as cute as ever. This was what Tom and Jillian had dreamed about. They wanted many children. They had even talked about moving to his ranch one day. Jillian hoped their first child would be conceived under their special tree; the one where they first made love.

"Father Michael," Tom called out. "We're going to cut the cake. Jillian wants you over here with us."

Father Michael was busy visiting with all the guests but was spending as much time with Morgan as he could. There weren't many reasons for Morgan to come to Sweetwater, anymore. This was where both he and Jillian had grown up under the watchful eyes of their mother and Father Michael, the local parish priest and family friend.

Their mother's house belonged to someone else now. A new family in town bought it, and the house was filled with an abundance of children. They knew their mother would have been delighted to know there would be kids growing up in the house that she loved so much.

There weren't many weddings in Sweetwater, so this one was an epic event. Virtually everyone that lived in town was there.

Mark Dobson and his lovely wife, Janet, came from St. Louis and Sarah and Dr. Reynolds, from Denver. A few of Tom's associates came to see New York's "most eligible bachelor" get married. Tom's mother, Elizabeth, looked lovely in her silk, emerald green dress, and matching jacket. She had cut her hair in a short bob, and it looked quite stylish. Jillian always thought that her long gray hair, braided, and up in a bun, made her look too matronly. While she always thought her new mother-in-law was beautiful, she liked this look so much better.

Tony Martelli was there, and he was such a gentleman. He kissed Jillian's cheek and shook Tom's hand. Jillian wasn't sure he would come, but she had hoped with all her heart that he would. Martha, Tony's housekeeper, could have easily accompanied the children on the flight, but Tony came with them and brought Martha as well. A part of her heart would always belong to Tony in a way but as a friend and only a friend. They shared a child together, after all. Her heart belonged to Tom, now, and it always would. It had been over ten years since Jillian and Tony had been high school sweethearts. Tony was two years older and had gone off to college. Jillian had been in her senior year in high school. It was after he had come home for a weekend that they took their relationship further and soon Jillian was pregnant. Shortly after that, Tony stopped coming home as often and finally stopped altogether. Jillian assumed Tony had stopped loving her, which was not the case. Tony had felt it was best that they didn't see each other as much. He needed to get through college and medical school and felt their relationship was getting too serious, too quickly. She never told him that she was pregnant and because she had stopped taking his calls, Tony thought she had found someone else. Both hearts were hurting, but neither knew the truth. It wasn't until years later after Jillian had met Tom that she accidentally ran into Tony and discovered his parents had adopted a child and were later killed in a plane accident. Tony adopted his little brother; later married and had a daughter. Jillian knew almost the instant when she met Danny that he was the child that she had put up for adoption.

The photographer had been scurrying around trying to get in all the celebratory shots and now came the part that Jillian was a little concerned about. Would Tom behave or would she be wiping frosting off her face?

"Alright you two," the photographer called out. "I want you to face each other and lift up a piece of cake. Tom, you will be first. Don't mess up her hair or makeup and watch out for her gown. I still have lots of shots to take."

Jillian was ready for him should he prove to be feisty. Tom lifted his piece of cake and aimed for Jillian's mouth. She opened wide and then she saw it. That look on his face that was, oh, so, Tom. He smiled that cute little half-smile of his, and she saw a twinkle in his eye. He smiled again and into her mouth the cake went. Jillian was surprised and relieved all at the same time. He had teased her with that half smile and those luscious dark green eyes. He looked pleased that she had fallen for it.

Tom smiled at his bride. "What? You didn't trust me?"

"Not exactly, but I'm so glad you'll be the only one with cake on your face," she announced, lifting her piece of cake and aiming straight for his lips. Trusting her completely, Tom closed his eyes and opened wide. Jillian was tempted for a brief second, but in his mouth, the tasty morsel went. With a small amount of whipped cream on his lips, he gently kissed her. Their guests applauded, and the newlyweds kissed again. By now, Danny's little sister, Julie Ann, was in between the newlyweds and Julie Ann looked up with her twinkling brown eyes and was tugging at Jillian's dress. Jillian loved this child. Not because she was Danny's half-sister, but Jillian had become very close to her as she came to get to know her son. She was precious and innocent. Julie Ann looked so sweet. She had lavender ribbons running through her brown hair, and she was wearing a cream dress with lavender trim. Julie Ann had made a picture perfect flower girl. She wanted to be part of the cake scene so Jillian raised her up. Tom held up another small piece of cake and told Julie Ann to close her eyes which made her squeal with delight. The photographer was clicking away.

Danny came closer and smiled that smile that Jillian loved. He was missing a tooth, and Jillian loved his lopsided grin even more. Danny was getting taller, and Jillian reached over to straighten up his hair. Danny looked so much like his father with his olive skin and dark hair and brows. He gazed up at her with those eyes that were as blue as a cloudless day. Eyes that were just like Jillian's.

Oh, how Jillian loved her son. She could have told the entire world at this moment that she was looking into the eyes of her first born child. She had to be careful, and she knew it. She had agreed that Danny would never know she was his mother. She had promised Tony never to reveal it. It was a price she would pay to have him in her life. Just knowing that he would be coming to spend time with her in the summer was a miracle. Of course, Julie Ann would be with him. She didn't mind that at all, as she loved his little sister very much.

They cut their cake and Jillian satisfied her sweet tooth with just a few more bites.

The guests were dancing as Father Michael took Jillian's hand and led her onto the dance floor. This would be the closest thing Jillian would ever have for her father-daughter dance. The dance floor was cleared, and the band played something soft. Not the traditional father-daughter music, but it was pleasant. Jillian hid her face in his broad shoulders, and the tears began to fall. Father Michael held her and whispered something that only Jillian would hear. This made her cry all the more.

"Father Mike, I love you so much. You are the next thing to having a dad. Thank you for this dance. It means so much to me. Thank you for telling me that you promised Mom you would do this.

"You are welcome, Sweetheart."

"I only wish she could see us here dancing at my wedding. I wish she knew that I married Tom like she wanted me to. I wish she knew I had Danny in my life. I miss her so much. I know you are still grieving for her, too. I know how much you must miss her."

Father Michael and Mary were high school sweethearts. They had known each other since they were small children. Father Michael made his decision in his senior year to become a priest, and his decision broke Mary's heart. She went off to college where she met, and eventually married, Daniel. They bought a house back in Sweetwater, Colorado. The town where Mary had grown up and they started their family. Father Michael was asked to come to Sweetwater a few years later.

"Jillian, all your mother ever wanted was for you to be happy. Did I tell you that you make a beautiful bride?"

"Yes, Father Mike, twice," Jillian said adoringly.

Jillian thought of her first husband, Peter and how Father Michael had danced with her at that wedding as well. She and Peter had looked very happy together, and Father Michael had told her what an amazing bride she had made on that day. She remembered what her mother had said.

"Jillian, you look so beautiful. You are the most beautiful bride God put on this earth. I love you so much, and I am so proud of you. Peter is the luckiest man in the world to have such a beautiful bride," she had said, wiping away her tears.

Jillian and Peter had met in college and in her third year, they began to date. After graduation, Jillian had gone to work for a well-known interior designer. She moved to Denver and Peter went with her. He had said that for him, it didn't matter where they lived as long as they were together. He wanted to get married, and Jillian finally had said, yes. After working as a designer for several years, Jillian found herself away from home too much. She liked it, but Peter complained, constantly. She would always tell him to come to wherever she was, but it just hadn't been that easy for him. One evening while having drinks with a female client, one thing led to another. It only happened once, but Peter felt he needed to confess to Jillian. She asked him to leave the house that night, and she filed for divorce the following morning. It wasn't until Jillian fell in love with Tom that she was able to forgive Peter and set him free from the guilt he had felt.

Jillian thought of her mother and how lucky she was to have had such a loving, caring mom. She thought about Peter for a moment and was glad they had worked out their differences and could be friends.

She and Father Michael finished their dance and Tom took her for a spin on the dance floor. He was an excellent dancer, and he made Jillian look fantastic. She had wanted to take lessons before the wedding, but Tom had taken her in his arms and danced with her every night at the loft. There was so much room, and the wooden floors were perfect for their dance rehearsals. By the time of the wedding, Jillian was his star dancing partner.

As the reception began winding down, Jillian tossed the bouquet, and the newlyweds said a few quiet goodbyes before changing into their honeymoon clothes. As they met in the hallway, Jillian smiled up at her new husband. "I love you, Mr. Bentley."

Tom leaned in to give her a sweet kiss. "I love you, Mrs. Bentley. Thanks for making me the happiest man on earth."

They walked out hand in hand, heading for the waiting limo with the crowd of well-wishers cheering them on and blowing bubbles. Leaning out the window, Jillian waved and blew kisses.

Chapter Two

The sand was warm beneath their feet, the smell of the ocean breeze was exhilarating. The seagulls were dipping down to pick up scraps left by untidy visitors. Children were tossing up pieces of bread and squealing every time a gull would dive down and catch something in its beak. Maui was always a beautiful place to be. Jillian and Tom shopped for souvenirs and gifts for the family. Jillian had made sure before they left for their honeymoon that she had the list of everyone's requests. Danny had asked for a Hawaiian shirt and Julie Ann had begged for a hula skirt. That was easy. But they had to ponder on what to get for Morgan's kids. They decided on some little sandals for Morgan Junior, and the girls would be delighted to see their new dolls with grass skirts. Father Michael was in for a treat. Chocolate covered Macadamia nuts. He had mentioned it several times that it was his favorite. He had hinted about Kona coffee beans as well, so they made sure to find him some. Jillian could barely let go of Tom's hand. She felt like it was still a dream and was so afraid someone would wake her. She said she felt like she was eighteen again. Tom seemed to be in the same frame of mind; for this was a day he had all but given up on months ago. Jillian had been with Tony, after finding out that he had their son. She felt it was the only way she could have her son in her life. Although she was very much in love with Tom, she did care for Tony. She was willing to give Tom up to keep Danny in her life. It had all become such a mess. Now, here they were on their honeymoon and their love was stronger–much stronger than before.

"I'm kinda hungry," Jillian said. "Do you want some lunch?"

"Yes, I'm starving."

"Let's go to our room and get rid of these packages, then we'll go eat."

"That sounds good to me. You know, I thought that we should book that dinner cruise for tonight, if possible."

"Sure, that sounds fantastic. Tomorrow we're going on the catamaran trip to Lanai Island. We'll be having lunch over there."

"I heard there will be lots of dolphins on the ride back."

"Really, they told you there will be dolphins?" Her bright blue eyes widened. "How cool is that?"

He chuckled. "Well, there are no guarantees, but they told me it looked pretty good."

As they walked back to their room, Jillian was impressed with all the flowers along the walkway. She wanted to bend down and pick some for their room but rationalized that it might not be the best idea.

Alone in their room, Jillian undressed out of her sundress and sandals. She pulled out one of the several new swimsuits and started to put one on. She looked up to find Tom watching her, and a hint of color came to her face. She stood there naked before him, and Tom shook his head from side to side.

"You are so beautiful. We have had a long, hard struggle getting here, you and me. It took more than we could have ever known in the beginning. You amaze me, and I love you so."

"Tom, do you want to make love?"

"I always want to make love with you."

"Then take me." She smiled. "I'm here for you, always. I am Mrs. Thomas Bentley, and I am yours forever. Nothing will ever come between us."

Tom took her in his arms and kissed her. This was the way it was supposed to be. This was what they both had dreamed of since the beginning.

After she had showered, Jillian went looking for the swimsuit she had tossed to the floor. She put it on and then tied her green flowered skirt around her waist. She pulled her long blond hair back into a ponytail and secured it with a bright green elastic band. Tom put on a pair of tan shorts and decided to wear his new Hawaiian shirt Jillian bought for him that morning. Jillian thought he looked very sexy. She was amazed she had such a handsome guy and told him regularly. Of course, the feeling was mutual. Jillian watched as he buttoned his shirt. His shoulders were broad, and his waist was slender. His brown hair was almost black at times, and his eyes were so green. Actually, they were a blue/green a great deal of the time, but they caught the green from his new Hawaiian shirt and made it look as if he had emeralds for eyes. The first night she met him she was attracted to his eyes. They had both attended an event to celebrate the completion of the offices of Mark Dobson from St. Louis. Mark Dobson insisted she come to the party and his wife, Janet, made sure she introduced Jillian to Tom Bentley. Janet Dobson had played Cupid a few times before, but it did her no good. Jillian wasn't interested in dating. She was busy with her work, and that was the way she wanted it. At the party that evening, Tom shook her hand and held it, slightly. Jillian had felt flush as they had lingered in that moment. She swore she felt a spark of electricity from his touch. Tom had asked her to come to New York to see his building that he wanted to be decorated. Later that night back at the hotel in St. Louis, Jillian found she was thinking about Tom and again on the flight back home to Sweetwater, she thought of Tom again, and it had made her blush. She would look back on those moments, etched on her heart forever, and smile.

Jillian and Tom went down to the restaurant and found a place to sit out on the patio overlooking the beach area. They looked like tourists, but neither really cared. They were having fun, and they were together. After lunch, they took a walk along the beach. Jillian took off her sandals and asked Tom if he would grab a few towels at one of the cabanas. Jillian found a couple of lounge chairs and placed her sandals under one of them. Tom came back with four towels, and they laid them out on the chairs. Jillian untied her skirt, and Tom took off his shirt. Jillian stared at his naked chest. He was in great shape for someone who didn't exercise. His stomach was flat, and his shoulders were broad. Jillian loved the way he looked. His hair was still dark brown, untainted with any gray. She amused herself with the thought that with all that she had put him through, she was amazed he wasn't completely gray; or bald. She flashed back on the day they had first made love under their tree at his mother's ranch. She had unbuttoned his shirt so boldly that day. That was the turning point in their relationship, but she had refused to accept it. Later that evening, she told him it had been a mistake. She had refused to talk about it any further. Tom had been crushed. Jillian shuddered as she reflected on that night. She didn't want to think about it. Not now, not ever again. He was the genuine love of her life. He was the calm she sought.

"Tom, I just thought of something. Do you realize this is the first time we have ever been swimming together? Seems odd we never have been in any water together."

Tom's face sported that little half smile she loved so much. "Not exactly, sweetheart, don't forget about the hot tub."

Jillian flushed as she thought about how many times they had made love in the hot tub in their New York City loft. She often wondered why they called it a loft. Back home in Sweetwater, a loft was the upper part of a barn where you stored hay. Here, in New York, a loft was a large open area on a second or third floor. Their loft took up the entire top floor with its four thousand square feet.

With even more color to her face, she smiled, "You got me there, my love."

They walked out to the water and let the small surf crash over their feet and ankles. Jillian never got fully in the water. She said it was a "sand thing", but Tom swam out and called to her. Jillian just waved and hollered for him to enjoy himself. She kept her sun hat on the whole time they were out by the water. When Tom came out, she slathered sunscreen all over his back and shoulders. He did the same for her then they both relaxed in the lounge chairs, holding hands like the lovers they were.

There were plenty of children running back and forth along the beach. They were chasing each other around and kicking up sand. When their play became close enough, the flying sand trickled down onto Tom and Jillian as they lay sunbathing. Tom sat up and gave the kids a stern look. They ran away, and Jillian laughed.

"They were just playing and having a little fun," she said. "You're such a bully."

Tom gave her his sexy half smile. "It's a 'sand thing,' Sweetheart." Jillian just shook her head, laid back and relaxed. Her heart was happy, and she was thankful. Thankful she had both Tom and Danny.

* * *

"Hurry, Tom. That horn they're blowing is for us. We're late. Run!"

Jillian laughed as she half ran, half skipped next to Tom, who laughed along with her all the way down to the dock. The big catamaran was loaded with people. Tom waved at a young woman wearing the uniform and hat. She saw him and waved back, acknowledging she had seen them, and they would hold the launch for them. As they dashed up the gangplank, Tom was out of breath. Jillian wasn't winded at all. She looked at Tom and laughed, reminding him that she was a runner. Tom gave the young lady their tickets and they found some seats near the port side of the catamaran. Jillian noticed the tarp just below the Captain's window and grabbed for Tom's hand.

"Honey, let's sit on the tarp. No one is there. How cool is that?"

It looked like the best seats on the catamaran, and no one wanted to sit there. Well, Jillian sure did. They took their towels and Jillian's new tote bag and climbed up to the top of the tarp and plopped down. It was very comfortable compared to all of the hard benches around the catamaran. Jillian thought it was almost like sitting on a trampoline. The Captain blew the whistle three times, and they were off. Jillian had on a long sleeve shirt over her swimsuit and shorts. Tom wore his khaki shorts and a short sleeve blue shirt. Jillian had applied a ton of sunscreen to his arms. She tied her hair up in a ponytail and attempted to tighten her sun hat down on her head. As they headed out into deep water, the breeze became much stronger. Jillian was forced to put her sun hat in her tote bag. Several more people joined them on the tarp and Jillian had to move closer to Tom, who put his arm around her and pulled her even closer. They were approaching Lanai Island. Suddenly, the catamaran came to a screeching halt. Water came surging up over the bow of the catamaran and right onto the tarp. There was no time to react. Jillian let out a scream, and the water went in her mouth and up her nose. She was livid. They were drenched. Their towels, Jillian's tote bag, and all the snacks she had packed were soaking wet. Tom was furious. Around the corner appeared the crew. With the biggest smiles on their faces, they began applauding and whistling.

"What is the matter with you people?" Tom shouted. "We are soaked to the bones. All of our stuff is wet. Why in the world are you clapping?"

"It's what we do. We come and applaud newcomers on every trip," replied one of the crew members in his native accent. "The Captain shuts her down on every voyage. Only newcomers and veteran 'cat' fans ever sit on the tarp. Most locals know what happens on the big catamaran."

"Well, we certainly didn't know. I want to see the captain right away," Tom shouted.

"I'll have her come see you."

"Her? Another woman did this to me?" Jillian shouted. "Look at me, I'm a mess! We're on our Honeymoon. I'm supposed to look good."

Tom took one look at her and began to laugh. Jillian's mascara was running down her wet face. She didn't even have a dry towel to wipe her face or hair. She was fuming.

"What is so darn funny, Mister?" she growled.

"We'll dry off. Why don't you go to the restroom while I speak with the captain. It'll be okay," he said, taking his wet bride in his arms.

When Jillian got back from the restroom, Tom was having a drink with the crew. They handed Jillian her drink, and she asked if it was hard or soft. It was delicious. She was rather fond of Mai Tai's. She wasn't mad any longer, but she was still a mess. They explained that she would be snorkeling soon, and they would provide her with dry towels. She could hang her wet things out, and her towels and clothes would be dry in an hour. It really was a custom of the "Big Cat." Tom couldn't help but laugh every time he looked at her. It wasn't long before she was laughing as well. Before they docked, the crew presented the newlyweds with a photo that was taken from the window of the pilot house as the wave came over the bow and one taken by one of the crew members just after the splash. Jillian was amazed to see how high the wave really was.

Their afternoon was enjoyable and exciting. Jillian had never snorkeled before, and there were so many places to enjoy seeing the fish. She was amazed by all the different sizes and colors. They were given a nice lunch complete with Hula dancers. The captain informed them that the water was going to be choppy on the way back, and the crew handed out pieces of ginger to the passengers saying it would help with motion sickness. The captain assured everyone that there would be no splashes on the way back, but no one trusted her, especially Jillian. The tarp remained empty. The water remained fairly calm, and Jillian was relieved. The last thing she wanted was to be throwing up on her husband's lap.

"Jillian, look," Tom called out pointing to the water. "The dolphins are swimming right next to the boat." He was leaning over the side as far as possible without falling overboard.

The captain shut down the catamaran, and there was hardly a sound except for the clicking of cameras. Jillian was glad she thought to put their camera in a plastic bag. Not one person spoke. It was an astounding and breathtaking experience.

Tom, mesmerized by the mere sight of the dolphins swimming alongside them, said to Jillian, "I think they are called Spinner Dolphins."

"Correct," said a young man in a uniform standing next to them. "They are Spinner Dolphins. They're here often, and they love to perform for the passengers. You picked an excellent day to sail with us."

"How many would you say there are?" Jillian asked.

"It's hard to tell, but hundreds for sure, Ma'am," the young crew member replied.

Jillian looked at Tom, who was about to come undone. Jillian wasn't sure if she was going to laugh or cry. Tom looked at his bride and then could not hold it back any longer. He put his hand to his mouth, but it did him no good. There was that half-smile of his, but Jillian wasn't laughing.

"Ma'am! Did you hear what he called me? Ma'am! I'm a Ma'am now? Just because I got married, that makes me a Ma'am? Oh, Tom, I got old."

That was it. Tom was now robustly laughing to the point of crying. He was holding his stomach and about to lose his breath. Jillian glared at him, and then, suddenly, she was laughing right along with Tom. They were making memories. These would be stories they would tell their children one day. Jillian was reminded of something her mother had told her once.

"Jillian, when the memories are precious, write them down. Keep a journal, and one day your children will get to read your words and see you differently. They will see you as human and not only as a parent. Write them down so you can fondly reminisce one day," she had said.

The Dolphins continued their show for about fifteen minutes longer. Then the engine came back on, and they headed for Maui. Jillian turned to look at the island of Lanai, often called the Pineapple Island. It was once home to the world's largest pineapple plantation. She had been surprised to see the big hotel, but progress was all around. She looked at Tom and sat back down and was a little dismayed that they had come to a close of such a beautiful day.

Back at the hotel, they took a little nap. All that fresh air, swimming, and snorkeling had them tired and worn out.

Laying on the bed reading the room service menu, Jillian said, "Let's have room service, okay? I'd be happy to stay in these shorts and relax and not go out for dinner tonight."

"So would I," he admitted. "I feel like I've been climbing mountains all day. Even the nap didn't do it for me. What's on the menu?"

"They have coconut crusted chicken. I'm going to try it with the Mango sauce. That sounds so authentically Hawaiian to me."

"Suit yourself, but I think I'll have a steak. For some reason, I'm starved."

"Good. I'll order our dinners then I'm going to take a shower. Care to join me?" She smiled slyly as she stood up and stripped off her clothes.

* * *

The flight home to New York seemed to take forever. Jillian had nothing left to read so after she napped, she gazed out the window looking down on the water. Tom had saved a book for the trip home and was really getting into it. Jillian looked over and stared at Tom, who gladly put his book down and gave her the attention she wanted. Tom watched as she wiggled in her seat as if he knew there was something on her mind.

When she didn't say anything he said, "Honey, what's going on in that beautiful head of yours?"

"Well, we haven't really talked about it yet, but well, you're not getting any younger, you know."

"What?" he said, interrupting her. "What are you trying to say? Are you already tired of my being six years older than you? I'm only thirty-four, remember." Thankfully he looked amused rather than angry.

"Of course, I'm not. You're the perfect age for me. I was thinking, well, I believe that we should start having children right away."

She was watching every muscle in his face. She waited for his half smile which didn't appear.

"You're right; we haven't talked about this yet. We aren't supposed to be making babies on our honeymoon you know."

"I'm serious. I think we should start making them right away. We both want a large family, and that takes time. Besides, it will be fun."

Tom smiled. "Do you want to get started right now?"

Danny

Chapter Three

Summer was coming to a close and Jillian wasn't pregnant. They had been trying since after they returned from their honeymoon. Tom assured her that two months of trying wasn't long enough to start worrying, and she needed to be patient. They had also been looking for a home to buy, but they hadn't been satisfied with anything so far. They were years away from moving to the ranch. Tom was starting to entertain the idea of becoming a country lawyer and coming home to a house full of kids every evening at the ranch. They both agreed that sooner, rather than later would be the plan. However, they also knew that their plans may come to fruition only in God's time. Jillian had many strong points, but patience had never been one of them.

Jillian was sitting on the couch idly petting Lucy when Tom came into the room. She looked up and smiled. "Let's take Lucy and go to the ranch this weekend before the weather turns cold. We can ride out to our tree and maybe we can get pregnant right there under our tree where it all began."

Jillian held Lucy up and looked into her adorable, flat Shih Tzu face. "Lucy, do you want to take a trip with Mommy and Daddy this weekend?"

Jillian moved Lucy's head up and down while grinning at Tom.

Lucy wasn't as independent as Sydney was, and there were times when Jillian missed him very much. He was with Danny now, and they were so good for each other. Lucy hadn't quite stolen her heart yet, but Jillian's relationship with Sydney was entirely different. He would be a hard act to follow. Sydney had been her constant companion, and when she gave him to Danny, Tom bought her the puppy as a surprise. Tom must have known it broke her heart to give Sydney up, but in a way it made her happy that Danny had a dog. Not just any dog. He had her beloved Sydney.

"So, what do you say? Do you want to go to the ranch?"

"Sure, but aren't Martha and the kids coming in a few weeks? I wanted to take them to see the ranch while they were here. I'm sure the weather will hold out for us long enough for us to have a special picnic under our tree and make baby number one."

"Oh, Tom, that sounds fantastic, but you know the children will want to be wherever we are."

"Of course, Danny and Julie Ann can go riding with us. On our special day, Martha can keep them at the house."

"I'm not sure Martha will want to come with us to the ranch. I better call and ask her. She mentioned that she wanted to go to the city and see a play."

"Call her and if she sounds apprehensive, use that charm of yours and coax her a bit," he said as he headed down the hall to his office.

Martha had been Tony's housekeeper since before his first wife, Tracy, had passed away. When Tony was left with two small children to raise, Martha became more like a part of the family. She cared for the two kids while Tony worked and took care of Tony, as well. She and Jillian had become friends after Jillian's mother passed away and Jillian was glad to have her friendship. In the beginning, Jillian had worried that after she left Tony to marry Tom, Martha would feel differently about her, but Martha remained friends and gave her support when needed.

That had been the hardest day when Jillian had gone to see Tony to tell him of her plans to marry Tom. She knew it would break his heart, but she had to be with Tom. He was the genuine love of her life. She thought about how frightened she had been that Tony might keep her from their son she had given up for adoption years earlier. Tony was a good and fair man and made it possible for Jillian to have Danny in her life.

Jillian grew excited at the thought of seeing Danny. This was to be his first trip to New York. Danny had said how excited he was to be flying on a big plane. Jillian had their rooms ready, and the refrigerator would be full of all their favorite foods. She had also learned how to make Danny's favorite chocolate cake and chicken tacos for Julie Ann.

Jillian wished Danny could call her mom, but that was the price she paid to be with Tom. When Tony promised to allow her to see Danny, he explained his concerns and that Jillian would just remain a good friend of the family. He didn't want Danny hurt or confused by things he had no control over. Tony knew Jillian loved the children; they loved her back, and that was enough. Tony had reminded her that Danny has a sister and where he goes, Julie Ann goes. Jillian had assured him not to worry. She loved Julie Ann and would never hurt or disappoint her. Tony said that Martha would accompany the kids until they were old enough to travel on their own.

"Sweetheart," Tom called out from his office. "When you call Martha, tell her we'll take her and the kids sightseeing. Tell her to bring her walking shoes."

"I will, but I'm sure she wants to ride one of those tour buses. She said she wanted to sit on top with all the tourists clicking their cameras and holding on to their hats," she said with a little laugh. "I can't believe that in two more weeks I'll get to hug Danny. It will be such fun to take them all to the ranch."

* * *

Monday morning, right after Tom had left for the office, the realtor, Meghan called saying she found just what they had been looking for. Jillian had heard the same story from the previous realtor so she wasn't getting too excited. They had given the realtor their criteria, but it wasn't looking very good. After twelve houses in the last two weeks, Jillian was getting discouraged.

"But, Jillian," Meghan gushed, "this one has a second story, and the balcony looks out over the most spectacular garden situated below the master bedroom. It doesn't have a pool, but it does have a beautiful gazebo with a huge hot tub. The kitchen is ultra-modern and spacious. There are three bedrooms on the first floor and a large office off the kitchen. The master bedroom takes up most of the upper floor, but there is also a workout room. The guest house is fantastic, complete with all the amenities you are looking for. It does need a little work, however."

"That sounds great," Jillian said. "What about the nursery? We're planning to start our family right away, and we need a nursery, preferably next to the master bedroom."

"Well, that was going to be my surprise. There is the sweetest nursery right off the master. You could make it into a small study after your family is complete. There's more than enough room for a crib, dresser and rocking chair."

"Okay, let's put this one first on the list for today. What else did you find?"

"After you see this one, I think you'll be calling Tom to come meet us. If not, then I have two more that you might like. Why don't you meet me at the office at ten o'clock this morning and we'll go have a look?"

"Sure, ten sounds great."

Jillian took a shower and ate a banana with a little peanut butter. She had given up caffeine right after they got back from Hawaii and she was eating as healthy as she could. Her doctor told her that a healthy environment for the baby begins before conception. Jillian was hoping to conceive right away, and she just knew it would happen soon. She thought about how easy it was when she got pregnant with Danny. She and Tony only had sex a few times, so how hard could it be? Jillian finished her breakfast and had another cup of tea. She tidied up the kitchen then drove to the real estate office. Meghan was at her desk, so Jillian waved to catch her attention.

"Let's go straight to the house you were telling me about. I have a feeling that if I don't like it, I won't like the other two, either. By the way, how long has it been on the market?"

"Five or six months. They had an offer, and it fell out of escrow. The owners were upset, to say the least. I'm sure you'll just love it. The neighborhood is lovely and quiet. Wait until I tell you about the schools. I'll drive you by the grammar school later if you would like to see it. Tom could take the train to the city or drive. I think he said he would prefer to drive, correct?"

Jillian liked Meghan. She reminded her of her friend, Sarah, from Denver. Meghan didn't have Sarah's dark green eyes. Hers were blue, but she did have long blonde hair and was tall and slender, much like Sarah. She was attractive and wore clothes to accentuate her lean figure. Jillian felt Meghan seemed more professional than the former Realtor. She appears to know what she was talking about.

Meghan was full of information, and she rattled on and on. Jillian's mind was wandering, and she found she didn't hear much of what Meghan had to say. She was thinking about Danny and having babies and eventually moving to the ranch. Jillian was thinking about how the loft could have worked for a few more years and maybe they were rushing into buying a house. She hated the way she went back and forth with her thoughts. They had discussed many times the pros of getting a house now. The loft was out of the way, and Tom had to go through extra traffic getting to the office each morning. He didn't like the traffic jams. Meghan said this house was much closer.

Jillian liked the neighborhood. It was quaint with all the brick, two-story houses. It was more of a country setting, but so close to the city. Meghan pulled up in front of a large home that was well manicured. The windows sparkled and not a leaf marred the immaculate lawn. Jillian liked it right away. It had a lot of "curb appeal" just as Meghan had said.

As they walked up the sidewalk to the front door, Jillian stopped to look around. The neighborhood was nice, and all the homes seemed to be as well taken care of like this one. She noticed a few bikes and toys around some of the houses, and she was happy knowing there were children in the area. Meghan had the key and Jillian followed her inside. The foyer was large, and Jillian liked that. She imagined a round table centered in the middle of the foyer with a huge bouquet of flowers. "Meghan, is this house empty?"

"Yes, the owners moved out shortly before it fell out of escrow. Actually, what happened as far as I know, is one of the buyers passed away, and that was the end of the loan. Come on, I'll show you the living room."

The house was large and nicely put together. Jillian's mind was already seeing it her way. She had decided when she met Meghan not to share with her that she was an interior designer. She didn't want Meghan showing them places that needed work. She would make any changes she wanted to, but not because she had to. Jillian loved the kitchen. She pictured Tom cooking his delicious Chicken Marsala, and there was a nice area over by the window looking out onto the backyard, where a highchair could be placed. So far, this was it.

There was a huge laundry room off the west side of the kitchen and a door going into the garage. Tom would like that. There was a walk-in pantry and a large spice cabinet. The granite countertops were tan and black with small gold flecks interspersed throughout.. Jillian liked the large tiled floor. The kitchen had large windows which brought in a lot of light.

The center island cook top was exactly what she and Tom had wanted. She was sure Tom would love this kitchen. It wasn't exactly gourmet, but very close. The only thing Jillian would want to replace was the hood over the cooktop. It was white and looked out of place. She thought the owners must have had white appliances. She envisioned a massive stainless steel hood to match the stainless steel appliances she and Tom had decided on.

They looked at the downstairs bedrooms and the office. Jillian thought Tom would like the office. It had an extra-large window, with a view of the tall trees in the back yard. They walked out the back door to see the gazebo and hot tub. The gazebo had a gate which was locked. Meghan fumbled with the keys until she found the right one. They took a quick peek inside then went back in the house to see the upstairs. The master bedroom was spacious with two huge closets, and the bathroom was spectacular. There were double sinks, and the shower had four showerheads. The Jacuzzi bathtub was so huge, Jillian wanted to climb in and see how she would fit. Jillian liked the mirrored wall alongside the tub. On one wall in the bedroom was a sliding pocket door, so Jillian opened it up. She stood there gazing at the little room. It was perfect. It was bigger than she had imagined by Meghan's description.

"I love this nursery! It's connected to the master and with this door, it could easily be used for something else, later. You were right, this might be it. I'll call Tom and see if he can break away. We can wait for him here."

Meghan smiled. It was written all over her face. Jillian could see that Meghan wanted to jump up and down for joy. This would be a hefty commission for her. Tom arrived forty-five minutes later. Within fifteen minutes they were following Meghan back to her office to make an offer.

Chapter Four

The days passed and soon it was time to go meet Danny, Julie Ann, and Martha at the airport. Jillian was running all around the house as she tried to get all the last minute things done.

Tom couldn't help but tease her, "Honey? You aren't excited are you?"

Jillian laughed and gave him a sexy smile. "No, Dear! Why do you ask?"

Tom reached for her and pulled her into his embrace. "Everything is perfect. The house looks great, and the refrigerator is so packed I'm afraid to open it for fear it will all come tumbling out," he said kissing the tip of her nose. "Let's go get the kids."

They decided to drive out to the ranch the next day so after hearing all the excitement of their flight on the big plane, they sat down together in the dining room for dinner. After everyone was showered and had on their pajamas, they watched a movie and visited then headed to bed for an early start.

The kids looked excited to be going to the ranch. Jillian tried to get Martha to sit up in the front seat with Tom, but she wouldn't hear of it. The car was small, and Martha wasn't a petite woman. The kids looked a bit squashed. Jillian kept looking over her seat in the car at Danny. He was precious in her sight, and he was growing so fast. Julie Ann was now missing a bottom tooth, and she made a little whistle when she talked. As they drove out of the city, into the country, the homes got bigger and bigger. The highway turned into a two-lane country road, and the kids were starting to see horses and cows along the way. Martha was looking out the window at all the large homes.

"My, oh my, I wouldn't want to be in charge of cleaning these mansions," she said clearly.

Jillian wondered what she was going to think when she saw the house on the ranch. Jillian remembered the first time she saw it. Her mouth had flown open at its splendor. She had guessed it to be close to twenty thousand square feet, and Tom had been impressed that she could guess with such accuracy. The ranch looked as if it was out in the middle of nowhere, with its sprawling pastures and grassland.

Jillian spotted the house and pointed with her finger. "Danny, look over to the left side. Right over there," she said still pointing towards the house. "What do you think?"

Danny's face was showing excitement. "But where are the horses? I want to see the barn!"

"Land's sake, this looks more like a hotel," Martha spouted.

Alice and her husband Hank, caretakers of the ranch, stood at the massive front door under the portico. Alice wore a huge smile and waved as they parked the car. They weren't used to having visitors and Jillian knew that Alice had probably prepared a special dinner for them. Her husband had been the caretaker back in the day when Tom's parents lived there. Tom's father had been a country doctor, and Tom and his sister were raised on the ranch. Hank and Alice had a small home in the back.

Tom reached for Alice and gave her a hug.

"It's good to see you and your lovely family," Alice said smiling. "I have all your rooms ready. I know you must be tired from that long drive. I have sandwiches in the kitchen, and I baked cookies for the kids. I understand someone really likes chocolate cake?"

By now, Danny and Julie Ann were both jumping and running around. They needed to stretch their legs after the long ride to the ranch.

"Where are the horses?" Danny asked again.

Hank offered to take the kids to the barn.

Tom nodded. "Oh, wait a minute, Hank. Could I have a word with you before you take the kids?"

"Oh sure, but if it's what we talked about–it's a done deal," he said, looking quite proud of his accomplishment. Tom waved them on.

Jillian was curious. "What was that all about?"

Tom smiled. "Hank picked up two 'extra gentle' ponies for the kids. They will belong to them from now on."

"You're the best. I love you so much," Jillian said.

Martha smiled. She seemed moved by their love. Her heart had broken for Tony, but she was happy for Jillian and Tom.

Alice took Martha to her room. It was light and airy. Tom had wanted Martha to feel pampered, and Alice saw to it that she was.

She put lovely bath salts in her bathroom and flowers in her room. She put a little tin of chocolate truffles on her bedside table and although it was late summer, she put a light afghan on the over-stuffed chair by the window. In front of the chair was a small ottoman. It would be perfect for an afternoon nap. Alice put the fluffiest towels in the bathroom, and she placed several candles around the bedroom.

Martha looked at her room and smiled. She walked over to the window and off to the left she could see the barn. She watched as the kids were leading their ponies around and Hank was showing them a thing or two.

"This is a lovely room. I appreciate what you have done for me. Thank you so much," Martha said extending her hand.

Alice took her hand and smiled. "Would you like some help unpacking?"

"Oh no, but thank you."

"Come down when you're ready. I'll put the sandwiches out in a bit, with a pitcher of lemonade. No rush, but it will be there when you want it. We have pot roast for dinner."

"Thank you for making Danny the chocolate cake. I'm sure that young man will thank you later, but he was so excited to see the horses; it was very kind of you."

Tom and Jillian were coming up the stairs as Alice was going down. She mentioned the sandwiches to Tom, who smiled at her and patted her on the shoulder as they passed by each other.

Jillian was looking all around their room. Alice had pampered them as well. "I love coming here. It's such a good feeling. I hope we can move here a little sooner than we have planned. I think you'll make a fantastic country lawyer."

"Thanks. I know it's rather big, but if we get all the kids we want, there certainly is plenty of room for them to run."

"There'll be no running in my house!" Jillian said with a huge smile. She reached for Tom and kissed him. "I can see it now. There will be children outside riding ponies and running all around this place. What do you think about setting a five-year goal for us to move here? Do you believe that we could do it in that amount of time?"

"We'll see, Sweetheart, we'll see."

Jillian went to the window, but she couldn't see the kids.

"I'm going to go to the barn and see what's going on. Did you bring the camera? I want to document all these memories we're making."

Tom reached into his bag and pulled out the camera, handing it to Jillian. "Here you go. Snap away." He chuckled as he reached for her giving her another kiss. "I'd like to keep you here in this room for a while, but I can see you need to be outside with the kids. Go on, scoot."

Jillian hurried down to the barn. Danny and Julie Ann were in one of the corrals and Hank was leading them around on their ponies. Danny had a straw cowboy hat on that Hank had picked up for him. Julie Ann had a pink cowgirl hat. Jillian was amused at the way she kept taking it off, then putting it right back on again. They looked very sweet as Jillian stepped up on the white rail fence to get a closer look. She took the camera out of her pocket and began to take pictures.

"Jillian, Look! No hands!" Danny boasted.

"Danny, you need to hold on to the reins and do what Hank tells you. Julie Ann, you pay attention to Hank as well."

"Oh, don't worry any, Miss Jillian," Hank said. "The kids will be experts for tomorrow's ride."

Jillian turned to see Tom coming up the walk. He had the video camera and had started filming the kids. Jillian was feeling very high as she took it all in. This was her first time having Danny without Tony, and it felt wonderful. How she wished she could have him always.

"Kids, are you two hungry? Alice has sandwiches in the kitchen. Tom and I will meet you there and after you eat maybe you can ride your ponies again," she assured them, glancing at Hank to make sure he had the time. Hank nodded and helped Julie Ann off her pony. Danny was off and running to catch up with Tom and Jillian. Martha was at the door to the kitchen when they all got there. She took Danny's hand and whispered something in his ear. He looked up and said, "Yes, Ma'am."

Alice was pouring lemonade into ice-filled glasses when Danny came to her and thanked her for making the chocolate cake just for him. She patted him on the head and smiled.

"What a nice young man you are. You have such good manners."

Jillian looked over with pride. He was a great kid.

After lunch, Martha said she wanted to go for a walk and the children wanted to go with her. Tom and Jillian went upstairs to grab a quick nap. Alice said she would love to walk with them and show them around a little. Martha thanked her for her kindness.

"I can see you're having a great time. I'm happy for you," Tom said.

He took her in his arms and kissed her. She moaned and moved in closer. Tom looked down at her, and she gave him her, *take me, I'm yours,* look. He laughed as he pulled her tightly.

The afternoon sun was warm and Martha, Alice, and the kids, came back after just a short walk. Martha hadn't brought her hat so she was delighted when Danny wanted to show her his pony in the shade of the barn. Julie Ann was excited, but she had her mind set on visiting with the baby goats. This was such a contrast from Denver. Danny missed his dog, Sydney. He remembered to bring Jillian lots of pictures, and when he gave them to her, she had cried. Jillian had told him they were tears of happiness. When she looked down at Danny, she could see tears of joy in his eyes as well.

Martha sat down and pulled out her cell phone. It was a good time to call Tony. She motioned for the kids to come over to where she was sitting, and they both talked with their father for a few minutes. Danny handed the phone to Julie Ann and went to find Hank. He wanted to ride his pony. Hank had instructed him not to attempt the saddle or bridle yet, but that he was expected to do it all by himself before he left the ranch in four days. Danny was excited. He wanted to practice before the family ride in the morning. Martha thought she would visit with Alice during the horseback riding festivities. She had never been on a horse, and she announced she wasn't about to start now. After Danny had finished riding his pony, he handed the reins to Hank.

"Danny, you'll need to cool this little gal down before you put her back in the barn. Remember, walk her slowly and when she cools down, you'll need to brush her. You take care of her, and she'll take care of you."

Martha watched as Danny did what he was told and afterward, he came and sat next to her.

"Martha, I'm tired. I want to go lay down for a little while. Is that okay?"

"Of course, it is," she said. Martha touched his forehead to see if it was warm. "You run on into the house and go upstairs and lay down. I'll come up to check on you in a bit."

Jillian was just coming down as Danny was sluggishly ascending the staircase.

"Hi, kiddo, what's up?"

"I'm plum tuckered out."

"Plum tuckered out? Oh, I see, you've been talking to Hank again, huh?"

Danny continued up to his room. A half an hour later he was back downstairs and out by the barn helping his sister catch the baby goats.

"Hey, I thought you were plum tuckered out?"

"Nope, not me, I'm a tough cowboy."

Jillian just shook her head. She was enjoying her time with the kids. She loved them both, but Danny was her little prince. Something happened to her every time she looked at his face. It was euphoric in a way. It was exhilarating to be with him. She finally understood what her mother had tried to tell her years ago when she had decided to put her baby up for adoption. Her mother had told her she would regret it for the rest of her life.

"The moment you see your child's face you will feel it. It isn't something one can describe, but you will feel it," her mother had said.

Jillian hadn't looked at her baby's face when he was born. She told her mother that she did, but she had lied. She had been afraid to see him. If her mother was right then how could she give him up? She knew that if she saw him or held in her arms, as the nurses encouraged her to do, she would not be able to give him up. She had always thought that somehow Tony would have found out and come rushing to the hospital. She had played it out in her mind many times right after the baby was born. Tony would come rushing into her room and tell her how much he loved her. That they would get married right away and raise the baby together. It never happened. Tony was not to find out until eight years later that Danny was his son. The fact that Tony ended up with his own child was a miracle. What were the chances of his parents adopting Danny and then dying in a plane crash? Then, Tony adopting his own son all the while thinking it was his adopted little brother? This union was meant to be. Jillian was sure of it. Danny looked so much like his dad. The darker hair and olive skin, but those blue eyes were just like hers. As Jillian continued reflecting back, so many emotions filled her heart. After a moment or so, she refocused her attention back to the present. She had Tom, the love of her life by her side, and her only child with her now.

Chapter Five

After breakfast, Tom and Hank saddled up the horses and the two ponies. Alice gave Hank a medium size basket full of fruit and bottled water. Entirely different from the basket she had packed for Tom and Jillian almost a year earlier. In that basket, Alice had packed wine and chicken salad sandwiches. Jillian smiled as she saw the basket. She remembered the day that she and Tom had made love under their tree. It was a moment in their lives neither would ever forget.

It was a beautiful morning. The sun was shining, and fortunately, there was a slight breeze. The sky was a beautiful cloudless blue that looked to be painted by the very hand of God himself. You could see for miles, and it felt to Jillian like a moment out of time. She pictured covered wagons, pioneers, and Indians. She thought about how hard it must have been for this to be the only mode of transportation. Clearly, she understood now, why people didn't move around as much back in the day.

Jillian ended her daydreaming and looked around, as she counted heads. "Come on, let's get going."

"Hold your horses, cowgirl," Tom laughed. "We have one more horse to saddle up then we're off."

Hank was fantastic with the kids. Danny was right up front with Tom and Jillian, but Julie Ann was falling back. Hank stayed with her and soon they were both up with the other three. Danny was now in the lead, and Jillian was beaming with pride. He was a quick learner. She pulled out her camera and began preserving more memories. She was planning to share some of the pictures with Tony. She knew how proud he would be, and in a way she was sorry he wasn't there to see his children on their first ride.

"I think Danny will outgrow his pony quickly," she said as she snapped another picture.

"I believe you are right. He's amazing, just like his mother."

Jillian beamed at Tom's praise. Off to the right was a familiar place. Coming up was their tree.

"Danny," Jillian said pointing to the tree. "Let's go over by that tree and have our snacks."

Tom wasn't quite as eager to share their special place and thought maybe they could ride on a little further. Jillian insisted, and so they all headed for the tree. In the basket was a blanket, and Tom spread it out on the ground under the shade of their tree. The kids were thirsty and downed some water before eating the fruit. Hank laid his body down and closed his eyes. Jillian looked at Tom and for a moment found she wished they were alone to reminisce about the moments they had shared under this tree. Tom smiled and gave her a hug. Danny stretched out like Hank and closed his eyes, too. Hank began to snore, and Julie Ann giggled. Danny sat up and looked over at Hank. He put his hand over his mouth to try to quiet his loud laugh. After Hank's fifteen-minute power nap, he was up and rearing to go.

"I'll be going back to the house pretty soon. Danny, would you like to go back with me?"

"Why, Hank, don't you want to ride anymore?"

"Sure I do, but I have some work to do. I'm going to pick up a few more little goats. Would you like to go with me?"

"Jillian, can I go with Hank? He's getting more baby goats. Can I, please?"

Julie Ann jumped up. "I want to go, too. I want to go with them. I love the goats. Can I?"

Tom looked at Hank and Hank raised his hands in the air.

"It's okay with me if the kids want to go. I'm just going to Perkin's barn down the road. It's no trouble if they want to come along."

"Please, Jillian? Please?" They pleaded.

Jillian looked at Tom and then back to the sweetest children in the world.

"Okay you two, but you listen to Hank and do exactly what he says, alright?"

They were on their ponies and waiting on Hank. Within minutes, they disappeared in the distance.

Jillian took off her shoes and lay back on the blanket. She closed her eyes and smiled. She could feel Tom getting closer, and that excited her.

"Tom?"

"Yes, my darling?"

"I think I am going to get my wish after all."

Tom smiled. "And what was that?"

"Remember, I wanted to conceive our first child under our tree."

"I remember," he said, gently touching her.

Jillian reached for him as she unbuttoned his shirt just like their first time under this tree. All that was missing was the wine. She looked up at the blue sky and felt a gentle breeze go through her hair. Tom took one glance around to be sure it was safe and then he kissed her.

Afterward, they slowly rode their horses back to the house. Hank and the kids were just getting back from Perkin's barn. They could hear the sounds of the goats as they got closer. Jillian just knew in her heart she was pregnant. She put her hand on her stomach and held it there for a moment. She was thankful and happy. She looked at her husband and smiled. He helped her down from her horse and touched her arm tenderly.

Then brushing the hair from her face, he smiled in return. "This will always be our special place. I love you very much. It only gets better from here."

She was almost in a waltz as she made her way to the house, as Tom reluctantly left her to return the horses to their stalls.

Jillian went in through the back door. Martha and Alice were busy in the kitchen; the aroma was exhilarating. Jillian felt a little giddy from her lovemaking with Tom. She wanted to announce to the world that they had just made a baby, but she held her tongue.

The kids, Tom, and Hank came in for dinner. Alice told them to go get washed up, and it would be ready in ten minutes. The kids ran up the stairs and were back down much too quickly. Martha looked over their hands and sent them marching back up the stairs.

Jillian was eating her second serving and enjoying every bit of her dinner. "Alice, I think I need to stay here and take some cooking lessons."

"Thanks, I learned from my mother. She was an excellent cook. Of course, Mrs. Bentley was always in the kitchen and together we made magic. Mr. Bentley, Tom's father, used to say that there was nothing better than coming home each evening to my cooking. We never told him his wife helped with many of the meals. That was our secret. If he thought she couldn't cook, I was assured a job here on the ranch."

"Why, Alice!" Tom teased. "I can't believe you and Mom deceived my dad like that. Shame on you. Well, to be honest, Dad wasn't the only one that loved coming home. April and I enjoyed your cooking so much we made a game of who could guess what was for dinner. Your spaghetti is amazing. I don't think I have ever had spaghetti sauce as good as yours."

"My dad makes great spaghetti and meatballs," Danny added.

"Yes, Danny. You are so right. Your dad does make the best spaghetti," Jillian said tenderly.

Danny was grinning from ear to ear.

"I'm not a good cook, but Tom knew that before he married me."

Martha leaned over to Jillian and whispered. "I would be happy to help you with some recipes when we get back to your house."

Jillian was touched. This was so kind of Martha. "I would love that. Thank you so much. So where is the leftover chocolate cake? I'm ready for dessert. Anyone else?"

Martha whispered something into Danny's ear, and there was no talk about who could make the best chocolate cake. Later she explained to him that most everyone thinks their family has the best spaghetti. Although his dad did make the best spaghetti, it wasn't polite to say. Danny asked who was having spaghetti, and Martha just shook her head. She tried one more time; this time using the chocolate cake as an example and Danny seemed to understand.

"Danny, I hear you are a Cub Scout?" Tom said after dinner.

"Yes sir, I am. I can't wait to show my troop the pictures of my trip. I might get a badge for riding a horse. Maybe I had better ride yours before we leave. I don't think ponies count."

"I have no idea," Jillian said. "Tom, do you know?"

"I was never a Cub Scout. That was always the one drawback of living in the country. Usually, the meetings were over in Bixby. It just never seemed to work out. We didn't mind, though. We had so much fun here with our horses until..."

Jillian saw his pain. She knew Tom was never comfortable talking about April.

Jillian touched his arm. "You don't have to talk about it. It's okay."

Tom smiled and told her it was alright. "Well, to make it short, my sister, April, was on her way to the Olympics when she had an accident and hurt her back. She wasn't able to continue."

"I'm so sorry, Tom. Where is April now?" Martha asked.

"Tom's sister passed away. It's been almost a year now," Jillian added.

Jillian looked over at Danny striving to change the subject.

"Don't worry, my Little Prince. We'll find out about the badge, and if you need to earn it on a horse, then that is what you will do."

Danny was smiling, and he went over to Jillian and hugged her. She held him tightly until he wiggled away.

Alice brought in the dessert. She had sliced the chocolate cake and served it on glass plates with a small scoop of vanilla ice cream and a few sliced strawberries. Jillian was thrilled to see the ice cream and said so. Martha asked for a smaller piece without the ice cream, and Danny offered to eat her ice cream for her. They managed to pull away from the table and went into the game room for a few rounds of ping pong. Danny was eager to play pool. Tom played a few games with him, letting him win. Danny was delighted, but he looked a little tired. Jillian said she thought it was time for the kids to go get ready for bed and she would come up and tuck them in. She looked at Martha, and she nodded in agreement. She took Julie Ann upstairs and helped her with her bath. It had been a long day for everyone. After she had got Julie Ann all tucked in she went into Danny's room. He was lying on his bed still in his clothes and fast asleep. Jillian wondered if this was typical for boys to do. She gently helped him into his pajamas and washed his face and hands. His teeth and the rest of him would have to wait until the morning. Yes, this was one plum tuckered out little cowboy.

Chapter Six

Once they had returned home, the loft looked so small compared to the house on the ranch. Danny loved all the room and was running to catch Lucy. He had taken to her right away. She was still a puppy, and Jillian explained that she had to rest in between playing ball and tug-a-war. Danny thought Sydney would really like her.

"How come we couldn't bring Lucy to the ranch?"

Jillian smiled at her son. "She's still so little right now, but she can go next time. Maybe one day I can even bring her to meet Sydney. We'll see."

There were only three days left of the vacation, and they wanted to make the best of it. Tom didn't go to the office so he could do the driving. Jillian was never comfortable driving around Manhattan and Martha had her heart set on seeing the Statue of Liberty and the Empire State Building. Tom took them to Battery Park where they all got on a tour bus. Martha was thrilled. She had wanted to sit on the top with all the other tourists. The bus drove around for several hours before the kids began to complain. One needed to potty, and the other was thirsty. Jillian was impressed that they lasted as long as they did.

Back at Battery Park, they got off the bus, and Tom drove them to Tavern on the Green Restaurant for lunch. Martha had this place on her 'to do' list along with a horse-drawn carriage ride through Central Park. After lunch, Martha was able to cross another item off her to-do list. As they left the restaurant, there were several carriages parked in the front. Central Park was full of people taking walks and sitting on benches. Tom put his arm around Jillian, and she looked up and smiled. She whispered in his ear, and he told her she was welcome. Martha looked enchanted. Jillian was sure Tom had impressed her. She hoped she and Tom would become an extended family for her as it would be Martha that would be bringing the kids to New York on vacations. Jillian was anxious to call Father Michael and tell him how well it was going. She missed him terribly. Maybe it was time for a visit to Sweetwater, she thought.

* * *

The airport was busy. It was always busy. Jillian's eyes were filling up with tears. Every time she looked at her son, she tried to smile, but she couldn't stop the tears. Oh, how she wanted to keep him just a little while longer. Danny would be starting school soon, and Tony had been adamant about not changing any schedules as far as the children were concerned.

Jillian looked at Martha, who seemed to be holding back a few tears of her own.

"We both want to thank you for bringing the kids here to New York. We enjoyed spending the time with all three of you."

"I had a wonderful time with you and Tom. You seem so happy. I'm looking forward to our next visit to see you. Thank you for including me in all of the activities. I'm sure the children will miss you very much. Oh, by the way, you better search Danny's pockets for Lucy."

Jillian looked over to see a teary-eyed Julie Ann.

"Oh, Princess, don't cry. We'll see each other very soon, I promise. Give your daddy a big hug for me, okay? You be a good girl and listen to Martha on the way home. I'll miss you very much."

Julie Ann didn't handle goodbyes very well. This one has been particularly hard for her. She loved Jillian, but she would be okay once they were on the plane. She would be back to her old self, but for now, she couldn't stop crying. Danny looked like he was trying to be brave, but the minute Jillian reached for him he joined in with the tears.

"Danny, take care of your sister, okay? She's a little upset. You know how she gets when she has to say goodbye. I'll see you both very soon."

"When will I see you? I start school in two weeks and then I don't have any vacations until Christmas. That's a long time from now."

Jillian's heart was breaking. She was saying goodbye to her only child, and he didn't even know she was his mother. She didn't know what to tell him. She glanced over at Tom, and he lovingly came to her rescue.

"Hey you two, why all the long faces? What's the fuss all about? Danny, I'll bet you have a few days off at Thanksgiving, right? We need to have turkey day with my mom, but how about if we fly to

Denver on Friday and spend a few days with you? Would you like that?"

"Yep, that would be awesome," Danny said jumping up and down. His blue eyes were sparkling. As if by magic, the tears were gone.

Martha said it was time to go, and Jillian gave the kids one more hug. She watched as they went through the ticketed passenger's only area, and watched as they blended into the crowd. She looked up at Tom, and he hugged her tightly.

"It'll be fine, Sweetheart. You'll get used to having Danny coming in and out of your life. Be happy for the time you have with him."

"I know, I am glad for the time I have with him, but this was tough on me. I know Tom, I know. Thanks for telling Danny we would come after Thanksgiving. I didn't know we were going to your mom's for dinner. I'm glad we are, though. We're all she has. Maybe we'll be pregnant by then. Maybe we already are." She smiled through the tears.

* * *

Moving day had finally arrived, and Jillian was exhausted. She and Tom had packed up the loft, and the movers were there to pick it all up. They needed to take it all since the loft was going up for sale. Although Tom hated to get rid of it, the new house was actually closer to the office than the loft, so Tom saw no reason to keep it. Tom had to go into the office early that morning and Jillian was left to manage the movers. She wasn't very happy about Tom leaving, but something came up at the office, and he had to go.

Jillian drove over to the house and waited for the moving truck. She wasn't in the best of spirits after discovering the morning before that she still wasn't pregnant. She was disappointed she hadn't conceived under their tree the month before. She had suggested they go back and try again. Tom was amused but didn't have the time to spare. He told her they could conceive anywhere. Jillian seemed driven to get pregnant. She was keeping a diary and Tom was now on call. He was getting a little testy about it as it was spoiling the moment. They had discussed it many times. He wanted things to be more spontaneous. After all, they were still newlyweds. Jillian thought about a conversation they had the day before when Jillian discovered she wasn't pregnant.

"Sweetie," Tom had said, "we'll get pregnant. Why the big rush? We haven't even been married a year. You need to relax a bit. It just doesn't feel natural always knowing when we'll make love. You know what your doctor told you. You have to just let it happen. It will, you know. Just try and relax."

"I'm not uptight about it," she had replied, "I just want to get pregnant, that's all. Why does that bug you so much?"

Tom ended the discussion with a smile. Jillian knew she was pushing the envelope, but she wanted Tom to be as excited as she was about getting pregnant.

The moving van showed up, and Jillian spent the rest of the day trying to make sense of the mess. It didn't look hopeful, but by the end of the second week, all the boxes had been unpacked. Everything had a place, and if it didn't fit, it went in the garage. The garage was huge, and there was plenty of room for the things she didn't want in the house. Tom called a local charity, and they were happy to pick it all up. Jillian decorated the nursery and then she shut the door. Tom had asked her about it, but she told him she just wanted to be ready. She didn't want to wait until the last minute, but actually; she was hoping it would bring her good luck.

* * *

October was much colder than Jillian had remembered it being the year before. She went shopping for pumpkins and straw to decorate the front of the house. She found a few scarecrows and some ribbon that would look perfect for her autumn decorations, but couldn't find any straw. On the way home, she drove slowly through her neighborhood looking at what her neighbors had done to their homes. Some were lavish while other homes were more modest. Jillian was leaning towards the modest approach. As she passed by the house across the street, she saw a woman out in her front yard decorating with all the fall colors. Beside her was a stroller holding a small child all bundled up. She hoped that this time next year this would be the picture out in front of their house. Jillian waved, and her neighbor waved back. She hadn't met her yet but was planning on dropping by. In a way, Jillian was hoping her neighbor would come by with a plate of cookies or something. As she pulled into the driveway, Tom pulled up right behind her. They both pulled into the garage and Jillian waited for Tom to get out of his car. He had his briefcase and a box of files in his arms as he came to greet her. He gave her a kiss, then, with an odd tone to his voice he asked if they had anything going on for the evening.

"What do you mean? Oh, well, no, it isn't the right time of the month," she smiled.

"Good, I'm a little tired, and I have at least two hours of work to do after dinner. Did you cook anything?"

Losing her smile, she muttered just loud enough for Tom to hear.

"You can see I just got home. So no, but I can make us something if you would like."

"Jillian, I was only messing with you. I brought home a pizza. Extra cheese and easy on the sauce just the way you like it. I knew you were shopping, and I figured you were as hungry as I was. It's the kind we have to bake."

Jillian quickly changed her tone. "You're the best husband I've ever had. Here, let me help you with those files. Looks like you're on a big case, huh?"

"Not such a big case, just a difficult one. None of the partners are free to help so I'll need to do the research myself."

"Father Mike called this morning. He'll be flying in to see us in a few weeks. It isn't easy living so far away from my family. We need to make a trip to California to see Morgan and his brood. We haven't seen them since our wedding last June. Seems we used to see each other every few months before my mother died. Father Mike must be so lonely, too. We've all left Sweetwater. Strange, but he said he was stopping off in Denver to see Tony and the kids. He wanted to know what size shirt Danny wore."

"Really, I didn't know he was that close with Tony?"

"He isn't. Of course, he knew Tony when we were kids, but he wasn't close with his family. Back then, Tony's mom, Rose, and my mom were best friends, but Mike... Well, it's probably more Danny than Tony. Since we are like family, he probably wants to get to know Danny better. Oh, who knows? I'm just glad he's taken an interest in Danny. Go shower and I'll get the pizza in the oven. I'll put a salad together."

Tom grinned. "Pour me a glass of wine, will you?"

Jillian put the pizza in the oven and made a small salad. She went out to the garage to get the ribbon and the little scarecrows. Tom was finished with his shower and was sitting at the table in the kitchen in his sweats, drinking his glass of wine. He offered to pour her a glass, but she thought she better not.

"Are you feeling okay," he asked.

"Sure, but just in case I'm pregnant, I better not have any alcohol."

Tom smiled but said nothing. Jillian still wondered why he wasn't as excited as she was, but she thought she would speak to him later about it. She wanted to let him relax before he started working. Nonetheless, he had been oddly quiet since he got home. Usually, he was talkative and playful.

"How was your day? It must be nice not to have such a long drive anymore?"

"My day was very busy. Sweetheart, is the pizza almost ready? I'm starving, and I need to get to work."

Jillian felt confused. Tom had always wanted to chat with her and talk about his day or listen to how her day had gone. Something was wrong, but Jillian wasn't sure how to broach the subject. Maybe he was just exhausted. He did look a little tired to her so she decided to let it go. It certainly wasn't the end of the world. If he wanted to talk to her about it, he would.

After dinner, Tom went to his office and Jillian decided to read for a bit. She went in and undressed and looked for a pair of sweats and a long sleeve tee shirt. She plopped into her favorite chair and put a small blanket over her legs and feet. She opened her book and started to read, but her mind was wandering back and forth. She thought of Father Mike and how much she missed him. She was excited that he was coming for a visit. She missed their long talks and how, no matter what was on her mind, she could always share it with him. He was an amazing person, and she looked to him as her dad, not her priest. He had been there for her and the family for as long as she could remember. Jillian had no recollection of her own father. It had always been Father Mike that went to school to meet with teachers. He even helped her mother when it came to disciplining the children. As she looked back fondly, it was Father Michael that gave all her boyfriends the third degree. For some reason, her brother Morgan wasn't as close to Father Michael as she was, but then Morgan was older when their dad died. Jillian thought about the time she asked Father Michael to marry her mother. Mary and Father Michael tried to explain to her why that wouldn't happen, but Jillian would insist that it could. They had asked her not to mention it again, but at five years old, she wasn't about to let her dream disappear. She had hoped and wished for the impossible.

Jillian looked over at the clock on the mantel above the fireplace, and it was close to ten o'clock. She wondered if she should let Tom know what time it was, but she didn't want to disturb him. Jillian gave him another half an hour then looked in to find him asleep at his desk. She took her sleepy husband up to bed.

Chapter Seven

Tom was scrambling eggs when Jillian came down to the kitchen. She took a coffee mug out of the cabinet and turned on the electric tea kettle. Jillian put an herbal tea bag in her cup and waited for the water to boil. The aroma of coffee was delightful, and she gave it some consideration but stuck with tea.

"Good morning, the eggs smell great. I'll get the toaster out. I bought some of those English muffins we like," she said as she walked up behind him to give him a hug.

"Good morning, Sweetheart. That sounds good. I couldn't find any sausage in the freezer."

"Sorry, I didn't buy any. I'll get some the next time I go to the market. Wait until you see what I bought yesterday for the front yard. Any chance we could get a bale of straw somewhere? I have an idea for the fall decorations."

"I'll see what I can do. Actually, Hank is driving into the city in a few days. He and Alice are flying out to see their grandchildren. I'll ask him to bring a bale of straw."

"Really? That would be great!"

She took a breath and decided to just ask him. "Is there something on your mind you want to talk about? You don't seem yourself."

"I'm a little consumed with this case. I hate to suggest that you get used to it, but there will be times when work gets in the way. It comes with the job and the paycheck."

"It feels like it's more than just work. I've seen you through lots of tough cases, and you always have time for us."

Tom walked over and gave his wife a hug. He kissed her tenderly and with a smile assured her all was well. She still felt there was more, but if he didn't want to discuss it, she would have to let it drop and hope it went away.

"We didn't discuss going to California last night. I'd like to go see my brother. Can you get away next week or will you still have this case?"

"I'll still be working on it. Why don't you go by yourself? Hey, I have an idea. Why don't you fly to California then fly over to Sweetwater and meet up with Father Michael or vice-versa? If you met him in Sweetwater, then you could go on to California together to see Morgan. Then the two of you could fly to Denver together. You can both see Morgan and Danny then come home."

"That sounds fantastic, but it'll be expensive at this short notice."

Looking amused, he chuckled. "Sweetheart, we've got it."

"I'll call Father Mike and Tony to see what they say. Thanks for the great idea."

Jillian straightened up the kitchen, putting the dishes in the dishwasher and wiping off the table. She went upstairs to shower and get dressed. As she was drying off, she looked in the mirror. She stood there looking at her reflection then put her hands on her stomach. She tried to imagine what she would look like pregnant and it made her cry. Again, she thought about how quickly she got pregnant with Danny. Just a few times and it had happened. She wondered if maybe it might be Tom. She didn't want to think about there being a problem, but maybe that was what was bothering him. They would figure out a way; she was getting pregnant, and that was that. She had thought before she made the plane reservations she had better check with Tony just to make sure there wasn't a problem with her coming with Father Michael.

"Hi, Tony. It's Jillian. How are you?"

"I'm good. What can I do for you?"

The hint of indifference in Tony's voice surprised her. His attitude threw her for a moment. She wasn't expecting Tony to sound excited at the sound of her voice, but they did share a child and would be interacting for a long time. She had broken his heart by leaving him to marry Tom, but they had worked through all of that, or had they? Jillian swallowed hard and then as cheerful as possible she continued. "Tony, you know Father Michael is coming to see you in a few weeks. I would like to join him if that is alright with you."

"Father Michael was planning on staying here with us. I'm not sure it would be a good idea if you slept here. Let me think about it."

"I can stay at a hotel, but what would be the problem with me sleeping there? Honestly, what is the matter with that? I slept there for months, remember?"

"That was different," he said. "I'm seeing someone. Maybe both you and Father Michael can stay at a hotel then come over together. That would work best for me."

Jillian was stunned. It had only been just six months since they had been together and he was already seeing someone? She knew she had no right to ask him about it, so she didn't dare. Now she understood why he was standoffish. She was probably standing right beside him there making it uncomfortable for Tony to talk.

"Sure, I'll call Mike and arrange for us to stay at a hotel. It's not a problem."

She heard Sydney barking in the background, and it was difficult for her not to react. She decided to make light of it. All of it. "It's good to hear Sydney's bark, but he sounds upset."

"Martha just took the kids to school, and I guess he wanted to go along for the ride. She takes him with her almost every day, but it's too cold to leave him in the car, and she is going shopping. He makes no bones about being left behind. You know Sydney."

"Yes, I do. It will be good to see him. I'm looking forward to it. Please let Danny, I mean the kids, know I'm coming with Father Michael."

"I'll tell them. I'm sure they will both be very excited to see you. Call when you get to the airport, and I'll pick you up. Talk to you soon."

"Okay, talk to you soon," she said, hanging up the phone.

Jillian walked over to the window and looked out. They had a beautiful view from the bedroom window. It overlooked the front of the house, and she could see both ways up and down the street. As she gazed out the window, she was reminded of the night she realized Danny was her child. She had figured it out almost as soon as she saw his blue eyes. She thought about how she had said to Tony that his son looked so much like him. She thought about when she and Tony were kids, and Danny really did look so much like Tony when he was a child. She thought about how Tony had told her Danny was adopted. It just didn't add up. Why did he look so much like his dad if he was adopted? Why did this child have her father's first name? The name she gave her own child before putting him up for adoption. She was haunted by those eyes of Danny's. When Tony explained how his parents had adopted him as a newborn and kept the name his birth mother had given him, it didn't take long for her to figure it out. Jillian thought about how she had gone upstairs to see the kids that first night she had gone to Tony's house after running into him in Denver, and how she had whispered to her sleeping son that she was his mother. Jillian remembered the look on Tony's face when she confronted him with the fact that she was Danny's mom; that Danny was their child. Tony had thought Jillian was drunk or had lost her mind. The many months she stayed with Tony just to be near Danny. The many months they had made love, and she would cry silently as Tony held her. Jillian had missed Tom and was sick to have betrayed him like that. She gave herself to Tony, and he had been so happy. She thought about how Tony had asked her if she was in love with him and Jillian had replied that she loved him. He had told her that wasn't the same thing, and if she wasn't in love with him, she should be honest with her feelings. She thought about how she had hurt Tom, the love of her life, and almost lost him forever. She thought about the manner in which she hurt Tony as well. The amazing thing was that Tom had forgiven her for all that she had done and Tony, although heartbroken, had accepted her decision. It was a chilling memory that could have ended up so differently than it did. Jillian went downstairs and poured herself a cup of forbidden coffee. She sat down at the table and sipped the hot liquid, enjoying every drop. Putting away her melancholy remembrances, she picked up the phone to call Father Mike.

"Father Mike, I have a surprise."

"You sound excited. What is it?"

"Well, actually it was Tom's idea but if you agree it will make me so happy. What do you think about my coming to Sweetwater and then we can fly together to California to see Morgan and the family. Then, we can travel to Denver together to visit Danny. Say yes, please?"

"Yes!"

"Really?"

"Of course, isn't that what you wanted? It's a great plan."

"Yes, and then we'll fly back to New York together. Wait until I get home then we can schedule our trip at the same time. That way there won't be any confusing about tickets and seats. Oh, I called Tony, and he feels we should stay at a hotel so I'll make our reservations."

"That's odd? Tony invited me to stay at his house. I'm sure he wouldn't mind that you are there as well."

"Actually, he does. He is seeing someone, and I guess it might be a problem. It's okay with me, but that cuts into my time with Danny. I can't argue with him. Tony is keeping his word by letting me have Danny in my life. He gets to make up the rules."

"What does Tom say about it? Since it is a legal binding agreement, perhaps Tony would reconsider and let us stay at the house."

"Mike, we're staying at a hotel, and that's that. Our agreement didn't cover where I can sleep."

"Where do you want to stay?"

Jillian laughed. "I'll find us something with a pool."

"Call me when you make your reservation. I'll drive to Mountain City and pick you up. I just took over a load of firewood to your house the other day. I've been using it as my man cave."

Jillian smiled. "Right! Okay then, see you soon."

Chapter Eight

Heart-wrenching memories came flooding back as Jillian and Father Michael approached Burbank Airport. Jillian thought about the last time she flew to California with Tom and how she had barely made it in time to see her mother before she had died. She thought about how Tom had come for her that day at Tony's house in Denver and introduced himself to Tony as her fiancé. She remembered the shock on Tony's face and the hurt on Tom's. Just thinking about that day made her shudder. She had made so many poor decisions in the past.

They were waiting at the baggage claim looking for Morgan. Father Michael spotted him first. Rachael and Amanda came running.

"Auntie Jillian!" They squealed, "Auntie Jillian!"

Jillian knelt down and opened up her arms up wide enough to grab them both.

Jillian looked around. "Where are Melissa and little Morgie?"

"They stayed home. There wouldn't have been enough room for everyone in our car. Melissa is making beef stew. Hope you're both hungry. She's making enough for an army."

Father Michael smiled. "I'm ready for a home cooked meal. I can't speak for your sister, or maybe I can. When has she ever turned down a meal?"

"Father Mike. Don't quit your day job, honestly."

Jillian was laughing. She knew he was right. She loved eating. She missed her mother's cooking. It had been such a treat to come home after a long job and go to her mom's house for dinner.

The drive went by quickly, talking and catching up. When they arrived at the house, Melissa was waiting for them. She pried the baby off her hip and handed him to Morgan. Jillian reached for the baby, and Morgan gave him right over. Father Michael took their bags to their rooms. Father Michael had the guest room, and Jillian took Rachael's bed. Jillian thought about the time she brought Danny here, and he had slept in Rachael's bed. He was able to meet his grandmother and Sydney on that trip. What a day that was. She thought about how that had been the only time her mother would be with Danny. Looking back, she was so thankful to Tony for allowing her to take him with her on that trip. Jillian smiled. There would always be the good times to remember, even in the midst of tragedy.

They settled in, and Jillian went to the kitchen to give Melissa a hand with dinner.

"Morgan said you made enough stew to feed an army. That's the way you are supposed to make it. At least that is what Mom always said."

"Help me set the table and we'll call them in to eat."

"Great. I'm starving, and I know Father Michael hasn't eaten either."

They all sat down for dinner. Father Michael asked the blessing, and they began to indulge. Father Michael said it first, although Jillian was thinking the same thing. "Melissa, the beef stew is delicious. Reminds me very much of Mary's stew."

"It should Father Michael, it's her recipe. Mary was always helping out in the kitchen, and I learned so much from her. It makes my husband one happy man."

Melissa went to the kitchen and brought out an apple pie. Jillian took one look at it and her eyes filled with tears. She was sure the pie was her mother's recipe as well. Melissa looked at Jillian and turned back towards the kitchen. Jillian followed her and put her arm around her shoulder.

"Melissa, it's me, not you. I love you so much for wanting to make Mom's apple pie. It's okay, really. I'm just feeling emotional about everything for some reason. It is so hard being without her."

"We miss her, too. I loved having her here to help with the kids."

Jillian dried her eyes. "I can't believe it will be a year soon. I miss her so much."

"By the way, tomorrow we're having chicken enchiladas. No one could make them like your mother. We can make it together, and I'll write it down for you. I'll give you the stew recipe, too."

"I think I better hang out in the kitchen and learn a few things. I'd love to be able to make her apple pie."

"We'll make another one of her pies and by the time you leave, you'll have a part of her cooking to take home with you."

Jillian dried her eyes. "That would be wonderful. Tom will be so impressed. I don't do much cooking. Of course, Tom would never complain about it. He married me knowing I wasn't too adept in the kitchen. Come on, let's go back to the dining room and eat this beautiful looking pie. Do you have any vanilla ice cream to go with it?"

"Right here," Melissa said opening the freezer and pulling out a big tub of ice cream.

Both women were smiling as they went back into the dining room.

"Hey Sis, have you decided what you're going to do with your house?"

"No, Morgan, Tom and I have talked about it, but he says it's up to me. I just don't know. We sold the loft a few weeks ago, and I'm just tired of the real estate game right now. I did go by and see Mom's old house. Kids were playing outside, and it looks great. It's comforting to know a young family bought it. On second thought, no, I don't want to sell my house right now. You're welcome to use it anytime."

"Jillian, take your time." Father Michael said. "There isn't any rush when it comes to selling your house. I don't mind checking on it, and besides, I have been using it as my man cave once in a while. When things get crazy at the rectory, I slip away and go watch some football."

Jillian smiled. "So you said."

"We have an announcement," Morgan said, looking at his sister. "We're going to need a larger car."

Jillian and Father Michael looked at each other and then back at Morgan.

"That's nice Morgan," Jillian said. "What kind of car are you getting?"

Smiling, Morgan said. "We're thinking about a minivan."

"Well, with three kids I can see why a minivan might come in handy."

Suddenly, Jillian finally caught his drift. She looked at Morgan and then at Melissa.

"You're pregnant? Oh, Morgan, Melissa, I'm so happy for you both. Do you know what the baby is yet?"

"Too soon to know, but another boy would be very cool," her brother said, with tears in his eyes.

Jillian loved that about her brother. He was a strong man, but very sensitive when it came to his family. That was what had intrigued her about Tom as well. He had sounded so lost when he talked with her that first time at the ranch about having a family. She often wondered if her father was the same. Jillian tried to remember him, but all she could ever come up with was the picture of her parent's wedding on the mantel over the fireplace in the home she grew up in. She never had actual memories of him. All she knew came from pictures she had seen and stories she had been told.

Jillian was smiling. "When is the baby due? I can't wait to call Tom and tell him."

Morgan smiled, and he winked at his wife. "We think in May. Melissa goes back to the doctor next week. We won't have the sonogram until next month, but for sure, it's a baby."

Jillian was very happy for them. She hugged her sister-in-law and patted her brother on the back. Jillian helped Melissa clear the table, and they took the dishes to the kitchen. It suddenly hit her, and she felt the tears welling up. Jillian didn't want to damper the moment and tried to not let Melissa see her face. She went to the sink to rinse off the dishes and found she couldn't stop the tears. She put the dishes in the sink and held on to the counter. She began to sob.

"Jillian, what is it?"

"I'm sorry. I'm so happy for you. Honestly, I don't know what is wrong with me. I told you I've been a little emotional, lately. It's just that Tom, and I have been trying to get pregnant. I've put off taking any job offers, and we have been trying really hard."

"You've only been married six months for heaven's sake. You need to stop trying so hard. It'll happen. It took us eight months after we decided to start our family. We'd been married for three years before we started. What's your rush?"

"We want to have a large family. We talked about having four kids. Tom is six years older, and we wanted to get started right away. Well, the truth be known, I'm the one who wanted to get started right away, but Tom is going along with it. I have a schedule and..."

"Jillian," she interrupted. "Oh, honey, I don't mean to give you marital advice, but you're newlyweds. You're just getting used to living together. A schedule probably isn't such a good idea. You need to be spontaneous. How does Tom feel about this schedule?"

"I'm beginning to think he doesn't like it too well. He's made a few comments regarding it."

"See? You'll get pregnant when you least expect it. All we did was stop birth control. It still took eight months. Believe me; it will be better for both of you if you forget about getting pregnant. Forget about schedules. As long as you are not using birth control, it's bound to happen. Don't change anything except if your doctor wants you on vitamins or something. I even had a few glasses of wine once in a while. You need to be as normal as you can. The harder you try, the harder it gets. I have some friends that made their husbands miserable. It's the schedule thing. That's a last resort thingy, not right off the get go. Making love is an expression of your love. Getting pregnant is a result–not an action.

"What if we can't get pregnant?"

"Where is this coming from? Have you been told there's a problem? Honey, trust me, would you, please. Some couples get pregnant right away, but for others, like Morgan and I, well it takes time. We weren't even trying this time. I thought as long as I was nursing Morgan Junior, I wouldn't get pregnant so we skipped the birth control. Surprise…"

"You're kidding? I never heard of that."

"Well, I found out it's just an old wives tale for sure. I thought it was true. Anyway, this pregnancy is meant to be. Secretly, I'd love another girl, but room wise another boy would be perfect. He could share a room with Morgan Junior. Actually, it really doesn't matter. We've talked about either adding another bedroom or buying a larger house. I thought that if we added on a large master bedroom that would work out great. Ours is a little small and I would love to have a new modern bathroom with a giant soaking tub. The girls could share our old bedroom, and they would have their own bathroom."

"That sounds like a great idea. What does Morgan think?"

"We're discussing all our options right now. Morgan thought maybe it was time to build a new house. We'll see."

* * *

Jillian and Father Michael stayed in California for three days. Jillian made Melissa promise to call as soon as they had any news about the baby. Saying goodbye was not so hard. Jillian promised to come and visit in a few months. She knew it would be a lot easier for her to travel than for Morgan to bring a pregnant wife and three kids to visit her in New York.

She had considered the advice of her sister in law. It made sense to her, and if that was what was making Tom on edge, then she wanted to change it. He was her beloved, and she had fought hard to keep him in her life. She was not about to make him miserable now. She wondered how she could have been so selfish.

As soon as they arrived in Denver, Jillian called Tony from the airport. She told him they would take a cab to the hotel and call from there. They settled in their rooms, and Jillian said she would be ready in an hour. She wanted a shower and to call Tom. Father Michael told her not to rush and to give him a knock on his door when she was ready. They took a cab to Tony's house and arrived after dinner. Jillian could hear the kids on the other side of the door and Sydney was barking. It had been six months since she had seen her little dog. Would he remember her? She wondered. Tony opened the door, and Sydney stood there looking for a few seconds. He cocked his head to one side and then, suddenly, leaped into her arms. Jillian held on tightly.

"You're such a good little boy, Sydney," she sighed as Sydney smothered her with doggie kisses.

"Jillian!" Danny squealed. Julie Ann was right behind him with her arms in the air.

Tony held out his hand to Father Michael and ushered them in. Jillian was still holding Sydney and trying to hug the kids. Julie Ann asked her to put Sydney down, and Danny reached for his dog. This tugged at Jillian's heart as she relinquished Sydney. Behind Tony stood a woman that Jillian presumed was Tony's new girlfriend. She was beautiful. Jillian could see right away that she was Italian like Tony. Her hair was very dark, almost black. Her olive skin was stunning. She was medium height and almost, but not quite, slender. She had sexy curves and a full bosom. Jillian noticed her dark brown eyes and her face was flawless. She smiled, and her teeth were perfect. She looked as if she had just stepped out of a glamorous fashion magazine. Jillian was taken aback. Her smile was sweet and sincere looking. *Where did he find this beautiful woman,* she wondered.

"Jillian, Father Michael, I'd like for you to meet Angela. Ang, this is Jillian. We have been friends since grammar school, and Father Michael was, and still is, the parish priest in Sweetwater where we both grew up."

"It is nice to meet you, both," Angela said. Her eyes sparkled.

"Thank you, Angela. It's nice to meet you as well," Father Michael said, leaving Jillian the last to speak.

Jillian extended her hand. "Yes, it's very nice to meet you."

"Come in, come in," Tony said. "Kids, let Martha know Jillian and Father Michael are here. Have you eaten?"

"Yes, thank you," Jillian said. "We ate at the hotel,"

"Martha made chocolate cake, and we waited to have it until you got here. Danny was getting nervous."

"I'll go find Martha," Angela said.

"She's lovely. I'm happy for you. Where did you meet?"

Tony ignored her question and beckoned them towards the living room. Jillian had gifts for the kids and Martha. She brought a special chew toy for Sydney, who was romping around the house with Danny. She could tell they were even better friends than when last she saw them together. It was the right decision, but still, there was sadness in her heart. She had raised Sydney from a puppy, and she loved and missed him so much. Martha appeared and gave Jillian a hug. She said dessert would be ready in ten minutes. Jillian offered to give Martha a hand, and she accepted.

Once in the kitchen, Martha gave Jillian another hug. She gave her a knife to cut the cake, and she began getting out the dessert plates and some linen napkins. She watched as Jillian began to cut the cake.

"Jillian, I know this isn't easy."

"What? What isn't easy?"

"Imagine how Tony felt at your wedding. This is hard on both of you. Be happy for him, he deserves a happy life. I know you. I can see from the look on your face that this bothers you. I'm sure there is a twinge of jealousy, and that is to be expected. Angela is a good fit for him, and he seems to adore her. The kids like her. She comes from a big family, and she is a Nurse Practitioner. She loves children and dogs."

"I'm not jealous. Really, I'm not. It's just uncomfortable in an odd way. How did they meet?"

"I'm sure Tony will share all that with you. Meanwhile, do you want to gather up the kids? I'll meet you all in the dining room."

Jillian spent the evening with Danny and Julie Ann and, of course, Sydney. Danny showed her his latest badge he had earned in Cub Scouts. He shared with her that Sydney slept on his bed and that his dad said it was okay. Jillian looked at her son and touched his cheek.

"Danny, are you feeling okay? You look so pale."

"Sure, I feel fine. I get tired, but Dad says it's because I never slow down."

"Oh, I see. Some things never change."

Tony looked over at Jillian. "Danny is fine. He overdoes it as I'm sure you can remember."

"Yes, I remember."

"Okay kids, it's time to get ready for bed. School night," Tony said, clapping his hands.

Angela got up and took Julie Ann's hand. She walked her up the stairs and, as Danny ran past them, she gave him a swat on the behind. Jillian had hoped to do this, but she wasn't quick enough. Desolation was etched on her face as she watched the three of them disappear at the top of the stairs. Twenty minutes later, Danny came down to say good night and get his dog that was on Jillian's lap. There was no struggle. Sydney went willingly and happily up the stairs with his master.

Danny turned to wave and then he was gone. Julie Ann never came back down, and Tony went up to kiss her good night. Again, Jillian wanted this honor but was not invited to attend. They had moved on. What did she expect?

Chapter Nine

Jillian called Tom from Denver, and he assured her that either he would pick them up or send a car to the airport. Tom explained that he was busy and had court that afternoon but that he would try his best.

When Jillian saw Tom, she shouted and waved her hands wildly. Tom saw her, and he smiled. He held out his arms and Jillian almost knocked him down. She hugged him and held on tightly. Tom looked down at her, and she kissed him. Tom let Jillian go and shook Father Michael's hand, and quickly ushered them to the car. Arriving at the house, Jillian felt happy to be home.

"I missed you very much. I'm really sorry you weren't able to go with me. Next time, okay? Oh, I'm making dinner tonight so don't be late."

"You're making dinner? Fantastic, what are you making?"

"Beef Stew."

"Wow! I love beef stew, but?"

"Never mind. Go back to court and we'll see you later for dinner."

"Yes, ma'am."

After Tom had left, Jillian showed Father Michael to his room. He wanted to rest for a while.

"I hope you can help me with the stew... Will you?" She said, issuing the question more like a challenge. "Melissa gave me the recipe, and we both know what it is supposed to taste like, right? I'll run to the store and get some things while you catch a nap."

Jillian shopped for dinner and bought a bottle of wine she was sure would go well with the main course. She hoped Tom would be impressed with her new found culinary skills. Melissa had promised to send more recipes and Jillian was excited.

Jillian found Father Michael waiting for her in the kitchen when she got back from the market. He'd found the large Dutch oven in the cupboard and had the onions cut and potatoes and carrots peeled. He had pulled what spices out of the spice pantry he thought he would need, and there was a bowl on the counter with a kitchen towel over it. Jillian was speechless.

"Jillian, I went across the street and borrowed some yeast from Katelyn, your neighbor, so you owe her now. She's very nice and has a beautiful little girl named Stephanie. Katelyn told me you two haven't met yet. I think you will really like her."

"I was planning on introducing myself one of these days. I was hoping she would have brought over cookies or cake like they do in the movies."

"She's going to do that soon. It doesn't just happen in the movies."

"What's the yeast for?"

"Bread, I'm making bread. Come on now, we need to get this going. If you check the recipe, you will see the stew simmers most of the afternoon. Did you get the beef broth?"

"I got everything that was in the recipe that we didn't have here. I even got apples for apple pie."

"Perfect. As soon as we get the stew on we need to make the pie. The bread will go in thirty minutes before Tom gets home. Call Tom and ask him to call you when he leaves the office. Okay, come on now, let's get started."

Jillian was delighted. Not only was she about to have a real cooking class, but she was also having it with her favorite dad.

Later, when Tom walked into the kitchen, he took a deep breath then called out, "Hi, Honey, I'm home."

Jillian came dashing in the kitchen, laughing at his comment. "Hi, Honey," she purred. "Welcome home. I hope you're hungry. We have enough for an army. Father Mike is in the family room watching the news. Go on in and visit with him. I'll bring you a glass of wine."

Tom looked perplexed, but he also looked happy. Perhaps he was seeing the old Jillian. This was the woman who had stolen his heart, just a year before. He reached for his wife, and she snuggled in, allowing him to engulf her in his arms. She leaned up to kiss him and issued him a passionate, seductive kiss. He looked surprised. She was still purring.

"I never want the honeymoon to be over. Being away from you this past week has reminded me of how strong our love is. I'll show you later just how I really feel."

Tom looked at her with wanting eyes. "Now if you just had my slippers."

Jillian poured both men a glass of wine and one for herself. She brought the drinks into the family room on a tray. She sat down next to Tom on the love seat and put her arm through his. He glanced over and smiled. She knew he was looking forward to later. The anticipation was etched all over his face. They took their glasses into the dining room and began to enjoy their meal.

"Sweetheart, the dinner was fabulous. The bread was delicious. What more could a man ask for?"

"There's more. Actually, Father Mike made the bread, but I have one more surprise. Do you have time for dessert?"

Tom looked intrigued. "I didn't bring any work home tonight. I have all the time in the world."

Jillian gave him a sultry smile and raised an eyebrow as she looked into his eyes. Tom watched her as she disappeared into the kitchen and sliced the apple pie.

"So, who is this woman and what has happened to my wife?"

Father Michael laughed. "Trust me, Tom; the real Jillian is in the kitchen."

Jillian put a tiny scoop of vanilla ice cream on each plate then added the apple pie and brought the dessert into the dining room and set a plate down before a euphoric husband. After dessert, Father Michael excused himself and went to his room to read.

"If this is what life can be like when you aren't working then I beg you to not take any job offers for the next twenty years." With a seductive smile, he kissed her. "This has been an entertaining evening so far."

Tom never minded cooking, and they had discussed the subject of meals long before they were married. Jillian had promised to learn to cook, but Tom had said he didn't care if she ever learned to boil water. But after this meal, he said he was definitely reconsidering.

"Go relax and I'll clean up my mess in the kitchen."

Tom reached for her. "How about if you go relax, and I'll clean up?"

"We can do it together and start working on fulfilling that promise to you," she said.

Up went that eyebrow of his. Tom took her in his arms and held her tightly. He kissed her and caressed her shoulders with his fingertips. He leaned in and kissed the back of her neck. Jillian was melting in his arms. She felt like a teenager. Tom looked into her eyes, and they were begging for more. Tom was kissing her and touching her as if they had been apart for months. Jillian's legs began to tremble, and her heart was beating fast.

"I'll do the dishes in the morning," she said, taking his hand, she led him upstairs to their bedroom.

Tom gazed at her with a look of astonishment. Jillian knew he wanted her so much at this moment.

Tom reached for her with anticipation. "I don't know what's gotten into you, but I like it."

"I'm glad because I plan on keeping this fire alive. Prepare yourself."

* * *

Early the next morning, Jillian got up and rushed to the bathroom. She was throwing up and dizzy. She felt as if she had the flu and was so disappointed that she wasn't able to spend time with Father Michael, but by noon, she was feeling fine. The next morning was a repeat of the morning before. Again, by noon she was feeling much better.

"I'm so sorry. I can't imagine what is wrong with me. Let's go get a late lunch and then shop for Sister Martha and Sister Eloise. I know just what you can take back to them. Would you like to take a walk in Central Park this afternoon?"

"Yes, I think that's a superb idea. I have a few ideas for the sisters as well. Actually, they gave me a list. Can you imagine?" he said, lowering his eyebrows.

During lunch, Jillian felt a little queasy. She couldn't finish her meal and begged out of the walk through the park. They got a horse drawn carriage and, less than halfway through the ride, Jillian asked the driver to take them back. For some reason, the motion was making her nauseous. Her stomach was so unsettled. She was more than thankful she didn't throw up.

"Where's the nearest drug store?"

"What do you need Father Mike?"

"It's not what I need, but I think you need a pregnancy test."

"I'm not pregnant."

"Jillian, let's go get a test kit. Seems to me this might be morning sickness. I'm no expert, but something has your tummy doing summersaults. Perhaps you have a little acrobat in there."

Jillian drove to a small drug store not too far from the house. She was in and out in a matter of minutes and driving home as fast as she legally could. She flew up the stairs and waited for the results. She opened another package and took a different test and waited for the results. Soon, she was racing back down the stairs.

Tears were streaming down her cheeks, and when she reached the bottom of the stairs, she sat down. Father Michael got down on one knee to look her in the eyes. She nodded, and he handed her a tissue.

"I'm pregnant! We're pregnant! Tom and I are going to have a baby."

Jillian grabbed her phone to call Tom. On second thought, she decided it would be best to wait until he got home. She wanted to see the look on his face. She wanted him to take her in his arms and never let her go.

Tom was home by five-thirty. Jillian and Father Michael fixed pot roast and by dinner time, Jillian felt well enough to eat a small portion. They served biscuits on the side and later brought out strawberries and whipped cream.

Later that evening, Jillian couldn't take her eyes off Tom as he watched the television. Father Michael went to his room after the news was over. Tom looked at her and smiled. She wasn't sure how she was going to say it. Jillian had rehearsed it over and over, but each time she changed it just a little. Now that the time was here, she wasn't sure how to start. It had to be perfect. Tom got up and went into the kitchen. Jillian thought he was looking for leftover pie from the night before, but he came back with two glasses of wine, handing one to her. She took the glass from his hand and set it down on the coffee table. Now that she knew she was expecting there would be no more alcohol.

"I thought a glass of wine sounded good. Can I get you something else?"

This was it. This was her perfect moment. "Thanks, Tom, but I won't be drinking any wine. I'm... We're pregnant."

"We're pregnant? When? I mean, how do you know? We are? Really? We're pregnant?"

"Yes, Tom. I took a test today that I got from the drug store, and it was positive. I have been sick for a few mornings now, and Father Mike suggested I take the test today. Wow, was I surprised. I was so excited after I took the test. I almost called you. I just had to see your face when I told you. This isn't exactly how I had planned to tell you.

I wanted it to be very dramatic. You know, candles, soft music, the whole works."

"Soft music? I feel like a marching band just paraded through our living room! How's that for dramatic? This is enough drama for me, Sweetheart. I'm still trying to process this. Did you tell Father Michael?"

"He was right here when I took the test. Well, not with me when I took the test. You know what I mean. He was downstairs."

"Let's call my mother."

"I made an appointment with Dr. Aldridge. She wants to see me next week. Could we hold off telling anyone until we know for positive? I think these tests are accurate, but let's wait to make sure. Actually, I took two tests. I bought two different brands just to make sure. I know how excited your mother is going to be. I would like to tell her in person. Is that alright with you?"

"You took two tests? Well, then I am sure we are pregnant, but of course, we'll wait until it is official. So, when should we be expecting our little bundle of joy?"

"I have no idea. Let me look at the calendar. Let's see... This is the end of October, and I was not missing anything the first of September, so I must be no more than a month along. Tom, we're going to have a baby. Melissa was right. She said when we least expect it, but I didn't think she meant this month. Oh, Tom, we're having a baby."

Tom wrapped her in his arms as tears of joy fell from her eyes.

Chapter Ten

"Everything looks wonderful," the doctor announced. "According to my calculations, you should expect this baby on or about June fourteenth. How's the morning sickness?"

"June? That's perfect. June will be just perfect. The morning sickness went away about as quickly as it came. I only had a few days of it."

"That's good. You are very fortunate to have had only a few days. If it comes back and you need some help just let me know. You could try nibbling on saltine crackers if it rears its ugly head. Yes, you are very fortunate. Some women have it for several months. Let's get you on some prenatal vitamins and I want you to continue with regular exercise and stay on your normal routines. You're pregnant, not ill, so relax and be normal. I'll give you a list of dos and don'ts, and you'll have one sonogram unless we feel it's necessary for another. You are young and healthy. Just keep up the good work and no excessive stress."

Jillian was delighted. "This is a miracle, you know that, right?"

"Yes, I do. Babies are miracles."

Jillian drove to Tom's office. She was on a cloud, and it showed, as she floated into Tom's office.

"Hi Donna, it's so nice to see you. It's been awhile. I don't get to the city that often. Is Tom in?"

"Yes, Mrs. Bentley. I'll let him know you are here.

Donna Martin had been Tom's secretary for many years. She had been the receptionist for the firm for several years and when Tom found out she had secretarial skills he hired her when his former secretary quit. Last year when his sister died, it was Donna that held his office together. Tom was ever so grateful and vowed never to forget it.

"You can go in now, Mrs. Bentley."

"Thanks, Donna."

"Hi, Sweetheart. Well? Are we pregnant?"

"Dr. Aldridge said June fourteenth. We'll barely be married over a year. Can you believe it? I'm so happy."

"We can celebrate tonight if you'd like. How about if we have Chinese food, or would you rather have Sushi?"

"Ugh! Neither sounds good to me. For one thing, no raw fish for now, or when I'm nursing either, and Chinese doesn't sound all that appetizing."

"Are you sick again?"

"No, and I don't want to be either. Let's go to Henry's for steak and baked potatoes. That sounds really good to me. Tom? If I get too fat, you'll tell me, right?"

"It's not my job to tell you when you get fat. It's my job to tell you how beautiful you are. You are going to make the most gorgeous expectant mother ever created."

"Oh, Tom."

"I'm still so sorry I couldn't have gone with you this morning. Darn depositions."

Jillian couldn't have been happier. Her last pregnancy was something she tried to hide from everyone in her hometown of Sweetwater, Colorado. She hardly went out, and when she did, she wore baggy sweats, and since it was winter, she wore a big coat. When she got too far along, she moved away to live with her great Aunt in Durango. She went immediately to college after the baby was born and no one knew. No one but Tony's parents, that is. Jillian's mother, Mary, had confided in her dear friend, Rose Martelli, in hopes that she would tell her son, Tony, and he would come rescue her daughter. Frank Martelli was an Obstetrician and had known of many adoptions throughout the years. He was familiar with some of the procedures. When he discovered that Jillian had given birth to Danny, he contacted his lawyer, and he and his wife made provisions to adopt their only grandchild. Why they kept the name, Daniel, would remain a mystery. They neglected to tell their son that the child they had adopted was actually his, and for some reason, they had done so on purpose. If they had planned to share this with him after he graduated from medical school, that day never came.

"I guess we could invite your mother to have dinner with us tonight or should we wait until..."

"Until what? Is there a problem?"

"Oh, no. I'm sorry if it sounded like that. I was going to say until we have a chance to absorb it ourselves, that's all."

"You scared me for a second. Yeah, let's absorb it. I want to celebrate not having to be on a schedule anymore."

"Oh, Tom, you hated that, didn't you?"

"Yes, I really did. I felt like I was being asked to perform on call. I kinda like being the caveman," he said, lowering his brows and giving her that half smile.

This made Jillian laugh as he took her in his arms.

"Me Tarzan, you Jane. Don't need any schedules."

Jillian got his drift. She remembered what her sister in law had said. Melissa was right. Tom had been resenting it. They agreed to wait a few weeks before sharing the good news with Tom's mother, Elizabeth.

"I'm going home to change, and we can leave from the house. It's too early for me to wait around and I really would love a shower."

He kissed her. "I'll see you at home."

Jillian called Father Michael when she got home to fill him in, then dashed upstairs to take a shower. She undressed and looked in the mirror. She smiled as she looked down at her tummy. There was no outward evidence that she was expecting, but soon, very soon. Tom got home in less than an hour, and Jillian was waiting anxiously to find out where they were going.

"Tom, where are we going?"

"I think we should go back to where it all began."

"We're having dinner at Mark Dobson's building in St. Louis?"

"No silly, but close. Remember the deli we had lunch at the first day you were in New York?"

"Of course, I do. You were making me stutter and stammer like a foolish schoolgirl. Of course, I remember. Is that where we're going? You are such a romantic. You were flirting with me then, I remember."

"It's where I fell in love with you."

"No way! It was a business lunch."

"Well, technically you're right. It was a business lunch, but I fell in love with you the first day I met you and weeks later when we had lunch, I was sure of it. Do you remember that evening back at your hotel when we had drinks in the bar, and I told you I wanted us to be more than friends, and you gave me your little spiel about not mixing business with pleasure? Well, that's when I knew you would be mine someday."

Lowering her brows, she looked up at him. "Gee, I feel honored to be yours. What a chauvinist you've become."

"I have not."

Jillian put her hands on her hips. "You have. But you're my little chauvinist. Stop now, no more of the caveman talk."

She looked in the mirror on the wall to check her make-up. "I'd better run to the bathroom. I guess I should get used to this."

The delicatessen was crowded with suits of all sizes. Wall Street people, mostly. They made their way through the crowd, and as luck would have it, they found themselves seated in the same booth, peering out the same window, as they had a year before.

"Who would have thought last year we would be back a year later married and pregnant?"

"I did!"

"No, you didn't, Tom. Neither of us did."

"You're wrong about that. I had all but given up on finding someone to live out my days with. When I met you in St. Louis I knew you were the one. I wasn't even going to finish my building here. I had already received an offer for it and was planning to sell it when I met you. It was the only way I could think of to get to know you better. I fibbed to you that evening. Didn't you see Janet Dobson smiling? She knew. We were in on it together."

"Why you little sneak!" She giggled. "How can I ever trust you again after hearing this story?"

"That's just the thing. I believed this would work, and it did, so you can always trust me. You are my beloved."

Jillian knew how much he loved her. He was her beloved. After hearing his so-called confession, she loved him even more, if that was possible.

After dinner, Tom took her to the Plaza. They went into the bar and looked for the table in the back where they'd sat. The owners had remodeled and, to Jillian's disappointment, the table wasn't there any longer. They agreed that a nice walk would be good for Jillian and the baby. As they walked, mimes, dancers, and vendors, magically appeared, and the streets were full of life. Jillian always liked this about the city. They came out of nowhere and ate a late dinner, then played on the streets. They walked as far as Broadway then turned to walk back to the parking garage.

Jillian began to slow down. "Let's go home, Honey. It's getting late, and I'm kind of tired."

Tom gave her a sexy smile. "I was thinking the same thing, but I'm not so tired."

She got his drift and smiled. She was a happy woman and life was wonderful. She placed her hand on her tummy and smiled. She longed for the day she would feel the life in her body moving. It would be several months before her child would grow enough for her to feel the kicking and she would have to wait. She wondered how she would tell Danny. She remembered the first time she had felt Danny kick. It was a sad time for her. It was not as exciting then, and she had no desire to experience it again. She tried to put those memories out of her head. There were no regrets now. She was moving forward.

* * *

November was wet and cold. Snow had fallen, and it was just a few days before Thanksgiving. Tom and Jillian were planning to give Tom's mother the news about the baby at dinner. Elizabeth would be thrilled. Jillian was looking forward to seeing Danny on Friday afternoon. She wasn't showing but loved to push her tummy out a little. She would stand naked if front of the mirror and turn sideways. Tom said he wanted to take her picture as soon as she was blossomed out. This would make Jillian laugh just thinking of posing for a nude picture, especially being pregnant. Tom took a few days off so he would have Wednesday and Friday to spend with family. Thursday afternoon they drove over to spend the day with his mother. They enjoyed hors d'oeuvres before dinner. Elizabeth was well known for her tasty morsels.

Tom was carving the turkey while Jillian and Elizabeth sat waiting to eat.

"Tom, hurry up. I'm so hungry and..." she paused, turning towards her mother in law to catch the expression on her face. "You know I'm eating for two?"

"What? Did you say you are eating for two?"

Tom smiled and took his mother's hand. "Yes, Mom, we hope this makes you happy. We most certainly are."

"Oh, my, this is wonderful news. This is what I have been secretly praying for. When are you due, Sweetheart?"

Jillian was beaming with pride. "The due date is June fourteenth. We're having the sonogram in two weeks and then we will know if the baby is a boy or girl."

"Tom, Jillian, I told myself that if this day came while I was living, I would turn the house over to you at that time. Well, it has, and I'm still alive. So the ranch is yours now. I'll have Harvey, my attorney, finalize the papers and soon it will belong to both of you. It was always yours anyway, but I wasn't going to give it to you until I died. Now it will have children running through it again. May I call Hank and Alice to share the good news?"

"Of course, Mom, sure you call them. I know how happy they'll be for us. About the ranch, you don't know how much this means to me. Jillian and I have already been hoping to move there one day. We want to raise our children there. I promise I won't ever sell it. It will be passed down to our children just as you wanted."

"Come on now, let's celebrate and eat," Elizabeth declared, with a huge grin.

Chapter Eleven

The flight over Denver brought back harsh memories for both Tom and Jillian. The day Tom had come to tell Jillian her mother had suffered a heart attack and may not make it was a painful day for Tom. Knocking on Tony's door, and introducing himself as Jillian's fiancée. The look on Tony's face had confirmed Tom's suspicions.

Jillian would always remember the pain and betrayal on both Tom and Tony's faces; looks of pure torment that she never meant to inflict, yet couldn't erase or take back. She had made so many decisions, in her effort to make up for giving Danny up for adoption. She wanted so desperately to have him back in her life that she almost lost him forever.

As they touched down in Denver, Jillian closed her eyes. She was worried about the awful memories this place held for Tom. Striving to dismiss these thoughts from her mind, she opened her eyes and glanced over at Tom. He was smiling at her. She wondered how she ever deserved this man. She was delighted and very thankful that he loved her so much. She loved him just as much and would do all she could to replace the bad memories with happy ones.

They checked in at the hotel and drove a rental car over to Tony's house. Tom rang the bell and Angela opened the door. Jillian was surprised to see her.

"Come in," she said sweetly. "Come in where it's warm. We've been looking forward to your visit."

We've been looking forward to your visit? This is very weird. What does she mean, we? Jillian thought to herself.

"Tony and Danny will be home soon, and Julie Ann is still over at her grandmother's house. She'll bring her home in about an hour. Please, have a seat," she said taking their coats and disappearing for a moment.

Jillian looked at Tom and shrugged her shoulders with a perplexed look on her face.

Angela returned with a tray of hot tea and cookies.

"I could make coffee or hot chocolate if you would rather."

"Where is Martha?" Jillian asked.

"She's visiting her sister for the weekend. She said to tell you how sorry she was for not being able to see you this trip. She told me you would understand."

"Of course, I do. Thanksgiving is a time for families. Tom and I spent yesterday with his mother who lives alone. How about you, Angie, did you spend yesterday with your family?"

"It's Angela, and yes, Tony, the children, and I spent yesterday with his in-laws. Did you meet them when you were staying here last year?"

"No. Tony spoke of them, but we never had the opportunity to meet. Tom, Angela is talking about Tony's late wife's parents. They live here in Denver."

The tension was building, and Jillian was clueless. Tom seemed a bit amused as he watched the drama unfold. Jillian asked for water, and Angela went to the kitchen to get it. Tom enjoyed the tea and had a few of the cookies. Before Angela got back from the kitchen, Jillian heard the back door open and shut. Danny came running through the house leaping towards Jillian. She reached out to him and hugged him tightly. Sydney was right behind him pushing his way through to Jillian's lap.

"Jillian, guess what?"

"What Little Prince? What is it?"

"Daddy and Angela got married."

Jillian's face went pale. It wasn't jealousy she was feeling, but insecurity was more like it. She felt her heart begin to race as she looked at her son.

"How nice, I'll bet everyone is very happy," was all she could think to say.

"Guess what else?"

Jillian put on a false smile. "I don't know, Danny. What more could there be?"

"Me and Julie Ann are getting a brother or sister. Isn't that cool?"

Tony and Angela came in the living room just as Danny was telling them about the baby.

Tony looked at his son. "Danny, I was going to tell them, remember? Run along and feed Sydney then you can come back and spend time with Jillian and Tom."

"Guess what else," Danny blurted.

"Danny, do what your daddy tells you. Come on, I'll help you feed Sydney," Angela said as she took Danny's hand in hers.

Tom stood up and shook Tony's hand. "Congratulations."

Jillian smiled. "Yes, congratulations, we are very happy for you both."

"I'm sure this comes as a huge surprise," Tony offered up.

"Surprise is putting it mildly." Jillian stammered. "You could have called."

Tom took her hand and gave it a gentle squeeze.

Tony looked a little surprised, but his voice was calm and assertive.

"Jillian, this is my life. It doesn't concern you."

"It does concern me? Danny is my son, too or have you forgotten that?"

Again, Tom squeezed her hand, but more strongly than the first time.

"Jillian, you are not a decision maker in my life or his. You know that. You are here to see him because I allow you that. He comes to visit you because I allow that also. I take excellent care of our son, and my personal life does not affect nor concern you. I'm sorry, but it just doesn't. I care for you, but you made your decision and made your life with Tom. Be happy for me, won't you? I love Angela very much. She is a wonderful person, and she loves the children."

"He isn't calling her mommy. I mean it, Tony."

"He already does. I'm sorry, really sorry if this hurts you, but this is our life. You will always have Danny in your life, but you are no longer in mine. I chose to move on and make a life of my own and to be happy, just as you are with Tom."

Jillian was stunned. "Why the harsh attitude, Tony?"

Tom put his arm around his wife, and then looked at Tony. "Go a little easy on her. She'll come to terms with this, but I agree, you should have called her. It isn't like she's an ex-wife. You two are friends. She has emotions just like you do. You're treating her like an outsider."

"I'm sorry. I didn't want to hurt anyone."

Tom cleared his throat. "You're missing the point, my friend. Jillian is hurt. She is fearful of losing Danny. Having him call someone Mommy is something Jillian had longed for herself."

"Tom, Danny doesn't belong to her. It's that simple. She gave him up for adoption and gave up her rights to him. I didn't have to let her see him at all, but they love each other. I'm not a mean person, but she doesn't play a part in our immediate family. She is more like an aunt to the kids. They love her, and I wouldn't do anything to ruin that, but we need a strong family unit here in this house, and Angela is his step-mother now. If he wants to call her mommy, and he does, then I feel it is a positive, and Jillian needs to accept it. I'm sorry if I am defensive."

"Tony, let us not forget there is a legal agreement. We appreciate your generosity, but it would be best if you lost the attitude."

Jillian began to cry. "Tony..."

Tom turned to his wife. "Jillian, they're coming back. Please drop this for now. This is enough."

Jillian looked at Tom with disbelief. The tears continued as she excused herself. Danny and Sydney came running in trying to find Jillian.

"She went to the restroom, kiddo, she'll be right back. So, how was Turkey day at your grandparent's house," Tom asked tenderly.

"Grandpa gave me the drumstick, but I like white meat. Daddy said to pretend to like it, but Grandma heard him tell me and she took my drumstick and gave it to Grandpa to eat. They let me bring Sydney. They have a cat. That was so much fun. That cat didn't like Sydney, and she spit at him. She spit right in his face."

"Oh, Kiddo, cats are famous for spitting at dogs. It's just what they do."

"Oh? Well, Sydney didn't like it. It made him sneeze and then the cat ran up the stairs. Guess what happened then?"

Amused, Tom asked to hear more.

"Sydney ran up the stairs, too. That old cat can really scream loud!"

With that, everyone laughed, and both Tony and Tom seemed to relax. Jillian came back and asked what was so funny. Danny offered to repeat his story, and Tony suggested they go in the kitchen, and he could fill Jillian in while they got more cookies.

"My Grandma made them cookies," Danny announced.

"The cookies," Tony reminded him.

"The cookies," Danny said taking Jillian's hand and leading her to the kitchen.

Alone in the kitchen, Jillian sat down at the table to talk with her son. She was careful with her words, but she wanted to know how he was feeling about the marriage.

"So, Danny, what did you do today?"

"I went to the pediatrician, and she took some of my blood. Did you ever see that before? They stick a needle in your arm and pull out blood. It's awesome. It didn't hurt, and I got a whole sheet of stickers for being brave. Stickers are for little kids, so I'm giving them to Julie Ann."

"Danny, why would they take your blood?"

"Because the doctor said to, that's why."

"Oh, I was just wondering kiddo. So, tell me, when did Daddy and Angela get married?"

"Right after you left when you were here before with Father Michael."

"Did you get to be the ring bearer again like at my wedding?"

It suddenly hit her. She understood what Tony was trying to tell her. She didn't ask Tony's permission to marry Tom. He had nothing to do with any of their decisions. That was between Tom and her.

"What have I done? I am such an idiot sometimes. How could I be so insensitive? So selfish?" She muttered.

"Huh, what did you say?"

"Nothing, little prince. Now tell me about the wedding."

"Yes, I was the ring bearer and Julie Ann got to be a flower girl all by herself this time. It wasn't big like yours, but Angela has a lot of sisters and cousins. I get a new grandpa and grandma, too. Angela's mom and dad said I can call them what I want, but he said all the kids call him Papa. I have a gigantic family now. When I come to your house at Easter, maybe I will bring some of my new cousins with me. Okay?"

"We'll see, Little Prince, we'll see."

"Hey you two, where's the cookies?" Tony called out from the living room.

"I'll go see," Angela offered.

"No, Angela. They're okay in there. Really, let them have their time together," Tony sighed.

"Tom, Angela would like to have you and Jillian stay for dinner. She's a much better Italian cook than I am."

"I'll speak to Jillian about it, but I'm sure she would like that. When is Julie Ann coming home?"

"I'll call over there if they aren't here in an hour. Betty thought they would do some shopping first, then bring Julie Ann home. It's the big, after Thanksgiving shopping day."

Jillian, Danny, and Sydney came in with the cookies.

"Tony, may I speak with you for a moment please?"

"Sure. Let's go to my office," he said, looking over at Tom.

Tom smiled and gave Jillian a wink. "It's quite alright, he reassured them. I'll just visit with your wife."

Angela looked a little disturbed, but seeing Tom's expression must have settled her thoughts. She smiled at Tom and began to ask him about his family.

Once inside his office, Tony looked at Jillian with uneasiness on his face. "What is it?"

"I'm so sorry. Honestly, I get it now. I truly get it. You are so right. I know I am not part of the decision-making when it comes to Danny or any of you, for that matter. You have welcomed us into your home, and I am so embarrassed; so ashamed."

"Stop it," he murmured. "Don't be so hard on yourself. I'm sorry, too. I get defensive when I'm around you. Jillian, love me enough to let me move on. This will all work out. You have to trust that this is the best for Danny. Have some faith. Can you imagine how he would feel if he thought we had lied to him? He trusts me completely. I believe he has the same trust in you. It has never been about you and what you wanted. It has always been what was best for Danny, right? I will never tell him that you are his real mother. There is absolutely no reason to do that. Had we gotten married I might have considered it, but I don't believe it is best for him now."

"I understand this. I just want you to know how sorry I am. Please forgive me."

"Again, stop it. We don't need to put ourselves through this. I also want what is best for you. In my heart, I will always love you, but I am in love with Angela, and there isn't room for you there now. Angela is my wife, and I adore her. I am in love with her, and she is in love with me. Remember that day I asked you if you were in love with me?"

"How could I ever forget? I told you that I loved you, but you needed me to say I was in love with you. I didn't understand the difference. You said that you wanted the whole enchilada, and I wanted Danny. I remember all of it. I did love you, Tony, but I came to realize I was in love with Tom. I broke both your hearts."

"We can't go back, but please allow me to be happy as I allow you your happiness. I told you then, and I'm telling you now, you will have Danny in your life, but you will not always be in his. Does that make sense to you now? It is up to Danny and not us. I will never force him to accept you in his life. Knowing the way he feels about you, well, I don't think you have to worry. He loves you very much."

"I understand. I also believe that Danny should call her Mommy. That is what she is becoming to him. It's only right. I can do this. Honestly, I can. May I share a secret with you first before I tell Danny and Julie Ann?"

"Of course, Jilly, what is it?"

"Tom and I are expecting a baby. There will be a child calling me mommy one day soon. This makes me think more clearly, and I would do anything to protect this baby, anything."

Tony held out his arms and Jillian accepted it as a peace offering. She held him tightly, then released him and smiled. They rejoined the others just as Julie Ann came bouncing in the house followed by Betty, her grandmother.

"Jillian," Julie Ann squealed, reaching up with outstretched arms.

Tony scooped up his daughter and gently placed her in Jillian's arms. Jillian knew he was acting protective of her condition, and she gave him a look shared only between the two of them. After the introductions, Betty dismissed herself and hurried off to do more shopping.

Angela asked if they would stay for dinner and before Jillian could answer, Danny announced that they would, indeed, be staying. He wanted them to spend the night, but Jillian explained they already had booked a hotel room, and maybe they could stay another time. They made plans to go to the zoo in the morning, and Jillian invited Tony and Angela to tag along. Tony had work to do, and Angela was seeing patients. Jillian was relieved that they were both busy. In a way it was awkward for all the adults; each of them for their own reasons. Jillian wondered if Angela knew she was Danny's mother. Should she dare ask Tony? She wasn't sure what to do. It had never occurred to her before. As she sat there with Sydney on her lap, and Julie Ann hanging off her shoulder, she watched as Angela interacted with Danny. One would never know there was no blood between them. Her heart sank several times that day when Danny called Angela Mommy in front of her. Saying she understood and witnessing it was very different. She knew her focus should be on Danny, and she should be very happy for him to have a mother. She knew she would never hold that title. Not a chance in the world, so let her little prince be happy.

"Jillian, guess what?" Julie Ann spouted.

Oh, no. Now, what? Jillian thought. "What is it, Julie Ann?"

"Grandma called me Tracy two times today. Isn't that funny?"

"Real funny, but she misses her daughter very much. Seems I heard you look just like her when she was little, right?"

"That's right. Put Sydney down. I want to sit on your lap. Sydney, go over by Danny. It's my turn."

Jillian put Sydney down, and he ran over to Tony and jumped on his lap, much to Tony's surprise. Julie Ann was on her lap within seconds. She seemed to have a closer relationship with Jillian than Danny did. How odd that was, but she was much younger and required more attention. Angela smiled as she watched her new stepdaughter.

"Well, it's time for me to go to the kitchen. Excuse me, won't you?"

"Angela, Honey, should I come give you a hand?"

"No, Tony. Stay here and entertain our guests."

"Daddy, I'm going to take Sydney out for a run."

"I'm going, too," squeaked his little sister.

"Take your sister and keep an eye on her," Tony called out.

Jillian and Tom weren't sure what to do without the kids or the dog. It seemed odd, somehow. Tom spoke up first, breaking the ice.

"So, how are the kids doing in school?"

"Danny is brilliant. He gets only A's, and Julie Ann is just now in Kindergarten so we will see how she does.

"Tony, forgive me for asking, but I really want to know. Does Angela..."

"Yes, she does. I felt it only fair to her that she understands your relationship with Danny. She realizes how important it is to not share this with anyone else, and I trust her. I told her a few nights before I proposed. I asked her never to discuss this with you. She found the story heartbreaking as she put herself in your position. She promised to not tell a soul."

Danny and Sydney came leaping back into the living room, but Julie Ann lingered in the kitchen. Danny said she was helping Mommy cook. Suddenly there was a commotion coming from the kitchen. They heard Julie Ann yelling, and Angela was trying to calm her down. Tony got up and started in that direction, but now the two had made it to the dining room, and Julie Ann was angry.

"No, Mommy! That isn't fair. I'm sitting next to Jillian, not Danny," she yelled. "Daddy, Angela is being very mean to me."

"What in the world is going on?" Tony demanded. "Ang, what happened?" he said, abruptly changing to a softer tone.

Angela began to cry as she tried to explain. "Julie Ann was setting the table, and I had her put her plastic glass next to my chair and told her that Danny would be sitting next to Jillian. I have never seen her behave like this before. I can put Tom at the end and put the kids on either side of Jillian. I'm so sorry."

"Julie Ann, come here. You need to apologize to Mommy. Get over here, right now."

Julie Ann walked up to Angela and looked her right in the eyes. "I'm sorry, An-ge-la."

Tony sounded very upset. "Julie Ann! Go up to your room right this minute. You'll stay there until I come to get you. Do you understand me, young lady?"

"I hate her," she yelled, as she ran up the stairs. "I hate An ge la!"

Angela sat down and tried to dry her eyes, but the tears kept falling. Jillian wanted to do something, anything. She wanted to fix this. Tears were welling up in her eyes. Her heart went out to Angela at this moment, but she felt such pain for Julie Ann. This had to be very confusing for her. What a clever little girl she was to know how to manipulate her parents like that. Where did she learn such behavior? Jillian was disappointed in her, but it was coming from somewhere. Perhaps her grandmother had some influence over her. Could it be Betty wasn't happy about Tony's marriage? She wanted to bring up her suspicions, but she knew she had no place in this matter. She held her tongue and said nothing.

"I must apologize to you both," Angela said looking at Tom and Jillian.

Tom spoke up with tones of reassurance. "There is nothing to apologize for. That was mild compared to some of the things my sister would say to our parents. Girls can be so emotional. Don't give it another thought."

"Ang, Julie Ann loves you. She gets headstrong when Jillian is around. She is very attached to her. I'm sorry, Honey."

"May I go up and talk with her? I don't mean to intrude, and it is not my business, but please, I think I can help."

Tony looked at Jillian with a look of mild contempt. His face softened, and he agreed. "Go ahead."

Jillian reached the top of the stairs and knocked on Julie Ann's door.

"Princess, it's me, Jillian."

The door flung open then Julie Ann closed it behind them. She flew on to her bed and kicked off her shoes, sending them flying across the room.

"My little princess, I love you so much. You are very special to me, you know that, right?"

"Yes," she said with tears running down her little cheeks.

"I want you to listen to me now, okay?"

Julie Ann nodded.

"Sweetie, when I was a little girl my daddy died in a car crash. I don't remember him, but I remember being sad. I wanted my mommy to get married so I could have a daddy again."

"Did she get married again?"

"No, Princess, she didn't. My brother and I would have been happy for her if she did. Even though she had two kids, we knew she was lonely for someone her own age. We wanted her to be happy. She had to raise us all by herself, and that was sad. Now you have a wonderful new mommy, and your daddy is happy. I have my own husband, and I love him very much. It doesn't mean that I don't care for your daddy and it sure doesn't mean I don't love you and Danny anymore, but I will never be your mommy. You understand that, right Princess?"

"I understand. Why are you telling me this?"

"Maybe you thought that one day I would marry your daddy, right?"

"Maybe, but we like Tom. He's cool."

This made Jillian laugh, and she grabbed Julie Ann and gave her a little squeeze which made her giggle. Her tears had dried, and she was coming around.

"When you get mad at Daddy or Angela, you mustn't yell or say mean things to them. I know you don't hate either one of them. If you want to call Angela your mommy then that is what you call her all the time. That was hurtful when you called her Angela and stretched out her name like that. It was disrespectful. Do you know what that word means?"

"Yes, it means you want to be mean."

"That's right, Princess. You are such a smart little girl. Now, if anyone says mean things about your mommy you must tell them not to say it. Let them know how much you love your new mommy and they will stop saying mean things, but you must never do what you did again. Angela loves you and Danny very much. Promise me that you will be a good girl and never be mean to Daddy or Mommy."

"I promise."

"Okay, my little Princess, I'll go tell your daddy you are ready to come downstairs now. I think you need to say you are sorry to Angela and really mean it this time. I love you so much. I hope I have a little girl just like you someday."

"I hope you do, too. You can call her Silly Jilly, like me."

"Oh, we'll see about that Sweetie. I think Tom would like to call her April like his sister, but we'll see."

"How come Daddy calls you Jilly, sometimes like me?"

"When we were little children my nickname was Jilly. Only three people called me that. I am told it was my daddy, my brother, and your daddy. When you were born, your mommy wanted to call you, Julie Ann. Your daddy called you a Silly Julie one day, and that started you calling yourself, Silly Jilly because it rhymed. It had nothing to do with me. That was a coincidence. Do you know what that word means?"

"Nope."

"Well, it means when two things happen alike, but no one planned it."

"Oh?"

Jillian smiled. "It's okay, Jilly, you can ask your daddy to explain it."

Jillian went down to the living room and explained to Tony that Julie Ann was ready to come down, and she was ready to sincerely apologize to Angela.

"What did you tell her?" he asked.

"I told her about when my dad died and how I would have loved to have had a new daddy. Julie Ann told me that she really loves Angela," she said turning to look at Angela when she said this.

Angela smiled and thanked her.

"You're welcome, Angela. I think from now on your daughter will be a sweetie. She really does love you. Julie Ann didn't say, but I think Betty might have a part in this. We all know how much she misses her daughter, and Julie Ann told me that she calls her Tracy once in a while. Just my uneducated guess."

Tony went upstairs to see his daughter. Several minutes later he came down the stairs with Julie Ann in his arms. He put her down and she went running up to Angela. Angela picked her up and took her in the kitchen. Jillian prayed this would have a happy ending.

Danny came running into the living room with Sydney in tow.

"Jillian, Mommy is making lasagna because I told her it was your favorite. I told her you make famous garlic bread from Sweetwater, and she wants you to come in the kitchen."

Angela was at the stove when Jillian came in. She turned and smiled at her.

"I want to thank you from the bottom of my heart. I prayed and prayed that this would be a happy day for all of us. You are very kind, and I can see how Tony had fallen in love with you, twice."

"He told you that?"

"Yes, he did. We were sharing our feelings a few days before he proposed and it was important for us to get everything out in the open. He said that you come to visit and that the kids look forward to having you come. He told me that your heart belongs to Tom."

"My heart has always belonged to Tom; I was just too blind to know it."

"You could have made this a very rough day with the way Julie Ann was behaving. She told me that you said she should call me mommy. I know it must be difficult to hear Danny call me mommy, but I love him. He is very dear to me, and I will do my best to earn his love and trust. I know how important that is to you. I just wanted to tell you."

Jillian smiled. "Thanks, we are both emotional right now. May I ask? When is your baby due?"

"April thirtieth."

"You are just six weeks ahead of me."

"What? You're pregnant, too? How wonderful for you and Tom. You must be so excited."

"We are. It's like a miracle for us. I am longing for the day I feel my baby move. I haven't told the kids yet. Maybe we'll tell them after dinner. I told Tony when we talked earlier. Now, where's that bread?"

Jillian was content. So much had happened in just a few hours, and she felt as if they had all reached a point where everyone knew where they each stood, and she was comfortable with that. She never learned the third "guess what?" from Danny. With all the excitement she forgot to ask him.

Chapter Twelve

There was so much snow; Jillian couldn't get out of the driveway. Tom said he would send someone over to clear it. He told her that he would be home in time to drive her to the doctor for her afternoon appointment. The initial sonogram was inconclusive, and they were having another. Soon, they would know the sex of their child. Jillian was anxious. She was sixteen weeks along. She wasn't showing, but she was hopeful to see a big bulge very soon. Christmas was in a few weeks, and Jillian had finished her shopping and mailed gifts off to Denver. She included the whole family and even sent a gift for Baby Martelli. She was curious to know what they were having, but to date; no one had shared that information with her. She was hoping that when she called at Christmas someone would tell her. It didn't really matter, but, still, she was curious. Tom's mother was spending Christmas with her sister in Ohio, and Jillian and Tom were meeting Morgan and his family in Colorado to be with Father Michael. Jillian wondered where they all would sleep, but she had inflatable beds and Melissa was bringing sleeping bags for the kids. Morgan had called before Thanksgiving to let them know they were having another girl. He sounded delighted, but then that was Morgan. She remembered how he had said he wanted another boy, but she knew in his heart, it didn't matter. Jillian thought how odd it was that all three women were just weeks apart. Melissa was due the middle of April. Jillian would be the last to deliver. She knew that Melissa was feeling her baby move now and as she thought of how precious that moment would be. She put her hands on her stomach and rubbed it gently.

"Tom, have you left yet? I don't want to be late and have to reschedule the sonogram."

"I'm on my way as we speak, Sweetheart. I thought it was going to start snowing again, but so far, so good. Are you ready to go?"

"I've been ready for hours," she giggled.

* * *

"Well, looks like your baby has really grown in a month. I can see everything," Dr. Aldridge said. "Would you like to know the sex now?"

"Yes, please," Tom urged her.

"You're having a son."

Tom looked ecstatic. "It's a boy? Jillian, we're having a boy."

Jillian didn't speak. She closed her eyes and took a deep breath. She opened her eyes and looked at her husband, who was now crying with joy. He kissed her on the forehead and took her hand.

"Be careful getting off the table. You can get dressed now. I'll see you both in my office in a couple of minutes."

"Oh, Tom, this is our best day, isn't it? I want to call Father Michael from the car and tell him the news. He was hoping we would have a boy. Oh, I know you were, too. I'm so happy."

Jillian got dressed, and she and Tom went into Dr. Aldridge's office.

"Everything looks good. Your baby is healthy and growing. You should be feeling something soon. Be sure and write it down so you'll always remember the day he first said hello to you," Dr. Aldridge said endearingly.

"Thank you so much, Dr. Aldridge."

"It is my pleasure. Go home and celebrate. I'll see you next month. Be sure and call the office if you need anything."

Jillian and Tom walked out to the parking lot arm in arm. Tom held her firmly so she wouldn't slip on the ice. It was getting colder, and it looked like it might snow again at any time. Tom chose the safest route home, and Jillian looked through her purse for her cell phone.

"Father Michael, are you sitting or standing?"

"I'm sitting down. What is it? Are you okay?"

"I'm more than okay. We're having a boy. Can you believe it?"

"That's great news, Honey. I am so happy for you."

"We just found out ten minutes ago. We're on our way back home. Oh, Father Mike, we are so happy. I can still hardly believe it."

"I can't wait to see you and Tom for Christmas. It will be such a happy day."

Jillian was smiling from ear to ear. "Oh, will you go over to the house next week and make sure everything is okay for Christmas.

What fun we'll have this year with two pregnant women. I am…Tom? Watch out! Look out! Oh, no!!!..."

Father Mike bolted from his chair so fast it overturned. "Jillian? Jillian? What happened? Can you hear me? What happened?"

All he could hear was the loud screech of tires, crashing metal and breaking of glass before the call was disconnected.

Tom's face was covered in blood. It was dripping in his eyes. Everything was blurry as he tried to blink the blood from his eyes.

"Jillian!" He cried hoarsely. "Where are you? I can't see very well. Say something so I know you are alright."

Tom tried to reach around to find her. He couldn't get his seatbelt to open and then he realized he was upside down. He reached again for his seatbelt and was finally able to release it. He crumpled down in a ball resting on the roof of the car. He tried to turn around and get right side up, but he was disorientated. He was having trouble breathing.

Tom was crying out for Jillian. "Where are you? Please, Sweetheart! Say something."

He wiped his eyes with the sleeve of his jacket and then he saw her. He tried to reach for her, but his arm wouldn't work. It hurt. There was no way he could have known how badly his arm was mangled. With his other arm, he touched her. She was breathing, but unconscious. Jillian was dangling above from her seatbelt, and there was blood dripping from her hair. Tom tried to wake her up, but she wasn't responding. She was bleeding from her nose and mouth. Jillian had what looked like a gash in her head, and her leg was twisted, oddly twisted. She was very still.

The sounds of sirens grew louder, but still in the distance. Lights were flashing as the police car approached the scene. A fire truck was close behind. Tom was moaning from the pain.

"Please help my wife. She's pregnant. Please help her."

"Sir, don't move. We'll get you out as soon as possible. Please Sir, do not move," the officer commanded. "The ambulance is on the way. No sir, please– stop moving."

"My wife is hurt. Please help her. She's pregnant. Please help her," he said before losing consciousness. The Jaws of Life was summoned. It took over an hour to get Jillian out of the car. They were able to get the driver's door opened and Tom was rushed to the hospital. Jillian was later flown to the same hospital.

* * *

Father Michael was sitting in her room. She was still unconscious. Her endless moaning was breaking his heart. It had been eight hours since the accident. He had driven straight to the airport and was able to get on the next flight to New York after the joyful conversation turned to tragedy. At the time, he only knew they had been involved in an accident. When Jillian didn't call him back, he immediately took action. Being a priest had its benefits and Father Michael had no problem pulling his weight for a seat on the plane. He explained that it was an emergency, and there were no questions asked.

Father Michael was traipsing back and forth between Jillian and Tom's room. Tom was awake and asking about his wife. Father Michael came in, and Tom tried to get up.

"Tom, stay put. You have multiple broken ribs and a broken arm. Your left foot was severely damaged. They were able to repair it, but you have a cast up to your knee. Please stay calm."

"Jillian? Where is Jillian?"

"She is in intensive care. She's had a head injury and a badly broken leg. Her knee was injured, and there are a few other problems."

"Oh, no. I have to see her. The baby? Mike, is the baby okay?"

"I'm sorry, Tom. She lost the baby," Father Michael uttered with tear filled eyes.

Tom began to cry. "Please? I have to see her. Is she conscious? I have to be with her. Please help me. Can you get me in a wheelchair? Please, Mike, I have to see her!" Tom was becoming increasingly agitated.

"Let me call the nurse. I don't think with those broken ribs you could get in a chair yet, but maybe they could push the bed or something. Just don't move, Tom."

Father Michael went to the nurse's station and explained the situation. There was not a chance they would move him today. The nurse went in to explain to Tom, and he begged them to reconsider. He tried to get up from the bed, and the pain gripped him and he yelled out. It was difficult for him to speak.

"Mike," he said, almost breathless. "Tell her I love her and that I will see her as soon as I can. Don't waste your time in here with me. Please, go be with her. Tell her, Mike, tell her I love her."

"Tom, she is heavily sedated. She doesn't know when I am in her room or not."

Elizabeth Bentley came rushing in the room. With a look of horror, she rushed to his bed.

"Tom, what happened?"

Tears were streaming down his face as he looked at her.

"Mom, we had an accident. Jillian lost the baby. Our son is gone."

Elizabeth looked at Father Michael and then fell down into the closest chair; pale with shock.

"Where is she?"

"I'm going there now. Would you care to go with me? She is in intensive care."

"I'll be right back son. Let me go check on Jillian and I will be right back."

Father Michael took her upstairs and buzzed the nurse. The doors opened, and they walked into the second room on the right side. There was Jillian just as he had left her thirty minutes earlier. She wasn't moaning any longer. She lay there very still. Elizabeth let out a gasp as she saw her daughter-in-law. Her face was swollen and bruised. Her head was bandaged, and her leg was in a cast up to her hip. She walked up to the bed and bent down to kiss her forehead. She took her shaking hand and brushed strands of bloody hair away from Jillian's forehead. She looked up at Father Michael and began to cry.

"This is the love of my son's life. She is his world. She bent down on her knees and prayed right there at the bedside. Father Michael put his hand on her shoulder and closed his eyes. He prayed in silence, as he cried. He had lost Jillian's mother hardly a year before and now this. It was too much to bear. Elizabeth was still on her knees when the doctor arrived. She rose to her feet and watched as he looked in on Jillian.

Father Mike, I'm here, I'm here. Oh, don't cry. I'm okay. Elizabeth, it's okay. I can hear you. Where are you? Where am I? I hear you. I'm okay. Where's Tom? I can hear you.

"Doctor, is my daughter-in-law going to pull through this. Please, you must tell me," she gently commanded.

Pull through? I'm not dying. What are you saying? I'm okay. Why can't you hear me?

"Mrs. Bentley, Jillian has sustained some serious injuries, but we are hopeful that she will make a full recovery. We are planning to keep her heavily sedated for a few more days. We will start to bring her around little by little. She will be in pain, and her body needs this rest. She will be here several weeks, if not longer, and then we will send her to rehab. Her leg was the most severe injury. She'll need physical therapy. The head injury wasn't as serious as we first thought. The tests show very little swelling, and it continues to go down. She is doing much better than she looks. There isn't any reason why she won't be able to have more children."

No! What are you saying? No, I have the baby safe within me. He is safe. My baby is safe. No, Doctor, no Father Mike, help me. I'm here, I'm here. Don't let them take my baby.

Father Michael extended his hand. "Thank you, Doctor. We appreciate the information."

"I understand her husband was injured in the accident?"

Oh no, please. Tom is injured? Tom, where are you? Father Mike, please find Tom, please find him.

"Yes, Doctor, my son would be here right now, but he isn't able to leave his bed. He wants the nurses to push his bed to her room."

What do you mean? Why can't he get out of bed? Tom, I'm here. The baby and I are right here. Please, Tom, I'm begging you, please find us.

"As soon as Jillian starts to come around, we will get him in here to be with her. I'll be back in the morning. We have a few rooms available if you are planning on staying here at the hospital. The waiting room is very comfortable. Just let one of the nurses know that you would like a room where you can get some rest, and it will be provided. Good night."

"Good night, Doctor," Father Michael replied.

* * *

Three, very long, days later, Tom was helped into a wheelchair, and the nurse took him to see his wife. Jillian was awake but very groggy. When she saw him, she cried out, "Tom..."

The nurse pushed him to her side and asked Father Michael to give them some privacy. Tom was crying as he looked at his beloved.

"What happened, Tom? Are you alright?"

"Yes, Sweetheart, I'm fine. I have a few broken bones, but I'm okay. Honey, I don't know how to tell you this."

"We lost the baby, Tom. You don't have to say it. I know. I just want to go home. Please take me home."

Chapter Thirteen

Two months had passed since the accident. Jillian had been home for two weeks and using a wheelchair. Tom arranged for a service to take her to physical therapy until he was able to drive. He was still in therapy, but his therapist came to the house. Jillian wouldn't be ready for home therapy for a while longer. Tom managed to work from home, and Jillian basically sat by the window watching it snow. She hardly spoke to Tom. She just didn't have anything to say. She wasn't the only one that was devastated, but it felt like that to her. She watched as Tom put his energy, heart and soul into his work, and it reminded her of when Tom had lost his sister, April.

Her thoughts were always of the child she lost. She didn't want to think of Danny or anyone else. She was consumed with her grief and accepted no comfort. Father Michael called every day, but it was Tom who usually took his call. Jillian couldn't understand how life could still be going on around her when her world had been ripped apart. Her heart was torn in two.

"Father Michael is coming to see us in a few days. Won't that be nice, Sweetheart?" Tom said gently.

Jillian raised her eyes to meet his, but she just looked at him, without a response.

Tom reached for her hand and lowered his voice. "You aren't the only one that is hurting you know? I'm heartbroken, too, but you need to snap out of this. We need to move forward with our lives."

"If you need to move forward; fine, I'm happy for you. Tom–just go for it. I can't. I just can't. If you can move forward, then that's great. Don't you understand what this did to me? Can't you wait for me to feel something? I still love you very much, but I can't do what you want. I won't. I don't want to move forward."

Tom sorrowfully gazed at her. She wasn't making sense. He let go of her hand. He shook his head and slowly hobbled away.

"Please tell Mike not to come," she muttered.

She wasn't asking, and her tone confirmed it. Tom left a message for Father Michael and was about to call him again when the phone rang. Tom wasn't moving too fast yet, and he hadn't mastered the crutches. He reached for the phone and took it to his office.

"Hi, Mike. How are you?"

"Better now that you both are home. I have a surprise for Jillian. I think it might be exactly what she needs right now. I'm meeting Tony in Denver, and we are bringing Danny to see her."

"I don't know Mike. I don't know how she'll react. I worry she will hurt Danny. She isn't in a very good place right now. Let's wait awhile."

"We already have our flights booked. You need to trust me, Tom. I am trusting in Jillian's heart. She loves that child so much. I think it will do her good. I don't believe that you should tell her, though. I hate to surprise her like this, but honestly, I think it is best."

"She loves me, too, but I can't get her to come around."

Father Michael said compassionately, "It's different when it comes to children. Trust me, please."

Tom warmed up one of the many casserole dishes from the neighbors. They had enough frozen lasagna to last a month, and he wasn't exactly sure what he was warming up tonight. It looked good, but what it was, he had no clue. So many meals had been brought over after he was released from the hospital. When Jillian came home, the generosity was repeated. Katelyn, from across the street offered to straighten up the house, but Tom hired a cleaning service to come in. Tom set the table with his good hand and called Jillian to come in the kitchen. He couldn't push her with one arm, so she had to maneuver the wheelchair herself. The tiled floors were helpful. She had refused to eat many times, but tonight she came in the kitchen. They ate in silence. This tragedy was tearing them apart.

* * *

Jillian sat by the window watching the cars drive by when a car she didn't recognize pulled into the driveway. The first person to exit the car was Danny; then Father Michael, followed by Tony. Jillian froze. She blinked her eyes hoping it was a dream. Could no one understand her pain? Her need to be locked away? The baby she was responsible for that she carried inside of her had been ripped from her! Her one duty to protect her son; she had failed, yet again.

"Tom?"

He called out from his office asking if she was alright, as the doorbell sounded. Tom hobbled on his crutches to greet their guests. He opened the door and let the three in. Danny brushed the snow from his shoes and took off his coat. Tony and Father Michael handed their coats to Tom and walked towards the fireplace where Jillian was sitting. She lowered her head down into her hands and began to cry. This was too overwhelming, and she couldn't quite rationalize her feelings. Danny spotted her, and although he had been warned not to jump on her because of her injuries, darted towards her. He looked bewildered as he set eyes on her short hair and seeing her leg in a cast up to her hip which caused her leg to extend straight out in front of her. Tony tried to prepare him as best he could, but even he looked shocked to see her looking like this. She was thin and frail. Danny started crying, which turned to sobbing, and Jillian called out to him.

This touched Jillian in a way only a mother could understand. She couldn't bear to see Danny in that kind of anguish.

"Come here, Little Prince. Come over here and give me a gentle hug. It's okay, Danny, I look worse than I really am. Come here, Sweetheart."

It was the sound of anguish in his cry that touched her heart. Her protective instincts were stronger than any pain she felt. She held out her arms, and Danny slowly came over to her. She held him and let him cry for her.

Danny would not leave her side. Tony had been watching them, and it was obvious the bond they shared. Not having Julie Ann there to come between them was an impressive sight. Jillian had been suffering for several months, but just the sight of Danny brought her back. She smiled for the first time, and her tears of grief turned to those of joy just from the sight of her son. This bond was very powerful. Father Michael had been so very right.

Danny was staring at her uneven locks and touching to see if there were pins holding up part of it. "Who cut your hair crooked?"

Jillian smiled. "Kiddo, I hit my head really hard when we had the car accident. They had to shave part of my hair off so they could give me some stitches. I had the other side cut, but it still doesn't match up yet. I know it looks silly, but it will all grow."

"Silly-Jilly," Danny smiled.

Reaching for his hand, she smiled. "Yes, Little Prince, you've got that right."

Tom was overjoyed. "Will you all excuse me for a moment? I have to hobble into my office and do one thing and then we can call for pizza."

"Let's get pepperoni. That's Jillian's favorite," Danny announced.

Tom looked at Jillian. Her favorite was easy sauce, extra cheese.

Jillian looked at her husband and smiled at him for the first time in such a long time. "It's a long story. Pepperoni is just fine."

Tony looked at Father Michael. "Why don't you show Danny around the house? It's his first time here."

"Of course, Tony, but it's your first time to see the new…"

"Father Michael, please."

"I would be happy to give Danny a tour. Come on Danny, which way do you think the kitchen is?"

"Jillian, I have so many things I want to say to you."

"Tony, please. I don't want to talk about it."

"Not that. It's about Danny. Just seeing how much he loves you. I have been harder on you than necessary. I want to tell you that I'm sorry. I want you to know that you can have a bigger part in…"

"Don't do this. Not to me. Just don't. Things are fine the way they are. I have been through a lot, but what could you give me as far as Danny is concerned? I really don't think under the circumstances I need to be a part of the decision-making process. Besides, that might cause a problem in your marriage. If you were single then maybe I could be more involved, but not now. Leave it the way it is. Don't look at me with pity and offer me a bone. Not when it comes to Danny, please. I'll be well soon and then what?"

"Jilly, that wasn't what I was doing. I was going to say that I'll keep you more updated on him, that's all."

"I'm sorry, Tony. I understand. Thanks. I would like to be more in the loop. Just the big stuff, though, okay? Danny loves to fill me in on all the little things in his life when we talk on the phone. I wouldn't mind a copy of his report card once in a while," she said. "Is there something more? I get the feeling you have something more to say about Danny."

"No. That's all. It just melted my heart when Danny saw you. To hear him sobbing for you broke my heart. There is a special bond between you and him. It's undeniable."

Danny came running in the living room. "Where's Lucy? I can't find her anywhere."

"Oh Kiddo, Tom's mother took her for a while. We can't take the chance that she will trip Tom, but as soon as he gets to put weight on his foot, we will have her back."

Jillian didn't want to tell Danny that it was her idea that Lucy left the house. She always needed attention and Jillian had none to give. Perhaps now she could come home.

"How long can you all stay?" Jillian asked.

"We have plenty of room," Tom added.

"Another three days, if that is alright with the both of you," Father Mike cheerfully said. "We can go to a hotel if that would be better."

Jillian looked at her son. "Danny, did you see the room with the twin beds and the big dinosaur on the wall?"

"I sure did. That's a cool room," he beamed.

"Well, that room was decorated just for you. That is your room whenever you come to see us. You and your daddy can sleep in your room."

"Wow, I get my own room at your house? Cool! If Lucy comes home can she sleep in my room?"

Tom smiled and patted Danny on the head. "We wouldn't have it any other way. I'll call my mother and have her bring Lucy home right away."

"Father Mike, we still haven't fixed up the guest house so you can have the den. Tom and I are in the guestroom. Neither of us, of course, can climb the stairs."

"That'll be fine, Jillian."

"The pizza is here. I saw out the window," Danny hollered, running towards the door.

"Danny..."

"I know, Daddy. I'm waiting."

The next morning, Father Michael took Tony and Danny to see some of the sights. Tony had not been to the city, and Danny wanted him to ride the tour bus and go for a horse drawn carriage ride like he did when he was visiting last summer. It would be too cold for that, but they would soon find that out.

Jillian and Tom sat together in the kitchen sipping on coffee and sharing a sweet roll.

"Sweetheart, I was afraid that this wasn't going to be a good idea. I'm so happy seeing Danny make you smile again."

"You knew?"

"Yes, it was Father Mike's idea. I told him not to bring them yet, and he gave me his, trust me routine, and I did."

"I'm glad they came. Seeing Danny is wonderful medicine for me."

"That was entirely obvious. That child loves you so deeply."

"Tom?"

"What, Sweetheart?"

"I'm sorry. I'm so sorry I shut you out like I did."

"It's okay..."

"No, it isn't okay. That was wrong of me. You are my beloved. I live for your love and I shut you out. The pain was so deep. I was dying inside, and I didn't want anyone or anything. I had even forgotten about Danny. I was so lost. I know what I felt wasn't exclusive, but to me, for me, I was so deeply wounded. I wanted to just stop breathing. How could one day be so powerful? Just one day? Do you forgive me?"

"I already have."

Tom put his arm around her and gently kissed her. As she responded, tears of grief, and those of joy, overcame both of them.

Chapter Fourteen

It had been six months since the accident, and both Jillian and Tom had, for the most part, recovered. Jillian needed to keep the pins in her ankle for another two months. Her knee was still sore, but she was walking. So was Tom, his arm was completely healed. The surgeon had released him from wearing his walking boot, and he was very comfortable with that. The broken ribs had healed nicely, without any problems. Tony had been very kind and sent Danny for visits every month. If he weren't able to bring him, he would send Martha along. It was usually a quick trip over a weekend, but Jillian treasured every moment.

Julie Ann had accompanied Danny a few times, but she was bonding with Angela and her new baby sister. Morgan and Melissa's daughter was now three months old. They named her Mary. Jillian was doing better emotionally, but she still didn't want to talk about losing the baby.

"Sarah Reynolds called this morning. Her sister, Madison, just built a new home near Dallas, and you'll never guess what?"

"She's coming to visit?"

"Sure! Why not? But seriously, she asked me to decorate their new home. I was thinking, it might be fun, and it shouldn't take me too long. She knows I only do commercial, but given that I did Sarah and Phillip's house, how can I say no? What do you think?" She said with a smile.

"I think if it is what you want then go do it. It's about time you went back to work and started helping with the bills around here."

Jillian lowered her brow. Her pouty lip emerged into a smile. It was time for her to get back to work. She hadn't even thought about work in over a year.

"I hope I haven't lost my touch," she giggled. "I'll call her then and let her know I'll fly out either Wednesday or Thursday. I'll only be there a few days and then go back when the orders come in. Want to go with me?"

"I'd love to, but I can't. I have to be in court the end of the week."

"Tom, I think we need to go out to the ranch. What about when I get back from Dallas? If we took your plane we could spend less time driving and more time ranching."

Tom looked pleased. "We'll go for a three day weekend after you get back. I'll call Alice and let her know we'll be coming."

Jillian liked Texas. It had been years since she was last there. She did a huge job for Sarah Reynolds's father, John Thomas Parker. He was an oil man, and the sky was the limit for his new corporate office building. They hadn't seen eye to eye, and he had fired her, only to pay much more to get her back on the job. They came to an understanding, and she ended up with more referrals than she could use. Sarah still talks about how Jillian was the only woman that could "boss Daddy around."

* * *

Madison Jordan was picking Jillian up at the airport. Jillian was searching the terminal for someone who even slightly resembled Sarah as they had never met. Jillian spotted a tall, slender woman that looked nothing like Sarah, but Jillian was almost sure that this had to be Madison. Her auburn hair was long and straight. She had straight bangs that tipped her exceptionally dark eyelashes. From a distance, her face looked flawless. Jillian caught a glimpse of her enormous breasts and gasped. As she got closer, she could see a little more plastic surgery. Just as she was wondering if perhaps this wasn't her after all, the woman looked over at Jillian and called out.

"Jillian Connors, is that you?"

Jillian raised her hand and waved then reached down as her bag made its way around to her on the luggage carousel. Madison was only five years older than Sarah, but she looked much older.

"Hi Madison, it's nice to meet you. Your sister and I are great friends, but you must know that already?"

"We'll see who knows more about whom," she said, in an anomalous tone that Jillian wasn't quite sure of.

"I beg your pardon?" Jillian asked.

With a syrupy smile that never reached her eyes, Madison just smiled. "Oh, don't mind me. I have a car waiting out front, so we better go. It's very sweet of you to do this for us. Calvin will be so pleased. Daddy told him all about you, and he can't wait to meet you this evening."

Outside the door was an exquisite stretch limousine. The driver immediately got out of the limo and opened the trunk. He took Jillian's suitcase and placed it carefully inside and quickly closed the lid. Then he hastened to open the door for the two women. It was luxurious and expensive. Jillian climbed in, and Madison was right behind her. She told the driver to take them out to the ranch.

"Maybe I should check in at the hotel first before I see your new home."

"Sorry, Dear. You'll be staying at the ranch with us. We wouldn't have it any other way. Cal wants to have a cookout tomorrow. James, no pun intended, will be our driver until you are ready to leave. We want you to see our style and what we like. We want the house to represent who we are."

Jillian was amused. This woman tickled her. "Who are you?"

"Oh, you're funny, Jill. We're going to get along just fine."

Jillian swallowed hard. She couldn't remember anyone ever calling her Jill. Why she didn't correct her, she wasn't sure. She let it slip by, this time, making a mental note that she would say something if it happened again.

"Daddy is coming for the cook out tomorrow. He loves our beef. Well, I think he secretly is in love with you, you know?"

"No, I don't know. You're kidding, right?"

"Jill, would I kid with you? James, stop off at Henderson's and run in and get my order. We can't have a cookout without whiskey."

As they waited for the driver to accommodate his passenger's request at Henderson's, Madison began asking Jillian a ton of questions.

"I'm surprised Sarah didn't mention anything about me getting married last year. She and Phillip were at our wedding."

Madison smiled a wicked smile. "Oh, Daddy will be so jealous."

"Really? Your father was such a ladies' man. I can't believe I made such an impression on him. Actually, we fought like cats and dogs."

"That's what he likes about you. He said you were feisty. He told me you got under his skin. I can't wait to see the look on his face when he learns you got married. He might stop by today. We'll see," she said with that evil smile of hers.

James got back into the driver's seat and headed for the ranch. It took several hours to get there, and Jillian now understood why she would be staying there rather than a hotel. It looked like something out of an old western movie. From the window of the limo, Jillian could see expansive pastures that appeared to have no end and herds of cattle grazing off in the distance. The house was enormous. Standing near the front door was J.T. He looked the same as he did six years ago. He was tall and lean with just a tiny hint of a spare tire in the front. His gray hair was short, and he wore a sizeable cowboy hat. He appeared as if he had emerged from an old time western. He sported blue jeans with a western dress shirt completed by a blazer, bolo tie and cowboy boots. Sarah had his huge blue eyes, but she feared Madison had his disposition. She was a forceful woman, and Jillian could sense that this was a woman who always got what she wanted.

The limo pulled in under the portico and parked. James helped the two women out of the limo and carried the packages around the back to the kitchen. Jillian walked toward the porch to reacquaint herself with J.T. He reached for her suitcase.

"Jillian, lands sake, you are skinny, girl. What happened to that luscious figure of yours?"

Luscious figure? Crap, he must be drunk! Sure I've lost weight, but I'm not that thin."

"J.T., it's good to see you, too. You haven't changed a bit."

With that, J.T. scooped her up and gave her a hug. Jillian didn't smell any alcohol on his breath but thought it was unusual behavior, even for him.

"J.T., you can put me down now, please. What's gotten into you anyway?"

"Daddy put her down! Stop clowning around. She's a married woman."

J.T. looked a little unsettled. He set her down and looked her straight in the eyes.

"Is that true? You got married?"

"Yes, J.T., I was married a little over a year ago."

"Who took you away from me?"

"His name is Tom Bentley. I only use Connors professionally now."

Jillian wondered why she had said that. This was her first job since she and Tom were married and she had never thought about what name she would be using. It didn't matter unless J.T. or Madison were planning to give her referrals. She would cross that bridge when she came to it. She wondered why J.T. seemed so disappointed that she was married. He had never shown any noticeable interests in her romantically in the past. She hoped this wouldn't become an issue. Madison seemed to be enjoying this and that bothered Jillian. Somehow this situation just wasn't very comfortable, and she found herself wanting to go home. She wanted to forget she ever met Madison and this misguided reunion with John Thomas Parker. Jillian had an uneasy feeling in the pit of her stomach.

Madison ushered her into the house and up the massive staircase to her room. Jillian, again, felt as if she had stepped onto an old western movie set, as she quickly looked around her room.

Jillian unpacked her small suitcase and took a shower. Afterward, she went downstairs and looked around. Everything about this place was so dreadfully overdone. The furnishings were massive, and she thought a bit ornate. The colors were hideous. Was this what Madison was referring to? Did she hear her correctly? Did she say they wanted the new house to represent who they were? Did she even want credit for bringing this repugnant reflection to their new home? There was no way she could turn them down now. This was a favor to her dear friend, Sarah. Maybe she should call her. No, she couldn't do that. Sarah would tell her to do what she felt was best, and she didn't want this to come between them. Jillian let out an audible sigh, as she glanced at the paintings on the wall. Her thoughts were disrupted when she realized she heard footsteps behind her.

"Pretty terrible, isn't it?"

Startled, Jillian whirled around, only to come face to face with an incredibly attractive man.

"What?"

"Hello there, Miss," tipping his hat to her. "I'm Calvin. You must be Jill. It's dang nice to meet you."

"It's Jillian," she smiled. "It's very nice to meet you as well, Calvin," extending her hand, encouraging an introductory handshake. "I was just looking around at your lovely home."

Calvin began to laugh. "My wife thinks the bigger, the better. Trust me; this will not carry over into the new house. We'll be entertaining more there, and I'll be danged if it will look like the ranch house."

"Oh? Well, you two work it out and let me know."

His tone changed slightly. "I'm telling you now, it isn't going to happen."

Jillian felt as if she had stepped into someone else's nightmare. She wanted no part of this battle, let alone being in the middle of, what she saw as, an upcoming war. They should have worked it out long before she got there.

"Would you excuse me? I need to call my husband."

Jillian quickly found a patio door and went out to call Tom. It was good to hear his voice.

"Hi, Sweetheart, how's the Lone Star state?"

"Tom, I don't think this is going to fly. At least not right now. Madison and her husband are not at all in agreement on what they want. They are both determined, and I won't be caught in the middle. You know me, fight or flight, and I feel like running. I'll see you tomorrow if I can get a flight out."

"I'll ask Donna to perform a miracle or two and get your flight changed."

"That would be wonderful. But if she's too busy, I'll find a way to bide my time."

"I'll have her call you when she gets back from lunch. Honey, is it really that bad? I know you were looking forward to getting 'back in the saddle' again," he said, laughing at his own lame joke.

"Oh, please, Tom. Back in the saddle? That's funny. You have no idea."

"Sweetheart, I need to be back in court at one-thirty. Try to enjoy yourself. I love you."

"Okay, I love you, too."

J.T. was sitting in a chair on the patio when Jillian noticed him there. She was embarrassed, knowing he had overheard her conversation with Tom. She was thankful she hadn't said much, but she wasn't sure just how much he had heard.

"J.T.?"

"Are you having trouble with my son in law? I wouldn't worry too much about what he tells you. And as far as Madison is concerned, she only thinks she has the final say."

"I don't work this way. I'm a commercial designer as you well know and not a residential decorator. This isn't my forte. They aren't on the same page, and that leaves me in the middle of an awkward situation that I would much rather not be in. You know me, J.T., remember?"

"Yep, how can I forget? When I think of how much I had to pay you..."

"'Had' to pay me? I was worth every penny. Or, at least, that is what you told everyone. You even gave me a huge bonus. Remember?" She snorted. "What about all those referrals? Remember what you told all of them? You said I was the best at any price."

Jillian was feeling rather lofty, and suddenly she realized she hadn't lost her touch after all. Up until a year ago, she was one of the most sought after designers in the country. She wasn't giving up that title now. If she could go up against John Thomas Parker, she could most certainly handle his spoiled daughter and son in law.

"You are. You are the best. I'm sorry, girly."

"Girly? You have been drinking? What in the world? Girly? Really?"

"Why do you limp? I don't remember you ever limping."

"I was in a pretty bad car accident. It really messed up my leg. My ankle and knee suffered the worst. I'll get the pins out of my ankle soon, and there should be no more limping. Thanks for asking," she said wondering why she said anything at all. Her flight had turned to fight.

Jillian went storming in the house. She found a woman wiping off the window sills and asked where Mrs. Jordan was. The young woman said she could find her in the kitchen.

"Where's the kitchen?"

Madison was at the sink rinsing out a large mixing bowl. Jillian calmed her voice. "Oh, there you are. I'm a little confused. I'm getting mixed signals from both you and your husband. I just had a conversation with Calvin, and you both have different ideas about what you want to be accomplished. We're definitely not on the same page. We can sit down and work on it, or I can come back some other time."

"Jill..."

"It's Jillian, please."

"Jillian, there is some misunderstanding, I'm sure. Calvin will go along with whatever I want. Let me go find him."

Jillian wasn't in the mood for this "he said, she said" stuff. Moments later, Madison and Calvin appeared in the kitchen.

"Calvin, I want you to tell Jill, crap, I mean, Jillian that whatever I want for the house is alright with you," sounding peeved.

"Maddy, I already explained to Jillian that whatever you want is fine with me. If y'all will excuse me, I have things to do."

The smile on Madison's face was one of pure evil. Jillian looked at Madison and then over to Calvin, who was quickly and quietly exiting the kitchen.

"So, we'll go over to the house after lunch, which I made by myself by the way. Oh, and Jillian, the sky's the limit–Daddy's paying."

Jillian's cell rang just in time for her to exit the kitchen. It was Donna, Tom's secretary, calling about changing Jillian's flight.

"Never mind, Donna, It looks like I'm staying in Texas. Thanks so much for calling me back. I'll call Tom later. I really appreciate you wanting to help me, though."

After lunch, they piled in the limo and drove to the city. The house in Dallas was breathtaking. Madison and J.T. were showing Jillian around. It was a large home and, under different circumstances, it might have been a fun project.

"I can see all the possibilities in this beautiful design. Did you have a local builder?"

"We used Daddy's builder."

"I see. Well, let's start upstairs on the master bedroom."

"Wait a minute," J.T. stammered.

"Maddy Girl, you run along now. I told you that Jillian will do it all. If you don't like it, you can tear the damned house down. I paid for this house, and I'm paying Jillian because she will give it what it needs. She is the best. You butt out!"

"Butt out? This is my house!"

This was getting stranger by the minute. Jillian's flight instinct was reminding her again that this was not a good idea. Had she misjudged Madison terribly? She was certain she always got her own way, but J.T. had her buffaloed. J.T. was calling all the shots, and Jillian was very surprised. Madison just stood there not saying a word. Finally, she walked over to the door without as much as a whine. She said she would be back in three hours, and they had better be done. Jillian was so stunned she could hardly believe her ears.

"I hate what she did to my ranch house. What did you think?"

Jillian looked surprised. "That was your ranch house?"

"Well, who did you think it belonged to? Did Maddy tell you it was hers?"

"Well, no, I just assumed," she fibbed. "So they are living at your ranch? Where are you living? In Dallas?"

"It took over two years to build this house so they moved to the ranch and brought all that crap with them. I bought a condominium, and that is where I've been living. I'm done with the ranch. I'm planning to sell it. I told the kids they could use it until this place was finished. So let's get this place done," he said in a gruff tone.

"I don't understand your attitude towards me. Honestly, I don't."

J.T. let out a cowboy yelp and took off his hat. For a second Jillian thought he was going to slap her on the butt with his hat. She scooted away with a surprised look on her face.

"Jillian, don't pay me no mind. I'm just a little peeved that you went and got married. I was planning to take you out on a date.

"J.T., you weren't?"

"Yes, I was. I've been thinking about you for years. Hey, you want to fool around?"

"No, J.T., I do not."

"I didn't think so."

Chapter Fifteen

Flying over New York City was always an amazing sight. The huge buildings, and the way the water looked from the plane. Jillian never got tired of seeing the city from the air. Tom had sent a car for her. He was still in court, and Jillian thought to surprise him with dinner, but she was exhausted. She longed to take a nap and couldn't bear to hear one more "Y'all." The driver took her home, and she came in through the kitchen. On the counters and the table were vases filled with red roses. A banner taped to the refrigerator read, "Welcome Home!" Jillian was touched. Tom was sentimental, and she loved that about him. Seeing all these roses reminded her of a sad day. Tom had been getting ready to fly to London after his sister's accident. Jillian had gone to the loft where she had stayed while she was in New York working on Tom's building. Tom had an apartment near his office. They'd had a terrible disagreement the week before, and Tom had assumed their relationship was over. Jillian had gone back home to Sweetwater. Tom had ordered hundreds of yellow roses and had them sent over to the loft, hoping she would return and find them. He offered his apologies in a note and wished her well. He had hoped they could remain friends, and the yellow roses were a peace offering. Jillian had come back to New York in hopes of reconciling; knowing that she really did love him. When she saw all the roses, her heart sank as she thought it was too late. Their love was meant to be. Only weeks later, they were back in each other's arms.

Jillian went upstairs to take a bath. The scent of more roses met her as she reached the door. She felt as if she had just entered a rose garden. Bouquets of roses had been eloquently placed throughout the bathroom as well. She sat down on the edge of the tub and smiled.

Alone with her thoughts, she tried to relax in the hot, steamy water. She and Tom had been through so much and yet they ended up together, after all. She closed her eyes and drifted off. The coolness of the water woke her, and she shuddered from the cold. She let out some of the water and replaced it with just enough hot water to warm it back up. She had no idea how long she had slept, but her skin had definitely had enough soaking time to be wrinkled. Climbing out of the tub, she glanced down at her leg. There were the scars to remind her of the accident. She put on her bathrobe and stepped into her slippers. She went down to the kitchen to fix a cup of tea. She loved the quietness of her home. She loved having all her favorite things around her. Some of which were, at one time, her mother's favorite things. She thought how nice it would be to sit here and have a cup of tea and chat with her mother. She thought about how they had laughed and cried and then she thought about the argument they had over her pregnancy with Danny. It was just like it had happened yesterday.

Tony had gone off to college and didn't even know she was pregnant. How upset her mother had been. Her mother wanted to call Tony's parents so Tony would find out about her pregnancy. She thought about how mad she had been at her mother for wanting to do that. She thought about how she never told Tony. Look at where they all are now.

Jillian thought about calling Father Michael, but she was just too tired. She texted Tom to bring home Chinese food, and she went to the living room to relax and read a book. Lucy jumped up on her lap, and she stroked her silky coat.

The jarring ring of the phone disrupted the world she had entered as she was reading. She reached for the phone and found Father Michael on the other end.

"Hello, my psychic priest. How do you always know when I need to hear your voice?"

"Jillian, those are two words you should never put together," he sighed loudly. "So you needed to hear my voice? How was your trip to Dallas?"

"It was educational, to say the least. I learned more about the Parker family than I cared to. I had no idea... Sarah seems so normal. How can two sisters be so different?"

"So you had a good time I take it?"

"Yes. It was good," she laughed. "I'll need to go back in a few weeks when my deliveries come in. Tom said he might be able to go with me and spend a few days. That would be great. We're going to the ranch in a few days. Tom was supposed to be done with court last Friday, but it carried over until today. We'll probably leave on Thursday. We need this time together without interruptions. We're going to fly out in his plane and bring Lucy along with us. What's going on with you? Is there anything new happening in Sweetwater?"

"Not much with Sweetwater, but I'm thinking about retiring."

"Priests don't retire. They work until they… Oh, I can't even say it. No, I can't think it either."

"I'm not sick, and I'm not dying. I'm just thinking about traveling a little. You're so dramatic," he chided. "I discussed it with the bishop, and he needs me to stay on in some capacity. We'll see what the future brings."

"Well, it's good you aren't dying," she giggled. "I was really missing Mom right now. I know you do, too. I thought misery might love some company, that's all. That's why I wanted to hear your voice. Oops, Tom's home; I've got to get off the phone. We're having Chinese food, and I need to set the table. I love you."

"I love you more."

Jillian swallowed hard as the tears filled her eyes. "Mom always said that to me."

"I know, Honey. Now it's my turn. Call me when you get back from the ranch that I have never been to see."

"Oh, brother," she giggled, "or should I say, father? We'll get you out there one of these days. Talk to you soon."

Tom was already in the kitchen with their dinner in his hands.

"I missed you," he said reaching for her. "I have a surprise. We can fly over to the ranch first thing in the morning."

Jillian leaned in for her kiss and lingered, teasing him. "That's super, I can hardly wait. I guess I'll cancel the doggie day spa for Lucy tomorrow. I'll give her a quickie in the tub tonight so she smells pleasant for our trip."

Lucy looked up at Jillian and cocked her head. She began to jump up and down and ran to where her leash was hanging.

"No Lucy, we aren't going anywhere. Oh, look what I've done. I'd better get her a cookie or something. She thinks she is going to see the groomer."

Tom looked amused. "She got all that from, doggie day spa?"

Lucy continued to jump and bark until Jillian diverted her attention with a cookie.

"She isn't much like Sydney, but she looks more and more like him now that she's grown up. Her hair is silky like Sydney's, and she has his black and white coat, but that is where it ends. Sydney seemed to notice my feelings. He was always there for me, but Lucy is not so intuitive. I really wish she were."

"Sweetie, Lucy is her own dog. The more you compare her to Sydney, the more she will fail in your eyes. Give her credit for who she is. I know there will never be another Sydney, but Lucy is pretty special, too. Just now she proved how smart she is. Oh, and she follows you all through the house. When you are home, she wants nothing to do with me. She sits by the door when you aren't home and sulks. So like it or not, that dog adores you."

Jillian picked up Lucy and gave her a gentle hug. "I'm sorry, Lucy," she said patting her head. "You are very special. We should have named you Oreo. You look like a big chocolate and cream cookie."

Lucy cocked her head again then licked Jillian's face. She was tiny compared to Sydney. They were always mindful of her size, and always on the lookout as to where she was. They didn't want to accidentally step on her.

"Hope you don't mind, but I went to Antonio's for our dinner. It just seemed easier on the way home. I got you your favorite, lasagna and garlic bread."

"Yum! What an excellent choice."

Jillian smiled as she took out the plates and napkins. She kissed her husband again then put the food on the table.

"Thank you for all the beautiful roses, and the banner was very impressive. I'm a spoiled woman. Don't ever stop, please?"

Things were becoming more normal between them. They still hadn't talked about the accident and perhaps they never would. Tom had tried a few times, but Jillian always stopped him. She just wasn't ready. They hadn't discussed trying to have another baby, but they weren't using any birth control either.

"When's the last time you talked with Morgan?"

"Just before I left for Dallas. He and Melissa were thinking about making a trip to see us. Morgan was worried the new baby would upset me. I can't believe little Mary is almost four months old, and I haven't seen her yet. Of course, the baby wouldn't upset me. It certainly wasn't her fault. They're sending pictures in a few weeks. I'm happy they named her after Mom."

"It wasn't anyone's fault. You know that don't you? It most certainly wasn't our fault either. That truck skidded on some ice, and we just happened to be in his way."

"I'm not blaming him. It's just... I really don't want to discuss it."

Tom honored his wife's request and changed the subject.

"When is Danny coming again? Maybe we could arrange it at the same time as when Morgan comes to visit."

"What a great idea. I'll call Tony when we get back from the country. I wish I had time to do the guest house. We're running out of room inside."

"We could hire someone if you don't mind."

"No, I really want to do it myself. I have a few plans drawn out. After I get back from Dallas, I'll give it a go."

They sat down to enjoy their dinner and after they had eaten Jillian told Tom to go relax while she straightened up the kitchen. Tom didn't argue. He was beat from being in and out of court all this time. He went in, and literally, plopped down in his easy chair. Twenty minutes later, Jillian appeared wearing only her apron.

* * *

The weather was perfect for flying. They were in there in less than an hour. Hank picked them up at the small airport and drove them to the ranch. Alice was waiting with lunch and the promise of a delicious dinner. Both Hank and Alice were pleased to hear that the ranch now belonged to Tom and Jillian.

After a light lunch, Tom and Jillian left Lucy with Alice, and Tom saddled up two horses. They rode slowly out passed the corrals and headed for their tree. Alice sent a little snack with them. They tied the horses to the tree and spread out the small blanket. Tom looked into the basket and laughed.

"Sweetheart, do you want cookies or cheese and wine?"

"We have cheese and wine? Why that Alice is such a romantic," she giggled, "I'll have the wine, a la carte."

Tom took out the plastic wine glasses, poured some for each of them and handed a glass of wine to Jillian. They were reminiscing about the day, where under this tree; they had made love for the first time. This was only their third time out to this spot, and Jillian couldn't have been more pleased.

"Tom," she said in a teasing voice, with a seductive smile. "Can we just build a hut right here and stay forever."

"Sure, Sweetheart, whatever your heart desires. It might get a bit nippy in the winter time, though."

Leaning in to kiss him, she whispered. "Oh, I'm quite sure you will keep me warm."

"I promise to always protect you from the wind and rain. I will shelter you with my body."

"With your naked body? I love you so much. When we share times like this together, it's like before we were married. We don't tease each other as much as we used to. I miss that. I remember the endless hours on the phone when I was in Colorado, and you were in New York. Those were playful times for us. Sharing our love and talking about how much we missed one another. The phone sex we used to have."

Tom grinned. "Oh, I remember that very well. It all seemed so easy then for us to be together and love each other. I remember how excited we would be after being apart. Wow, do I ever!"

"Tom, remember when we were in Atlanta? That was such a turning point, but looking back, it had some really funny parts to it."

"Sweetie, I'm not sure I can go so far as to say any of it was funny. All I remember is how distressing it was in the beginning."

"Well, yes, the first part was miserable for us. We hadn't seen each other for several months, and we both thought it was over between us. I was with Tony to be near Danny, and you, very lovingly, stepped aside. There was never a day that had gone by that I didn't regret my decision to be with Tony just to have Danny in my life. I should have tried to figure out another way. It was so wrong of me and selfish, but I felt like I had no choice. I missed you more than you could possibly ever know. I even started resenting poor Tony for it. Every moment with Danny was precious for me, but I longed for you. My body would ache for your touch. I wanted to hear your voice. I thought I would never see you again."

A disheartened look came over Tom's face. "There was never a reason for us to see one another after we parted. I missed you so much. I was so badly hurt, but I was willing to move on without you. I let you go because I loved you so much. I knew that being with your son meant everything to you, and it had nothing to do with you not loving me."

"That is so true, but when you showed up in Atlanta, I felt it in my heart. By the time you left my hotel room that night, I knew that it was you that would always hold my heart. I could never be happy unless your arms were around me. I wanted so much to make love with you that night. Just to be in your arms and feel your love, one more time. When you left that night, I ran after you, but the elevator door was already closing. I turned around to find the stairs and ran right into some poor woman knocking me to the floor. I picked myself up and found the stairs. By the time I got down to the lobby, you were on your way back up to my room to fight for me. Remember?"

"How could I forget? I was knocking on your door half yelling and half begging you to open it up. I had no idea you weren't in the room. Then I went back to the elevator with my tail between my legs, thinking you refused to let me in."

"Meanwhile, at the same time, I was running all around the lobby looking for you. When I realized you were gone, I was devastated. I didn't even know where you were staying. Then I took the elevator up to my room, crying my eyes out, only then to discover I didn't have my key. Back down I went to the front desk. That poor front desk clerk didn't know what to think. She took one look at me and wasn't sure what to do. I had mascara running down the streams of tears on my face, and I had smeared it trying to wipe the tears away. I was a mess. Then you showed up, and the rest is history. My hero! You were so funny when you told the clerk I always got upset when I couldn't find my key. She looked at both us like we just escaped from the mental ward."

Tom was laughing now. "Yes, her face was priceless. A moment we can definitely share with our children."

Jillian went from laughing to crying at the mention of children. Tom looked at her with such tenderness.

"I'm sorry, Sweetheart. Forgive me."

"It's okay, honestly," she said, reaching for him. "Atlanta will be a great story to tell our kids one day. I'm really okay. Losing our first child was horrible. I know it was no one's fault, and there is no one to blame. I have to believe that God has a plan for our lives, and He gave me time to heal. I want to move forward now, and I love you so much for giving me the time I needed to grieve and to get beyond what happened. We have each other and, together, we will be happy. I love you. You are the best thing in my life."

Tom set his glass down and held her. She kissed him and her kisses became more passionate until there was no space between them. Jillian slowly and seductively unbuttoned his shirt.

Susan Vance

Chapter Sixteen

Jillian and Tom flew to Dallas a few days before she planned to start working on Madison and Calvin's home. They went to visit some old friends of Tom's and did a little sightseeing mixed with shopping. Tom flew back to New York Sunday afternoon, and Jillian called Madison that evening to let her know she would need a driver first thing in the morning to take her to the house. She assured Madison that she would be delighted to see her, and asked her to come by at the end of the week. Madison had expressed wanting to be there Monday morning, but she reassured Jillian that Daddy had explained to her that she needed to stay out of her way. When Jillian reiterated; it appeared Madison got the message. That didn't seem to stop J.T., however. He stopped by every day without fail, and Jillian was losing her patience with him quickly. He was starting to annoy her to the point of her walking off the job. She wondered if he was getting a little senile or was he just more pig-headed than she had remembered. Jillian tried to be polite; however, it just wasn't working. She was just going to have to tell him how she felt. She knew it was going to bruise his ego. She found his behavior rude and, even more so, very distracting.

"I appreciate you stopping by, but you are getting in my way."

J.T., looking indignant, snickered at her. "Oh, here we go again, right?"

"Oh, come on J.T. You know how I am. I can't have disruptions when I work. I need to be able to give the job my fullest attention. I appreciate your wanting to help, but don't you have an oil well to pump or something?"

"Now that's funny, Jillian, very funny. If you're a good girl, maybe I'll leave you one when I die."

"Oh, J.T., do you promise?"

"You think that's funny, do you? Well, just for that little missy, I've changed my mind."

"Little Missy?"

Jillian was laughing now. Even J.T. must have realized how ridiculous that sounded.

"Okay, okay, I'll leave you to your misery if you have dinner with me tonight."

Jillian wanted to turn him down, but she didn't know how to refuse him. She had just stabbed his ego right in the heart and to turn him down for dinner seemed like adding insult to injury. Her cell rang just in time to rescue her from the moment.

"Hello?"

"Hi, it's Sarah. Guess what?" She asked without waiting for a response. "I'm in Dallas. Let's get together tonight for dinner. The kids are in Denver with Phillip."

"I would love to. Come by the hotel and we'll plan it out from there. I'm so excited to get to see you."

"Okay. I'll see you later. I'm on my way over to see Daddy in a little while. Then I'll be by to get you. Well, that is if Daddy gives me a driver. I'm in a cab right now. What hotel are you staying at?"

"Oh wait. I have a driver. Where are you staying? I'll come get you."

"I'm going to stay at Daddy's condo; do you know where it is?"

"No, but I'm sure my driver does. See you around six o 'clock."

J.T. approached Jillian with a sullen look on his face. "Hey, I asked first."

"I'm having dinner with your daughter J.T. That was Sarah."

"Sarah's here?"

"Yes, and you better get going. She is on her way over to your condo to see you right now."

That was all it took for J.T. to leave her alone. He was on his way out the door. She finished up at the house for the day and went to her hotel. Jillian took a hot shower and got dressed. She put on a pair of jeans and a tee shirt. She was so slender, and for the first time in her life, she really liked the way she looked. She never minded her shape so much in the past, but she always carried a few extra pounds. Since the accident, the weight hadn't returned. Her hips were still curvy, but her waist was small, and she looked very slender. She knew Sarah would be surprised to see her new figure. Alone in the hotel room, she suddenly thought of her mother. It was always times like these that would remind her that her mom was gone. This would have been the time of the day she would have called her. Just to confer and talk about their day. So much had changed. She would have always called

Father Michael, too. She still called him, but just not as much. Everything was just so different now. She sent Tom a text letting him know of her plans with Sarah then was about to go downstairs to find her driver when the phone rang.

"Don't be mad, my friend. Daddy insisted he come with us to dinner. He's paying. Sorry, it wasn't in my plans. I really needed some girl talk tonight."

"That's okay, but is there something wrong?"

"It can wait until later. Maybe we can talk tomorrow."

Jillian was curious. She wondered if Sarah had some troubles. Sarah wasn't shy. She was sure she would get around to telling her what was going on eventually. It was odd to hear Sarah sounding so ominous.

Jillian went downstairs and asked the driver to take her to the condo. Ten minutes later, they were parked out in front of a large condominium complex. The driver entered a code to open the wide gate, and he pulled up to the door. The driver keyed into J.T.'s unit, and they came right down. J.T. climbed in first, then Sarah, putting J.T. in the middle of the girls. Jillian could smell liquor on his breath, and hoped they weren't in for too wild of an evening.

Jillian smiled and reached to embrace Sarah, but with J.T. in the middle it was impossible. Sarah laughed, waved a little wave and smiled back.

"Where are we going?"

"Daddy said since he's paying he got to pick. I hope you're hungry."

The driver pulled into a very busy parking lot. The building was overly impressive for the sign they boasted; "Larry's Steakhouse." It looked a little too fancy for jeans, but it was too late to change now. Sarah opened the door as the driver came around and he held it open as he helped her out. J.T. got out and took Jillian's hand to help her out. She looked at him and lowered her brows. He wasn't going to take no for an answer. The aroma from the steakhouse was very tantalizing. Jillian felt bad for the driver as he was staying in the limousine. Sarah looked radiant, as always. Her long blonde hair was dancing to the rhythm of the slight breeze. She was wearing a rather short skirt and a slinky top. Jillian remembered her being more conservative. Jillian's jeans and tee shirt were more Sarah's style, but things seem to be changing more every day.

As they walked in, Jillian could see people waiting for tables, but they were taken immediately into the dining room. It was a large booth with plenty of room. Jillian was relieved. The idea of being cooped up with J.T. all evening at a small table was nauseating, to say the least. She wouldn't hurt Sarah for the world, but the rest of her family was a bit over the top for Jillian. J.T. ordered for all of them right down to the salad dressing. Jillian told the server to bring her ranch dressing on the side as she smiled brazenly at J.T. She had never been a blue cheese fan and wasn't about to start now. Jillian's steak was done to perfection, and her baked potato was creamy and fluffy. She was surprisingly delighted that J.T. had ordered extra butter and sour cream. They had all chatted during dinner and J.T., much to Jillian's surprise, behaved very well in front of his daughter. After dinner, J.T. said he was taking the limo back to his place and would send it back to the restaurant right away so the girls could go bar hopping. He was only kidding, but Sarah gave him a look which made him apologize. He kissed his daughter and looked at Jillian, who quickly thanked him for dinner. He took her hand and kissed the back of it. Jillian gave him one of her looks, and he quickly released it. The waiter came over and said the driver was finished eating and would be waiting for him out in the front. Jillian was impressed that J.T. had ordered something for James and had him come inside to eat it. That was the J.T. she had remembered.

"I'm sorry about that. I don't know what's gotten into Daddy. He has never been like this."

Jillian smiled. She decided not to share with Sarah what a pain her father had become. She didn't want to hurt her. What would be the point anyway? "Don't give it another thought. So, what do you think your father ordered us for dessert?"

Just as Sarah was going to render a guess, the server brought in two small slivers of cheesecake.

"I adore cheesecake," Sarah said, barely touching her piece.

"Sarah, talk to me."

"I don't know how to start, but I've met someone," she said lowering her head.

"What? Sarah? What about Phillip?"

"Don't judge me."

"I'm not judging you," Jillian said slightly irritated. "Go on."

"I never meant for this to happen. I'm not even sure exactly how it did happen. One minute I was helping a friend with an internet dating site and then next thing I know I'm chatting with some of the members of the group."

"Chatting? I don't understand. What are you talking about?"

"Just listen and I'll tell you what happened," Sarah said. "I was helping a friend get acquainted with this guy, and he started chatting with me instead. I don't know why I didn't just close the screen, but I was curious. My friend, Jessica, decided this wasn't for her, but he was more than happy to just chat with me. I thought I would just say hello, and the next thing I know we are chatting for hours. We did it again the next day and the next."

"Why did you keep this up? I mean you're not single, you're happily married. I'm confused. It sounds like more than idle curiosity to me."

"I'm trying to tell you. Hush and let me go on."

"Okay."

"The next day, I peeked just to see if there were any messages from him, and there were lots of them. I replied to all his messages then suddenly he came on the chat screen. His picture came up, and he was gorgeous. He lives in New York City and works on Wall Street. He has never been married and is thirty-six. He reminded me of your Tom. He told me that he hadn't found anyone he wanted to spend his life with. I posted my picture..."

"You didn't? Oh, Sarah, why would you do that?"

"It just felt right. I can't explain it. He said I was beautiful."

"Well, you are beautiful. That shouldn't have been any surprise."

"Jillian, we have been talking online for four months, and he wants to meet me in person. He said he would fly to Denver in a few months, but was very tied up with some investments. He said we are soul mates. He wants me to divorce Phillip and marry him right away."

"No! You don't even know this man. Sarah, wake up! He could be a serial killer for all you know. Soul mates? There isn't any such thing. Love comes from mutual trust and respect. Oh, Sarah, no..."

"Oh, my sweet innocent friend, Trevor isn't a killer. He is so wonderful. He even wants me to share in his latest investment that he has kept all to himself. I haven't agreed yet, but if this works out we will be millionaires together."

Jillian suspected this was one of those internet frauds, and Sarah had fallen victim to it. She had been emotionally reeled in and from what she had read about these things; there would be no convincing her otherwise. She didn't know what to do. She wanted to call Tom for advice, but then what would he think of Sarah? As she looked at her friend, she knew that Sarah was treading on dangerous ground. She was in trouble, and it could only lead to disaster. She had a wonderful husband that adored her and their two beautiful children. This was not going to have a happy ending. Jillian was certain of it.

"This is wrong. You have to end this."

Sarah's face grew red. "No!"

Jillian softened her tone. Please, just hear me out."

"Okay, I'll listen, but you don't know him. We are so suited for one another. He knows me so well. Okay, I'll listen."

"Would it be alright if we had Tom look into him a little? Just to make..."

"No! That isn't why I am telling you. I had to tell someone, and you are my friend. He is who he says he is. Why do you think he would lie to me?"

"I don't know. You're probably right. I jumped to the wrong conclusion. I am very sorry," she fibbed. "Can I see what he looks like?"

Sarah was happy to show her his picture that she had on her cell phone. She went to the website, which Jillian took special notice of, and pulled him up by his profile. Jillian took a mental picture of his face and name. Together with the name of the dating service she would give Tom all the information.

"Hold on to his picture for a minute, I have to run to the ladies room. I'll take a better look in just a minute."

Sarah seemed to hardly hear her as she stared at her online soul mate. Jillian took her purse with her, and Sarah didn't seem to notice. As soon as she got to the bathroom, she wrote down everything she saw. She hoped it would be enough. She would call Tom and fill him in. She knew he could get an investigator on it right away. She had to do something. If she could expose this creature without Sarah's husband finding out, perhaps Sarah could return to her life with Phillip without too much damage. It would be, of course, up to Sarah how much, if anything, she would tell her husband. Jillian felt it would be better for her to just tell Phillip everything. Sarah would have a lot to deal with and keeping this secret would wear on her.

When Jillian returned to the table, Sarah was texting a message. She was relieved when she saw she was sending a message to her sister, Madison. Afterward, Sarah was happy to show off her prize again to Jillian, who was mentally confirming the notes she had made for Tom.

"So what do you really think? Isn't he handsome?"

"He is very handsome. Sarah, don't you love Phillip? What about the children?

"I haven't thought that far. I don't know how I feel about Phillip. Of course, the kids will be with me."

"When are you sending him the money for the investment?"

"Not for a few weeks. I need to borrow the money from Daddy until the divorce, but the way he is acting, I decided not to ask him for a few weeks. Like I said, I haven't seen him like this before and if he is coming down with something I better wait."

Jillian chuckled under her breath about J.T. but was relieved Sarah didn't have the money to send to this guy. Yes, J.T. was coming down with something alright. The girls finished their dessert and Jillian had James take Sarah back to the condominium.

Later in her room, she called Tom.

"Hi, Honey. Are you still up?"

Chuckling, Tom confessed, "I just finished a few cookies and a glass of milk."

Jillian explained what Sarah was going through, and Tom promised to get right on it. She decided to call Sarah in the morning and invite her over to the house while she worked. She hoped to keep her mind off Mr. Wonderful, if only for a few hours.

* * *

Jillian's driver was there right at nine o'clock as requested. She handed him a cup of coffee and a chocolate covered croissant. She had two more stuffed in her bag for later. She carefully set the box holding the two other cups of coffee on the floor of the car. She missed the croissants she used to get at Ernie's Bakery back home in Sweetwater. She and Sydney would take a walk, and she would eat her croissant. *Those were the days*, she sighed.

"Thank you very much."

"It's my pleasure, James. The chocolate covered ones are my favorite," she said with a hint of color to her face. "Today will be a short day. If you want to hang around, I should only be a few hours. We're picking Sarah up on the way, and then I'm meeting the carpet installers at the house. It's up to you. I mean, if you have something else to do; go ahead, but I'll need you back by noon."

"I can run a few personal errands if that is okay?"

"Sure, that will be just fine with me."

Jillian was hoping to hear from Tom, but it was probably too soon for the investigator to dig anything up. Sarah wandered around the house complementing Jillian on what she had done. After the carpet was installed, the last room would be the kitchen. The appliances would come in through the garage, and that would be it. Tomorrow would be the revealing day, and then she would go home over the weekend.

As she and Sarah sat down to drink their coffee and eat their croissants, Jillian's cell rang.

"Hi, Honey. Sure, what do you have? Oh, I see. Well, that doesn't sound good. Oh, well I was wondering about that as well. Can you fax that over to the hotel? Oh, Honey, you are the greatest. I love you. What? Well, if that's what you think is best," she said, under Sarah's watchful eyes. "Okay, Honey. Call me later. I love you, too."

Sarah looked intrigued as she appeared to wait for Jillian to hang up. "I assume with all those honey's, that was Tom?"

"Yes, we are buying a new car, and Tom wants me to decide while I'm here. He is faxing me the details," she lied, trying hard not to let it show.

Sarah brushed the blonde hair from her face as she picked at her croissant. It was as Jillian suspected. This man did not exist. How was she going to tell her friend that she had been scammed? Tom offered to send his investigator to Dallas. Jillian wasn't convinced that was the best idea but decided to trust Tom on that decision. Jillian knew that Sarah would be quite upset. She was hoping that this internet fraud hadn't cast his spell so deeply, that Sarah would accept the facts for their face value and rejoin her in the real world. Mostly, she didn't want the outcome of this situation to damage their relationship, but this was Sarah's future at stake here.

"When James gets here, let's go to lunch. I'm done here for the day. I can't believe tomorrow is the end. I thought it would be more like the first of next week."

"Sure, I could eat a light salad or something, but that croissant was a bit rich, don't you think so?"

Jillian laughed. "I love them, so you are asking the wrong person."

While Sarah was in the bathroom, Jillian called Tom. He told her that Brent had been in the air for several hours and should be at her hotel in another few hours with all the information he uncovered.

"It was a simple job," he explained. "These types of people don't worry about covering up much. Most people are so embarrassed about being scammed, they rarely call the police. Brent found the same picture on over twenty-five profiles, and that was in the first hour of his search. This group has been swindling women all over the states. They most likely live out of the country. There are too many protective laws here in the US."

"Sarah is going to be devastated. What do you mean, they?"

"Sweetheart, it is probably a network of people. They use pictures that they find on the internet. There is no Trevor. He doesn't exist."

"You're kidding?"

"Sarah is lucky Phillip hasn't found out. Brent told me that many women are careless about what is on their computers, and it wouldn't take long for him to see what she has been up to. In a way, Phillip is more the victim than Sarah."

"We can't judge her, okay? She got caught up in something, and, well, let's not go there for now."

"I'm just saying this might not turn out very well." Tom offered.

"We're going to lunch and then we'll go back to the hotel and wait for Brent. When he calls, ask him to wait for us in the lobby. Okay, here she comes; I'll talk to you later. I love you."

James drove them to one of Sarah's favorite soup and salad places. She picked at her food while Jillian sampled up and down the salad bar.

After lunch, they went to the hotel so Jillian could be dropped off. Sarah had asked for the driver so she could do some shopping that afternoon.

"Please come up for a few minutes. I want to talk with you," Jillian said taking her arm and leading her into the lobby. Jillian went to the front desk and picked up her fax, then looked around for Brent. She spotted him sitting on a couch looking at some papers. He looked up, and Jillian gave him a nod.

Brent gave the two women a few moments, then he knocked on the door. Jillian let him in. Sarah looked confused.

"Sarah, this is Brent Jacobs. He works for Tom. I ask him to come here to tell us what he found out."

Sarah smiled. "Found out what?"

"I'm a private investigator, Sarah. I have some information for you."

Sarah had a peculiar look on her face. "For me?" She whirled around to face Jillian.

"Oh, I see what's going on here! This is about Trevor, right? How dare you! I thought you were my friend. How dare you!" She said heading for the door.

"Please don't leave. If you go now, you will never know what I found out. You need to know about this," Brent said in a calm voice.

Sarah was crying as she looked at her friend. She shook her head in disbelief. Jillian was heartbroken and her eyes filled with tears.

"I'm so sorry. I know it feels like I betrayed you. I'm so very sorry. Please, let's sit down and hear Brent out. We really don't know what he has to say, please?"

Sarah glared at Jillian as she sat on the edge of the bed. Jillian took a chair at the table with Brent.

"After only three hours of investigation, I have found that this person does not exist. The face on the profile has been used on several dozen profiles on many different sites."

"No. That can't be true. I don't believe you."

"It's very true. I now have statements from four women that have been personally taken by this fraud. It is most likely a group of men outside the country that prey on women of all different backgrounds. They eventually ask for their victims to invest money in a secretive way, telling them they will both be rich and live happily ever after. Once the money is sent, they never hear from them again."

"No! Trevor wouldn't do that to me. He said we were soul mates. He wants to marry me."

Brent looked at her with great compassion. "I'm very sorry, but this is exactly what he–they told the other women. This is what they do. Some of the others weren't as lucky as you."

"Why do you say that? How am I lucky?"

"A few of them actually sent the money, and another woman told her husband she was leaving him. It was a disaster for all of them. Some may never recover from the pain of betrayal. You are lucky to have such a good friend as Jillian."

Brent handed Sarah the files. Sarah stood up and walked to the door. She never turned around. She opened the door, still holding on to the papers, and walked out of the room. Jillian stood up to run after her, and Brent suggested she let her go.

"This is very humiliating for her, and she might not want to face you or perhaps she doesn't believe you, but either way she needs some space."

"You're right. Thank you for coming, Brent. Did Tom get you a room?"

"I have business in Los Angeles, so I need to catch a flight in a few hours. This was just a stopover for me. Take good care. It was nice to see you again. I hope this works out. I'll leave this other file here for you. If you get a chance, you can give it to Sarah to read. There is plenty of information in the file I gave her, but she may want more. I'll be going now," he said, extending his hand.

Jillian sank down in the chair. She wanted to reach out to her friend, but Brent was right. She needed some space. Jillian tried to call Tom, but he was still in court. Needing someone to talk to, she dialed Father Michael. He wasn't available either. Needing some kind of release, she took a shower and ordered up a glass of wine. She was spent and wanted to go home. She called the airline and got an earlier flight. She would be finished before noon and after the walk through, she could fly home. She wished she could go home at that very moment, but tomorrow afternoon would have to do. She called downstairs and booked a massage.

Chapter Seventeen

Two weeks had passed since Jillian left Dallas and not one word from Sarah. Jillian was beginning to think she would never hear from her again. Even though she tried to understand her hurt and embarrassment, she missed her friend and prayed that one day things would work out. Jillian wondered how Sarah and her family were doing.

Morgan and his family were flying in, and Jillian was getting the house ready. Danny wasn't able to come, and Jillian fretted a little about it, but Tom reassured her there would be plenty of other times when they would all be together. She was looking forward to meeting baby Mary. Tom sent a van to the airport to pick them all up. Father Michael was arriving the following day. Everything was ready. Jillian and Tom decided to put Morgan and Melissa in the master bedroom upstairs. They could use the nursery for Morgan Junior and put the crib in the master with them. She and Tom would take the guest room downstairs, and the girls would stay in the room Jillian fixed up for Julie Ann. Father Michael would sleep in Danny's room, or he could sleep in the guest house that wasn't finished. The bedroom in the guest house was complete, but the kitchen still needed some work.

Jillian was beginning to worry where they were when the doorbell chimed. She ran to open the door to see the most beautiful baby in the world sleeping in her father's arms. Clinging to Melissa's hip was, a very chunky, Morgan Junior. Amanda and Rachael looked tired.

"Come in, come in everybody. The baby is beautiful. How sweet she is. I'm so happy for you both. Tom will be home soon. He's bringing hamburgers and cheeseburgers and fries. Juice for the kids, and we can have what we want to drink."

"Sounds good to me, we're all a bit hungry. It's a shame they don't feed you on the planes anymore. Well, you can buy a meal, but it isn't the same," Melissa said.

"You look fantastic. Who would ever have known you had a baby just a few months ago. Look how slender you are."

"You would be too if you had four kids to care for," Melissa said as her smile left her. "How thoughtless of me; I'm so sorry. Please forgive me?"

"For what? Let's not walk on egg shells around me, okay? I'm more than okay. It's been eight months. Tom and I have moved forward. There will be children in this house one day. Come on; let me show you the house. We have the upstairs fixed up for you and the little ones, and the girls can sleep down here with us. Is that okay with you, girls?"

"Yippee! We're sleeping with Auntie Jillian!" Rachael roared.

"Wait a minute, Rach. We aren't sleeping together, but we have rooms next to one another. You and Amanda are sleeping in the girly room."

"Anybody home?"

Amanda ran into the kitchen and was the first to see him. "Uncle Tom! Uncle Tom! Pick me up."

"Uncle Tom! Me, too!" Rachael squealed.

Morgan took the bags of hamburgers from Tom's other arm allowing Tom to scoop up Rachael. The girls were kissing him and touching his hair. Melissa got out her camera as quickly as she could and was able to get several of shots of Uncle Tom and the girls. They adored him, and it was a sweet sight as Jillian looked on. She tried to imagine for a moment their children happy to see their daddy when he got home from work. It was a bittersweet moment.

Jillian and Melissa set the table in the dining room. Melissa was munching on fries as they put the food out on the table. She turned to her sister-in-law and smiled.

"What was that for?"

"I love you. I just wanted to say that," Melissa said with tears in her eyes.

"It's okay, honest. Sure, it hurts, but it's okay. Sometimes I let it get to me, but I can't stay in the past. When I came home from the hospital, I could hardly get up in the morning. It was like I had no reason to do anything. Tom is the love of my life, and he couldn't break through. I wouldn't let him. Then one day, Father Mike brought Tony and Danny out to surprise me. When I saw them, I wanted to run and hide. Tom let them in, and Danny looked so shocked to see me in the condition I was in. Tony had tried to prepare him, but he started to cry. Then all of a sudden he began to sob. It had been so painful for him to see me looking the way I did. It broke my heart. The pain I felt did not compare to the pain I saw on my child's face. It was as if nothing else mattered. I reached out to him and held him tightly. Can you believe that was what snapped me out of it?"

"Of course, I can. Something happens to a mother when they see their children in pain. It's powerful; more so than any drug. When your child is hurting, you can think of nothing else except how to make the pain go away."

"I know how right you are, Melissa. It was so very powerful. Then, when I released him from my arms, he stepped back and looked at me. He was staring at my uneven hair. You know, I needed stitches, and they shaved one side. I had the other side cut, but I didn't want to have it shaved. I figured it would all even out eventually. Actually, at that particular time, I didn't really care. Then Danny got this silly smile on his face, and then he asked me why I let someone cut my hair crooked? This made me smile for the first time in months. It was a moment with my son I will never forget."

"So, why did you let them cut your hair crooked?" Melissa said, drying her eyes.

The two women embraced and laughed.

After dinner, they all sat around in the family room. The girls played with their new dolls Jillian had bought for them, and Morgan Junior was down for the count. The baby was on the couch between Morgan and Melissa on a quilt they had brought from home. Tom and Jillian were cuddled on the love seat as they sat around chatting. The phone rang, and Tom got up to answer it. Jillian could hear him talking, but she couldn't make out who it was. She thought it was probably Father Michael. Tom looked over at Jillian, and then she saw it. The look on his face told her something terrible had happened. Cold chills traveled down her spine. Her chest tightened as she stood up.

"What is it, Tom?"

Tom handed her the phone. "It's Tony, Sweetheart."

"Tony? What's wrong?" she asked.

"It's Danny, we need you here. Danny is very ill."

* * *

Jillian stared out the window of the airplane. She was thinking about the first time she saw Danny. How just looking at his eyes told her so much. How could this be happening? She thought about the time at the ranch when Danny got so pooped out that he went upstairs for a nap. That wasn't the only time. She thought about the blood test he said he had, and she wondered if that had anything to do with it. She remembered that Danny had said, "Guess what?" a third time while they were there after Thanksgiving. Was he going to tell her he was ill last November? How long had Tony known Danny was sick? She thought about the many times Danny told her he was tired. Jillian thought that was normal, but thinking back, Julie Ann never complained about being tired. Why didn't she recognize this as a warning or an indication that there was something that wasn't right? She was his mother. Why didn't she sense something? Now her only child needed a kidney transplant. How could a ten-year child be in kidney failure?

"I am his mother. If I am a match, we need to talk about this. Tony said time is of the essence, and I might be his only chance. Tony said he wasn't a match. They put Danny on the transplant list, but that all takes time. I have to do whatever I can."

Tom was quiet for a few minutes. Jillian knew he was processing.

"Sweetheart, of course, you have to help your son. You can't blame me for being worried about you, though. Danny may be your first concern, but you are mine. I know you have to do this. I will be right by your side, always."

Jillian put her head on his shoulder and closed her eyes. It was surreal. There were times she wanted to scream and other times she felt so incredibly numb.

After landing, they took a cab and went straight to the hospital. They rushed to Danny's room and there he was. Jillian could hardly look. His eyes were closed, and he had tubes running everywhere. Tony was asleep in a chair. Jillian touched his arm, and Tony leaped to his feet, startling her.

"Tell me how this happened, please?"

"He has been sick for some time. We didn't know what was wrong. He had test after test. He has been so tired. He is in end stage renal disease."

"But what happened to cause this? I don't understand."

"It's called Glomerulonephritis. It affects the kidney's ability to properly filter out waste and can lead to swelling, blood in the urine, and a reduced amount of urine production. At first, the doctors thought it could be treated with medication, but now he has to be on dialysis. He needs a kidney transplant. Both his kidneys are failing."

"Who will test me to be a donor?"

"You can be tested to see if you are a match right here in this hospital. You have to be a match. We can't lose our son."

"Why didn't you call me sooner," she snapped.

"It came on rather suddenly. Don't be mad. You're here now, and you can save him. One of us has to be a match, and I'm not."

Jillian looked at Tom. She was scared. Tom took her in his arms to comfort her.

"They won't be here to test you until tomorrow. You're welcome to stay at the house and use one of the cars," Tony said solemnly.

Jillian was frantic. "I'm not leaving this hospital," she snarled. "Tom, we have to stay here. See if there are any overnight rooms here in the hospital. Some hospitals have a room where you can get a shower and rest. I just can't leave. I'm not!"

"They do," Tony said. "Tom, just give them Danny's name and room number and they will find something for you and Jillian."

Tom turned for the door. "Thanks, I'll go see what I can find out."

Jillian's heart was breaking as she looked at her son. Her sweet little prince looked so tiny in that big bed. She wasn't feeling well. Realizing she hadn't eaten since burgers with the family yesterday, she looked in her purse for the pretzels she was given on the airplane. She couldn't find them, but she felt she needed something.

"Tony, have you eaten anything today?"

"I haven't eaten since breakfast, yesterday. Angela is bringing something over later. The hospital has a good cafeteria. It's down in the basement. You look a little pale. Maybe you should get a bite to eat."

"I'm staying right here for now. Tom can go get me something. Where's Angela?"

"She will be here soon. Martha is taking care of the baby and Julie Ann went home with Grandma Betty."

"Did I tell you we named her Bella? Well, actually she is Isabella, but we love the name Bella," he rattled on. "I can't take this. He is the sweetest kid in the world. How can this be happening?"

Tony was still rattling on, and Jillian could see how tense and worried he was. She touched his shoulder, and he stood up. Jillian put her arms around him and together they cried softly. When Tom returned, her arms quickly fell from around Tony's shoulders, and she gave Tom her full attention.

"I got a hold of the head nurse, and she arranged a room for us. It has two recliners and a shower. I'll take our bags there, and be back in a few minutes."

"Would you find a vending machine and get me some crackers or something salty? I don't want anything sweet, but my stomach feels so odd. The stress, I guess. I just need to eat something."

"Sure," Tom said picking up their bags.

"Daddy, I'm thirsty."

"Hi, Little Prince, I'm here, too."

"Hi," Danny said in a weak voice.

"Can he have water?" she asked.

"Sure, whatever he wants. He doesn't stay awake much for some reason."

Jillian went out into the hall to find the nurse. She wanted to let her know Danny wanted some water. By the time she returned Danny was sleeping again. Suddenly Jillian remembered she had forgotten to call Morgan. She had promised she would call as soon as she saw Danny. Morgan and Melissa agreed that they would stay at the house for a few days and then fly back to California. It was hard enough to travel with four children as it was. They needed a few days to relax, and Father Michael was coming. Jillian went to a small seated area in the hall to call her brother. She felt dizzy from the constant worry. She looked around for Tom, who was still out looking for the vending machine.

"Hi, it's me. I don't know what to say. For one, I don't know much except Danny has... Wait a second, I wrote it down. It's in my pocket."

She searched her pockets until she found the piece of paper that held the name of her son's condition. "Here it is. It is called Glomerulonephritis."

"I know what that is," Morgan said. "I'm so sorry."

"Why do you say it like that? He can stay on dialysis until he gets one of my kidneys. They will test me for a match tomorrow and the sooner, the better for Danny's sake."

Jillian saw Angela coming down the hall with a large bag and a small suitcase. Angela saw her and gave a wave. Jillian acknowledged her and returned to Morgan.

"What do you know about this illness?"

"I don't know much, really. I've just heard of it."

"Did Father Mike get there yet?"

"No. He called from the airport to say you forgot to send him a car so he called a cab. He's on his way. I didn't tell him about Danny yet. I thought I would wait until he got here."

"Tom must have forgotten to have a car there for him. Tell him we're really sorry about the car. Once you tell him what is going on, he'll understand."

"Don't worry about any of this stuff. Just get some rest and call us when you can. We love you."

"I love you, too. I'll call you tomorrow."

Jillian walked back down the hall to Danny's room. Tony was in the bathroom changing into the clean clothes that Angela had brought him.

"Are you okay?" Angela said.

"Thanks, I don't really know how I am."

"I brought sandwiches, and there are plenty for you and Tom. I'm sure you haven't had time to stop and eat. Come over here and sit down and have a sandwich. I brought juice also. You need to eat, and this will encourage Tony to eat as well. Come, sit down with me and I'll have one with you," Angela said sweetly.

Jillian could see why Tony loved her. She was genuinely concerned. Jillian sat down and took a few bites of a sandwich. By the third bite, she began to feel ill. The stress was too much. She put the sandwich down and sipped on some juice. That only seemed to make her feel worse.

"You need to keep up your strength if you want to be a donor. You have to be well. May I ask you some questions?"

"Sure, go ahead."

"Do you have high blood pressure?"

"No."

"What about diabetes or heart disease?"

"No."

"Have you had any issues with mental illness?"

"No, just stress," she said trying to smile. She knew Angela was just getting some questions out of the way.

"They will be doing HLA-typing or, what is called, tissue typing. It is a blood test that determines the major antigens or proteins that make each person different. Six antigens are important in kidney transplant. Tissue typing will let them know how many antigens you share with Danny or what the match is. Do you follow so far?"

"I think so. All I want to know is, are we a match? I mean, why shouldn't I be a match? You understand what I mean, right?"

"Yes, but family members are not always a match. Look at Tony for example. The term 'match' is often misused when referring to a recipient and donor. A clearer way of describing the evaluation process between a recipient and donor would be to use the terms, 'suitable' and 'compatible'. A suitable donor is someone that is healthy enough to donate. A donor has to be compatible when all the tests are finalized. A person has to be suitable and compatible to donate to the recipient. All this will be explained again tomorrow, but I thought you might benefit from a heads up."

"Thanks, but you lost me a while back. I appreciate you trying to help, but I am too tired and stressed out right now to even begin to comprehend all of this."

Angela's face became serious, and her smile went away. "Then let me say this; don't let yourself get wiped out. You need to keep your blood pressure and blood sugars in check. You have to be healthy. Rest, eat and breathe. I understand how stressful this is, but if you don't appear healthy, even if you are a match, you may be rejected based on your health."

"What? I am so stressed right now I can hardly tell you my name."

"I know you are very stressed out and based on your relationship with Danny; they will expect a certain amount of stress related raises in blood pressure and blood sugar. But, if you get too high or low the red flags come out, which is why I brought the sandwiches. I know it is hard to eat right now, but..."

"Are you telling me that if I am a match they can still reject me?"

"Yes. This is a major operation for you, and when it is over you will have only one kidney. You have to be a good specimen. I'm just trying to prepare you."

"How do you know all of this?"

"Renal disease is my specialty."

Suddenly Jillian understood why Tony and Martha were reluctant to tell her how they had met. It all made sense now. Tony met Angela because of Danny's kidney disease."

"When I came at Thanksgiving, Danny told me that he had just had a blood test. Was that about this?"

"Yes, Danny has been a patient in our office for a while now. I have worked with Dr. McKinley for eight years. He is the top renal specialist in Colorado, perhaps, in the country. I haven't been on Danny's case since Tony and I were married because of the conflict of interest clause, but I am very close to knowing what is going on. I assure you, I have his best interests at heart as does Dr. McKinley."

Jillian was stunned into silence. She felt so betrayed. She couldn't even begin to explore the depth of her emotions. Her only child has been seriously ill for so long, and she wasn't made aware of it. She was sure her shock was apparent on her face but was unable to do a thing to erase it.

Tony came out from the bathroom and sat down to have a sandwich. He motioned to Jillian to eat. Jillian felt like the calf being fattened for the kill. She tried to explain that the food was making her sick, and Tony suggested she find Tom and go rest for a while. Jillian agreed but had to call Tom on his cell to find out where he was. She knew the next day was going to be a long one.

Chapter Eighteen

The morning began with one questionnaire after another. Forms and more forms. Jillian was feeling better and had eaten a good size dinner in the cafeteria the evening before. She was told to eat this morning, as the bulk of the physical testing would be done the following day. It was a long process, and it would be one test at a time. A routine chemistry and hematology panel ended the testing for the first day. She was scheduled to meet with the surgeon that afternoon. Jillian was feeling positive about being a good match. She had done some research on the internet, and she had learned that it can be a fifty-fifty possibility for each parent. Since Tony wasn't a match, Jillian assumed she would be.

"Mr. and Mrs. Bentley, it's a pleasure to meet you both," Dr. McKinley said motioning for them to sit down.

"Please, call me Jillian, and this is my husband, Tom."

"Danny has become a very special patient, and we are doing all we can to get him well."

"I'm his real mother, Dr. McKinley. His father isn't a match so I must be, right?"

"Jillian, you may or may not be a suitable match, but you cannot be a donor at this time. I'm sorry to be the one to tell you this. We will do all that we can to find a suitable donor for your son."

Jillian's face went pale. "What do you mean? I don't understand what you are talking about. I might be a match, but I'm not a suitable donor?"

"You cannot be a donor while you are pregnant. It's really quite that simple."

"Pregnant? I'm not pregnant!" she snapped, looking at Tom, who was looking at the doctor, who was looking at Jillian.

"You didn't know you were pregnant? Yes, you are quite pregnant. You'll need to see your doctor when you return to New York. These are extremely stressful times for you. You need to protect your unborn child."

Jillian stood up. She felt numb. This wasn't fair. This wasn't right. She was here to help her son. To save his life and they are telling her she can't do that? She wasn't taking no for an answer.

She had a very determined look on her face. "Why can't I be a donor? I still want to do it."

Tom bolted up from his chair. "Jillian!" He looked grief stricken. "You can't sacrifice our unborn child for another child, even if it is Danny. What is the matter with you? Didn't you hear the doctor? You are pregnant! It isn't safe for you or our unborn child."

Dr. McKinley spoke calmly. "Your husband is correct. There is not a surgeon in the country that would do this surgery on a pregnant woman. You need to face this. You will not be the donor."

"Can Danny stay on dialysis until this baby is born? Can we take it early?"

"Mrs. Bentley, we aren't even sure you are a match. Your testing has been terminated. We will find a match and a donor for Danny."

Jillian turned and left the room. She walked across the crowded parking lot to the hospital and went straight to Danny's room. She understood now why she was feeling sick. It wasn't the stress after all. It was a baby.

"Where's Tom?" Tony asked.

"Has Danny been awake?" she asked, ignoring his question. "Has he asked for me?"

"He has been awake on and off, but I think he's fairly confused. He was asking for Sydney."

"Then tell someone to bring Sydney here. If he wants his dog, then give it to him for pity's sake."

"What's wrong with you? What has happened? Where's Tom?" he asked her again. "Are you done with the testing for today?"

"Permanently!" she shrieked, beginning to sob out of control.

Tony took her out of the room and tried to calm her down. One of the nurses brought a plastic glass of water and handed it to Tony. He handed it to Jillian, and she knocked it out of his hands sending water everywhere.

"Stop it! What is wrong with you? Get a hold of yourself," Tony warned her. "If Danny wakes up he will hear you."

She looked at him with fire in her eyes. "Our son needs a kidney, and I can't give him one of mine. They tell me I'm not suitable. I could be a match, but I'm not good enough. Danny will have to stay on dialysis."

"Calm down, Jillian. He's been put on the registry. They'll find him a kidney."

"That could take up to two years. You go in there and look at him. Do you want him to be this way for two years," she snarled. She was more than livid; she was out of control.

"We were his only chance. Don't you get it?"

"Jillian, I know you want to save him, so do I. We'll find a way, but ranting and raving isn't going to get Danny a kidney. I was counting on you being a match as well. This is a huge blow for both of us. There has to be a way. I was just as positive as you were that it would be you."

"It could have been me. It should have been me. But oh, no, I'm pregnant, and the doctor refused to let me help our son."

"You're pregnant? Did you know?"

"No! What do you mean did I know? Did I know? Why would I start the tests if I knew I was pregnant? The doctors found out through the blood tests this morning. I never even started with any of the other tests. The doctor said it was impossible for me to have the surgery while I was pregnant. Maybe after the baby is born, I could do it, but now I don't even know if I'm a match. They won't even finish the testing on me. Why do I have to be pregnant?" In her heart, Jillian knew she was acting irrational, but she couldn't stop.

She looked up to see Tom standing there. She had no idea how long he had been there or what he heard, but the look on his face was painful. He turned and walked to the end of the hall then turned the corner.

"Tom? Is that you?"

"Lydia?"

Tom walked over to a petite woman with auburn hair. Her azure blue eyes sparkled as she gazed at him. He opened his arms and embraced her small frame. She lingered slightly.

Lydia took a few steps back and looked at Tom. "What are you doing in Denver? It's so good to see you. I've thought of you often and, really, it's good to see you."

She was as beautiful as when he saw her last.

"I'm here because of a sick family member," he said, not offering to explain the situation. "What are you doing here? The last time I saw you, you were living in San Francisco."

"I'm an RN, and I was offered a job here several years ago. I miss Frisco, but I like it here. Can we get together later? I'm off duty in an hour. I'd love to catch up," she proposed, with an undaunted smile Tom remembered all too well.

"Lydia, we could have coffee downstairs in the cafeteria later, if you would like. I'd enjoy catching up. I need to be available so I would prefer to stay in the hospital. But sure, let's meet in the cafeteria in an hour."

Lydia smiled and touched his arm. "Okay, Tom, but make it in two. I have a little charting to do."

Tom watched her walk away. He wondered what her life was like now. There was one thing he knew for sure, and that was he had better let her know right away that he was a married man.

It had been six years since they had first met in a New York courtroom. Lydia's brother, Henry, had been a junior partner with Tom's firm and needed help on a case. Tom offered to assist, and Lydia was there every day observing her brother. She'd been visiting from San Francisco. She never missed a day in court, and would have lunch with Henry and Tom often. Tom had felt brave one day and asked her out. Before long they were a couple. Lydia had seemed adamant about living in San Francisco, and Tom's practice was in New York. They dated for the six months she was in New York, but when it came time for her to leave; that was what she did. Tom had no idea she would have stayed had he asked her. They tried to maintain their relationship; long distance, but before long their separate worlds led them back to their separate lives. Henry moved on to another firm, and Tom lost contact with both of them.

Jillian was sitting in the hall when Tom returned.

She lowered her eyes. "Where have you been?"

"I was walking around. We need to talk."

Seemingly annoyed, she curtly replied, "Not now. I'm tired, and I haven't eaten. Can we go to the cafeteria? You haven't eaten either, I'm sure."

"Alright, let's go get something to eat."

On the way to the cafeteria, Jillian's cell phone rang. It was Morgan. She wanted to talk to him, but she wasn't prepared. She let it go to voice mail; planning to call him after they had finished eating.

"Aren't you going to answer that?"

"No, I want to eat," she said unwaveringly. "That is all I need to do right now is eat."

"Her phone rang again. It was Morgan. At this point, Jillian felt she had no choice but to answer.

"Hi, Morgan."

"Jillian, are you okay? I've been calling you."

"I'm just so tired, and Tom and I just sat down to eat. Are you all okay? Did Father Mike make it in?"

"We're good, and Mike is here. I'll let you eat, but just tell me how did the testing go?"

"It appears that I am pregnant, so I can't be a donor. So, it went badly. Win one, lose one, kind of thing."

"I'm coming to Denver. Father Mike will stay with Melissa and the kids. We've talked it all out. I'm coming to get tested."

"No..."

"Don't waste your breath, I'm coming. I'll be there in the morning. Melissa agreed that if you weren't suitable, which now you aren't, I'm the next best choice since I am your sibling. I'll see you in the morning. If I'm a match, Danny will have one of my kidneys. Melissa said to tell you that if something should happen to my other one; you owe me one of yours," he said. "We're family, and Danny is my nephew. We're family." As they hung up, Jillian thanked him.

"Morgan is coming to get tested. We are full siblings, so this could be the answer. Melissa agrees that this is what needs to be done. Let's eat and go share the news with Tony."

Tom developed a serious look to his face. "I hope he understands what he is doing. He has a family to care for."

Jillian looked annoyed. "He's a dentist. He knows what the risks are."

Tom picked up their food, and they ate in silence. As soon as they were finished, Jillian wanted to hurry back to Danny's room to find Tony. When they got there, Angela was sitting on the edge of Danny's bed. She was wiping his face with a washcloth and speaking softly to her stepson. Danny was awake, and they seemed to be having a conversation. Angela did not move when Jillian came in the room. Jillian wanted to sit with him and talk with him, but Angela did not budge. Jillian walked around the other side of the bed and took Danny's hand.

"Mommy?" Danny murmured.

"Yes, Little Prince, I'm here," Jillian said.

"Jillian, he's speaking to me," Angela replied quietly.

Jillian felt enraged. She glared at Angela. Tom came around and took Jillian's arm. He motioned for her to come out in the hall and he led her in that direction.

"What? What, Tom?"

Tom looked at her tenderly. "She's his mother now. Let them have their time. She is protective of him as she should be. He is frightened, and he wants his mommy. You have to step aside. Don't confuse him right now."

"I can't believe you are taking her side?"

Tom's tone changed quickly. "Be careful, Sweetheart. You're not thinking correctly. I always have your best interests at heart."

Tony came from down the hall. He asked what was going on, and Tom explained that Danny was awake, and Angela was comforting him. Tony started to go in the room when Jillian stopped him.

"Morgan will be here in the morning. He wants to be tested."

Tony looked at her and tears began to well up in his eyes.

"I am so grateful for Morgan. As kids, we would always say that we were there for each other. I never imagined in my life that he would be there to try to save my son. I can only pray that he is a match. He has to be."

"He is my brother. He will be a match. I'm positive."

"Don't get your hopes up. Let's wait until he can be tested," Tom reminded her, reaching out to offer her a comforting hug.

Jillian glared at him; stepping back. "He'll be a match. You'll see."

"I know you are in a lot of pain, but you're not thinking clearly," Tony said, "No need to take it out on Tom."

Tom didn't look happy. The situation kept changing too quickly, and mixed emotions were cropping up all over the place.

Tom smiled. "You don't need to defend me, but thanks."

Jillian and Tony went back to Danny's room, and Tom stayed out in the hall. He looked at his watch and walked over to the elevator.

Lydia was waiting for him when he came into the cafeteria. She waved, and he walked over to the table where she was sitting.

"Come sit down. I got us some iced tea. I remembered you like that better for afternoons."

Tom smiled. It was nice that she remembered.

"So, did you say you have been living in Denver for two years?"

"Yes. I live in a suburb. I just bought a house a few months ago. I would love to show it to you," she chirped. "How is your sister? It isn't her that is sick, is it?"

"April died a year and a half ago. She was in an accident."

"Oh, no, I'm so sorry," she said, touching him on his arm.

"Not your mother?"

"No. Mom is fine. She lives in the city now. It's a long story, but let me just fill you in briefly. It's my stepson. He is almost ten, and he has end-stage renal disease."

"I'm so sorry. Did you say, stepson?"

"Yes, I got married a year ago last spring. My wife, Jillian, had a son before our marriage."

"I can't believe it. Tom Bentley, the most eligible bachelor in New York, got married? I just can't believe it. Congrats," Lydia said with a smile.

"It's not that hard to believe. If you remember, I always wanted to get married, but I never found the right one," Tom blushed.

"You mean, besides me, right?"

"Lydia, you never wanted to marry me."

"Yes, I did. You never asked. If you had, I would have said yes."

This caught Tom off guard. He didn't know what to say. Lydia just smiled. She stared at him, and he felt nervous. She was just teasing him; or was she?

"Have they found a donor for your stepson?"

"No, Danny is on dialysis. His father wasn't a match, and we didn't know if my wife was going to be a match, but she is pregnant and can't be a donor."

"Really? You're going to be a father? How wonderful for you. How far along is she?"

"I have no idea. We just found out this morning. She was having the first blood test when they discovered it and told us. Her brother is on the way to see if he is a match. He'll be here in the morning."

Lydia looked at Tom tenderly. "Are you happy? I mean, well, are you? I see this anguish in your eyes."

"Yes, I am. I am very happy, but this is a hard time for the entire family right now. We have no idea what will happen and then we find out we're going to have a baby. I don't think either one of us has processed it yet. It's something we have wanted, but it just wasn't the best timing right now."

"Tom," she said, putting her hand in his. "I need to run. I have plans this evening, but I want to see you again. Will you meet me here about this same time tomorrow?"

Tom seemed reluctant to agree to meet again. "Everything is so up in the air, but I'll try."

"Give me your cell number. If you aren't here, I'm calling you," she said.

"If I'm not here it is because I can't make it; not because I don't want to."

"Okay, Big Guy, I believe you."

Tom smiled. He hadn't heard those words in a very long time. He stood up and Lydia kissed him on the cheek.

"See you tomorrow, Big Guy."

Tom sat down to finish his iced tea. He watched as she walked away.

Chapter Nineteen

Angela drove to the airport to pick up Morgan. They were expecting him by ten o'clock that morning to be at the hospital. Tom was going to ride back to the house with Angela so he could pick up their other car. He had decided that they should move to a hotel very near the hospital. Jillian needed more rest, and she wasn't feeling well. She kept insisting on staying at the hospital, but Tom was able to persuade her to do otherwise. He got another room for Morgan, for a few days. If he turned out to be a match, he was going to need some decent rest as well. Morgan started right in on the preliminary paperwork and had the chest x-ray that afternoon. Tom spent some time with Julie Ann and held Bella while Angela did a few things around the house. Martha was shopping and would be back with the car, and then Tom planned to check in at the hotel. He would not be back in time to meet with Lydia. Considering that, he thought that was probably for the best.

"You are so comfortable with Bella. You're going to be a great dad."

"If you only knew how nervous I am to hold her."

"Babies sense these things, and Bella hasn't fussed once since you picked her up. She has been somewhat colicky. I worry about my milk right now with all the stress. If she doesn't calm down soon, I'll put her on formula for a little while and just pump."

Tom had a peculiar look on his face and Angela laughed.

"Sorry, is this too much information?"

Tom smiled, raising an eyebrow. "Just a little."

* * *

By the time Tom got back to the hospital, it was afternoon. He found Jillian sitting in her favorite place in the hall. There was no sign of Morgan, but Jillian had a hopeful look on her face. She looked up as Tom approached her.

"So far, so good," she cried softly. "Let's find Morgan and go to the hotel for some dinner, and I need to lie down for just a little while."

Her face was pale, and she looked tired. She needed to get some rest. They found Morgan and left for the hotel. During dinner, Morgan commented that he and Danny had different blood types. No one told him if the various types were compatible, so in the morning, he would find out.

"That's impossible. There has to be some mistake. Danny and I are both B positive like all the Connors."

"No, we're all A positive. Mom, Dad, you and I. We're all A positive. It can't be anything but that when both parents are the same."

"Morgan, you're mixed up. Believe me, after the car accident I know that I am B positive. You misunderstood. Besides, Danny is B positive, just like me."

Morgan smiled. "We can't both be right. I'll be typed again in the morning. If there was a mistake someone will pay for it, I'm sure. This could have had horrible results."

Jillian excused herself and went to the ladies room.

"I'm sure of my blood type, and I am just as sure of our parent's blood type. The reason being; when I was in dental school, I had a school project involving blood typing. We were to use our own blood type and our parents. Well, long story short, my mother sent me information on her and my dad and we all three had the same blood type. Jillian should be as well. The curious thing is, Tony and Danny aren't a match while Jillian and Danny are, but they are both B positive. I know it' been a while since Dental school, but this is a little confusing to me."

Tom looked puzzled. "I have no idea what you just said. I don't know a thing about blood types. I couldn't tell you what my blood type is."

"I don't want to upset my sister any more than she already is. This will have to stay a mystery. I told her I would be typed again in the morning and I will. Just because I said I would, that doesn't mean I'm expecting a different result. She's coming back so I'll drop it for now."

Jillian reached for Tom's arm. "I'm exhausted. Let's go to our room. Morgan, will Melissa come if you become the donor?"

"Yes, but her mother will fly to New York to be with the kids. Is that okay if she stays there at your house?"

"Of course, it is," Tom said. "I'm sure Father Michael couldn't handle it."

They all laughed for the first time in days. The very thought of Father Michael watching three kids and a baby was enough to break the tension for a moment.

Jillian had yet to even mention anything about her pregnancy. It seemed a topic no one wanted to bridge, especially Tom.

Alone in their room, Jillian showered. She put on a pair of sweats and a tee shirt and walked over to the bed. It was a lovely room with a view of the Rocky Mountains. The window was large, and Jillian stood there remembering when she had first come to Denver, to work For Sarah and Phillip Reynolds. She remembered how she had gone for a power walk one morning and was impressed with the splendor of the Rockies, as she looked up from where she stood. Who would have known that in less than a few hours from that moment, her life would have changed so drastically that day? She would go to Phillip Reynolds' office and pass by another office with the name of Dr. Martelli on the door. Who would have known it would have been her high school sweetheart and the father of the son she had put up for adoption. What were the chances of that? She had often asked herself. Suddenly, in the quietness of their room, she put her hands on her stomach and held it. Tom came in from the bathroom drying off his hair with a towel. He walked up behind his wife and wrapped his arms around her. She began to cry softly and then, without warning, she broke free of his hold and went to bed leaving Tom standing there. She wasn't blaming Tom for anything, but she was just so frustrated with everything. Jillian wanted to have another baby with all her heart, but why now? Why now, was all she could think about. Tom was still standing where she had left him.

"I know what you are thinking, but I swear, I'm not mad about the baby. I'm not. You, of all people, know how much a child would mean to me."

Tom walked over and sat on the edge of the bed. He stroked her hair and touched her face. He climbed into bed and turned out the light. He whispered softly, "I love you."

"I love you, too. Good night."

* * *

They were all up early as Morgan was expected to meet with one of the doctors at seven-thirty. They agreed to meet for lunch later if Morgan was able to eat at all. Tom and Jillian went down to the cafeteria and Jillian opted for orange juice in place of coffee and ate a slice of toast. She was anxious to see Danny, and she knew Angela wouldn't be there that early.

"Before we go upstairs, I wanted to tell you something."

"Sure, what is it," she said in a more pleasant voice than she had been using.

"The other day I ran into an old friend. Actually, we were involved for a while. Her name is Lydia Jeffries."

"Really? Small world I guess."

"Well, I just wanted you to know. It doesn't really matter, I suppose."

"I guess it doesn't. We need to go up to see Danny now."

Tom looked wounded. Jillian couldn't see beyond her own pain, and she didn't even realize how she was hurting Tom. She was indifferent to everyone. That is, everyone but Danny.

Morgan met up with them at the elevator. Jillian instinctively knew by the look on his face that he wasn't a match. Her legs went weak, and she looked to Tom, who grabbed her and held her, as she glided to the floor. She was out cold. A nurse rushed over immediately and soon they had her on a gurney.

"She's pregnant, and she's under a tremendous amount of stress," Tom told the nurse.

Jillian was taken directly to the emergency room, and all precautions were taken to be sure she and the baby were both comfortable. They put her in a small exam room where she was resting and talking with one of the nurses who was being very kind to her. Tom was standing in the doorway due to the lack of space inside.

"What did you have to eat this morning?" The nurse asked her.

"What? Um, I don't know. Juice, I had orange juice and toast."

"That's good, dear, but you need more than that. I understand you are under a lot of stress, but to have a healthy child you need to feed yourself."

"That's why I am here. My son is sick, and he needs to get healthy. That's the most important thing to me right now."

140

"More important than the child you are carrying? Seems to me that you have two children to worry about now. If you don't get rest and proper nutrition you won't be any good to either of them."

Jillian said nothing. She looked around the tiny room for Tom, who was still standing in the doorway. Morgan was right behind him.

"I can't stay here any longer," she said sternly. "Tom, we need to be with Danny."

"I'll get your release papers in the works, but in the meantime, I'm having a meal sent over to you. If you eat it, I will process your release quickly, otherwise…"

"I get it. I'll eat it, but just so you know; you can't keep me here."

The nurse smiled, and Jillian began to cry. Tom came in and brushed by the nurse. He sat at the edge of the bed and held his wife.

"You have to promise me that whatever happens; you will think of our baby you are carrying. You can look out for both of your children. Standing by Danny and caring for our unborn baby. Don't throw one away for the other."

"Okay, but you don't know what I am going through."

"Actually, I do. Remember? We both lost a child, it wasn't just you. We lost our child. I'm not ready to lose another one."

Jillian began to cry harder, and Tom continued to hold her.

Morgan went down to the cafeteria to get a bite to eat and then he said he would look in on Danny. Jillian's meal arrived, and she picked at it until the nurse came in. She shoveled the rest down and got up to get dressed. She actually did feel better after eating her meal and thanked the nurse who handed her the release papers. She and Tom hurried up to Danny's room. Tony wasn't in the room, and so Jillian was able to sit on the bed with Danny, who was awake.

Danny looked happy to see her. "Hi, Jillian."

"Hi, Little Prince," she said. "I am so sorry you are sick. We came as soon as we found out. Uncle Morgan is here, too."

Danny looked at her oddly. "Morgan is my uncle?"

Jillian grasped for something to say. "Well, all the kids call him that. It's okay if you call him Uncle Morgan if you want."

Tony came in with a cup of coffee and a breakfast sandwich from the cafeteria. Morgan was right behind him.

"Here's your daddy. I need to talk with Morgan for a minute. I'll be right back."

Morgan followed her out into the hall.

"What happened? Did you get your blood re-typed?"

"I did. I told you I would, and it isn't a match."

"I don't understand this, Morgan? How can that be?"

"Sis, I have no idea, but it isn't anything for you to worry about. I'm not a match, and that is it. We need to find another. We will. Don't worry."

"I am worried. All the possible donors haven't been a match. Now we have to go outside the family, and that could take a very long time."

Jillian had a puzzled look on her face and then it hit her. "Morgan, does this mean we have different fathers? No, that's impossible. Mom wouldn't have cheated on Dad? Maybe I'm adopted? That has to be it. I'm adopted. I'm calling Father Mike. If anything, he will know. No, I'm not going to ask him. I don't want to know. I don't want to know."

Jillian began to cry and soon she was wailing uncontrollably. Morgan was taken aback at her sudden outburst. It wasn't just the blood type. It was everything. She just fell apart.

Tom came running down the hall.

"What in the world is it now?"

Both Jillian and Morgan looked surprised by his tone.

"I could hear you crying all the way down the hall to Danny's room. You need to get a hold of yourself," he said, sounding more irritated by the second.

A nurse came over and asked if everything was alright. Tom glared at them; shaking his head in disgust.

"I'm sure Tony heard you down here and maybe Danny did, too."

Jillian looked up with tears running down her cheeks. "I'm sorry. I didn't mean to be so loud. I'm sorry."

Tom was in the elevator and the door shut before Jillian could say anything more. He continued down to the cafeteria and got a sweet roll and a cup of coffee. He sat down at one of the tables and closed his eyes. Suddenly there was a hand on his shoulder, and he uttered Jillian's name as he opened his eyes.

"I'm sorry, it's Lydia. What's the matter? Is it your stepson?"

"No. He's the same. We're having trouble finding a donor, and my wife is beside herself. She is so upset, and I am not dealing with it very well."

"Hasn't it only been a few days?"

"Yes, but no one in the family has been a match, my..."

"Tom, these things take time. Haven't they explained all of this to the family? It could take up to a year or longer before the registry finds a suitable match," she offered, reaching for his hand.

"We were hoping someone in the family would be a suitable match. I told you Jillian is pregnant. She didn't take the news very well."

Lydia looked at Tom with tender eyes. "Which part? Not being suitable or being pregnant?"

"Both I guess. She is under a lot of pressure, and it is a long story."

Lydia looked at him. "I have an hour. Will that do?" She smiled and continued to hold Tom's hand. "Tom, talk to me. I can tell you need to get this off your chest. Please, I mean you no harm; you know that, right?"

"It isn't my story to tell, but all I can say is that her son lives with his dad and stepmother. They are all very happy, but Jillian isn't in the decision making... I'm saying too much now. I'll tell you this; I'm not handling this the way I should. I'm trying to be supportive, but I am losing my tolerance. He isn't my child, and I need to understand that Jillian feels differently. I do worry about Danny, but I'm worried about our unborn child. Jillian was pregnant last year, we had a terrible car accident, and she lost the baby. That tore us up and now during all this stress, we find she is pregnant again."

"Women can go through a tremendous amount of stress and not lose their babies. Have faith. Really, it is what it is, don't you understand this? She can't think about the baby right now when her son that is here in the flesh needs her. Does this make sense? Her pregnancy is just now becoming real to her."

"She isn't acting like herself at all. She's a strong woman and she is falling apart."

"Tom, you can't fix her. Obviously, her stress is different than yours. But keeping in mind that he isn't your son, you are worried more about her, than about the little boy, right?"

"His name is Danny, and yes, I guess you are right. She is more important to me, of course, is that wrong?"

"No! Oh, no, not at all. I would imagine you are at the top of her list as well, but I also would guess she feels like she is being torn in two, or more like in thirds now, with the new baby in the picture. Give her some time. Just step back if you need to, but give her some time."

Tom looked at her and was surprised she was giving him such good advice. He thought she would try to come on to him, and it was quite the opposite. He looked down and discovered she was holding his hand. He tried to wiggle his hand away, but it was too late. Standing right behind them stood Jillian.

"Yes, my dear husband, give your poor, fragile wife some space. Good advice. Perhaps your new friend could just hold your hand to comfort you. After all, this has been so hard on you."

Tom stood up and reached for her. "This isn't what you think. Please, this isn't what..."

Jillian turned and marched out of the cafeteria.

Tom ran after her. He caught up to her and took her arm. By the look on her face, she was devastated.

"Please, Lydia is a friend, and she was only trying to help. She's an RN, and I needed someone to talk to. I didn't go looking for her, but we just met in the cafeteria. It was quite innocent."

"It didn't look innocent," she said, a bit stoic.

"Sweetheart, please, I didn't even realize she had my hand. When I did, I was pulling it away when you came up. It was nothing."

"Whatever it was or wasn't, it doesn't matter."

Tom let go of her arm. "What do you mean, it doesn't matter?"

"I'm on edge, of course, but I don't think for one minute that you are having a thing with that woman. Honestly, I over reacted. I know you love me and only me," she smiled. "Let's forget it. I have more on my plate than I can handle right now, and I need you by my side."

Just then, Jillian's cell rang. She looked at her phone, it was Sarah.

"No, not right now. Tom, please answer the phone and quickly explain the situation. Tell her I will call when I can."

Tom took her phone and answered it. "Hello?"

"Tom, this is Sarah. I really need to talk to Jillian. Please? It's important."

"I'm sure it is, but Jillian is at the hospital. Danny is ill. She will call you when she can. She's just too upset to talk right now. Please understand," he said, gently. "Hello? Hello?"

Sarah hung up the phone without a reply.

Jillian forced a smile. "I need to talk with you. Let's go to the hotel. We had better find Morgan. He's trying to get a flight back to New York tonight. There isn't anything he can do here now."

Tom put his arms around her. "I'm sorry, Sweetheart."

Danny

Chapter Twenty

Alone in their room, Jillian sat down and looked at Tom. Her eyes filled up with tears. Once again, her world seemed to be unraveling around her. She felt so helpless.

Jillian reached for Tom's hand. "I love you more than life. You are my world, and once again, I have shut you out. Not because I meant to. I never intended for that to happen. I need your strength. I've lost my courage, and I don't know what to do. First, our unborn son, and that was so very hard, then, all of these events with Danny. Being pregnant and not being able to be a donor to save my own child. This is just so hard. With all my heart I want this baby. For some reason, I just couldn't process it. Finding out I was pregnant was just another setback for Danny. I know it should have been a joyous time, but because of the circumstances..."

"Sweetheart..."

"Let me finish. It has been so mixed up in my mind. For some reason, at this moment here alone with you, my heart is calm, and my thoughts are becoming more logical. Have I told you that I love you? I do, I love you so much. My behavior in the cafeteria was very inconsiderate, and I will apologize to Lydia when I can. If there is one thing I hold true in this life; it is that I trust you."

"I trust you, too. You are the love of my life. Sweetheart, I have faith in you. I have confidence in us. I know this has all been so hard on you..."

"There's more, Tom. Learning that Morgan isn't a match was one thing, but because we aren't the same blood type has opened up another door of distress for me. I believe I may have been adopted, and Mom never told me. We were so close. I don't understand why she didn't tell me. After what I went through with Danny, it might have helped me. It doesn't matter at the moment, but I need to talk with Father Mike. That is why I was crying so loudly when you found Morgan and me in the hall. I simply lost it and was out of control. I know I have to call Sarah back, too. She is in a lot of

146

trouble. You know that, right? I'm just not ready to deal with that, yet I know I have to help her. This is too much for one person to handle. I need you to help me stay strong."

Tom put his arms around her. "I'll do whatever you need me to do. I'm here for you. You have to know that. We'll do this together. Why don't you take a shower and I'll call room service. You can call Father Michael after we eat. Then maybe you should rest a little before we go back to the hospital."

"I will rest. I want to keep our new little one safe. I'm so overwhelmed, but the thought of having a baby is helping more than you know. I'm hungry, and a shower does sound incredible."

After her shower, Jillian sat down at the small table. The food hadn't arrived yet, so she picked up her cell phone and called Father Michael.

"What news do you have for us, Honey?"

"Morgan isn't a suitable match either."

Without any hesitation, Father Michael spoke up. "I'll fly over right away to get tested."

Jillian was taken aback. "Mike? None of us so far have been suitable donors. What are the chances?"

"I have to try, Jillian. The eligibility of me being a donor is as good as anyone else's out there. I love you dearly and would give my life for you. If I am a match, I would be honored to help your son. Besides, I am getting older, and it would be a great feeling knowing I was able to accomplish something miraculous in my time here on earth."

Jillian's eyes filled up with tears. "I love you so much for wanting to help Danny, but I think you might be too old?"

"I'm not too old," he said. "I'll make the arrangements right away. Let them know I'm coming."

"Thanks, Mike, I love you so much. Morgan will be back there later tonight. If you want, you could leave first thing in the morning. Be safe. I love you."

"Father Michael is coming to get tested."

Tom looked puzzled. "I wonder if he couldn't get tested in New York."

"Maybe so, I don't know, but I'm glad he's coming to Denver."

"I thought you were going to ask about being adopted?"

"I was, but it can wait. I think I'll call Sarah now," she sighed.

Jillian dialed Sarah's number, and Sarah answered on the first ring.

"Thank you for calling me back so quickly. I have to talk with you."

"Okay, tell me what is going on?"

"First, how is Danny?"

"We'll talk about Danny afterward. Tell me what has happened."

"Brent was right about Trevor. He is a romance scammer. There isn't even a real person named Trevor. He doesn't exist. The papers Brent gave me included some names and phone numbers of the other women that were almost scammed. One actually was. She lost her husband and her children. It is a terrible story."

"We tried to tell you all of this in Dallas. What changed?"

"I asked him. That's what changed. I told him I called the other women, and he hung up the phone. I haven't heard a word since."

"I'm happy for you. It could have turned out much worse, you know."

"I'm asking that you never tell Phillip. He can never find out. This would destroy him. Please don't ever tell him," she begged.

Jillian was livid. "Really? That is why you called me? You called to beg me not to tell your husband? Sarah, you owe him the truth, but it isn't up to me to tell Phillip anything about this."

"I don't know what I'm going to do yet, but I just need to hear it from your lips that you won't tell him."

"Sarah, I can see that we're not friends any longer. Friends trust each other and, evidently, you don't trust me. Have a happy life with Phillip or whoever," Jillian said disconnecting the call.

Tom looked stunned but curious.

"It's okay. She doesn't need me as her friend. She was worried I would tell her husband. I would have never told him, and she should have known that. We tried to help her. I guess she never really was my friend, but it all works out in the end, doesn't it? I never even got to tell Sarah about Danny. I suppose she will run into Tony at some point, and he can fill her in. You are my best friend and that is all I need."

The food arrived, and Jillian ate slowly. She managed to finish her sandwich and most of the fries. She pushed herself away from the table, and Tom stood up and kissed her. She hadn't been really kissed in days, and as she responded she felt herself loosen up even more. They lay on the bed and cuddled for a while. They were both too tired for much more than that, and Jillian fell asleep in the arms of her best friend. They awoke several hours later to a knock on their door. It was Morgan saying his cab was waiting, and he wanted to say goodbye. He kissed his sister and hugged her tenderly. Jillian told him about Father Michael, and she promised to keep him up to date. After saying goodbye to Morgan, they dressed and went back to the hospital.

Tony was standing out in the hall when they arrived. Angela was in with Danny. Tony looked terrible. He had lost weight and was very pale. He had dark circles under his eyes, and his cheeks appeared hollow. He hadn't combed his hair in days, and most likely just rinsed off in the shower. Angela brought him fresh clothes every day and he manage to change.

"Tony, let us stay with Danny tonight. You go home and get some rest. I promise to call if anything changes, but honestly, you need some rest."

Angela came out in the hall and put her arm around Tony's waist. She hugged him and said he should listen to Jillian. Tom spoke up in agreement with the ladies.

"Okay. I can't fight you all," Tony responded. "I really need a good night's sleep, and I am longing to see Julie Ann and Bella.

"Good, we will be right here in the hospital, and one of us will be with him at all times. Father Michael will be here in the morning. Would you please let the doctors know he is coming for testing?"

"What? That's great news. I'll let them know. Isn't he a little too old?"

"That's what I said, too. But Father Mike assured me he wasn't. I guess we'll find that out when he gets here."

"Angela and I will leave about seven, so you two go grab a bite to eat first."

"We just finished a late lunch at the hotel. Morgan already left for the airport. He said to say goodbye. If you want to leave earlier, go ahead," Jillian said.

"No, seven o'clock is fine with me. It's only a few hours from now."

"Tony," Angela said. "Let's go home now. Danny is sleeping, and I'm sure Julie Ann would appreciate more time with her daddy before she goes to bed. She hasn't seen you in days. I'll need to get going soon anyway. I only left one bottle with Martha, and Bella will be hungry soon."

Tony looked defeated. Not having the strength to argue, he gave in. "Okay... Alright... Let's go."

Together, they walked down the hallway and disappeared through the large double doors at the end of the hall. Jillian took Tom's hand, and they went into Danny's room. He seemed to be sleeping peacefully, and Jillian walked up and kissed his forehead.

"Mommy?" Danny murmured.

"No Little Prince, It's Jillian. Your mommy will be back in the morning. You just sleep, my little angel."

Tom put his arm around his wife, and she put her head on his shoulder.

"It is as it should be. He needs a full-time mommy, and Angela loves him. All I want is his happiness. He is very attached to her, and this makes me happy."

Tom looked at her with loving eyes. Jillian was coming to terms with the way things had turned out, and it seemed she had made peace with it.

* * *

Father Michael got to the hospital at six-thirty in the morning. He had taken the red eye, and he looked tired. He went straight to Danny's room and found Jillian and Tom sleeping in reclining chairs. He touched Jillian on her shoulder, and her eyes flew open.

"I didn't mean to startle you," he whispered, this time waking Tom. "Do you know where I am supposed to go?"

Jillian smiled at her dear friend. "Good morning, Mike. How was your flight?"

"It was okay. I didn't eat, though. I wasn't sure if I should or not."

"They won't do the glucose test until tomorrow, and I didn't get past the first day so I don't know for sure. We can ask the nurse to be sure then we can get a bite downstairs after Tony gets here. When I came for testing, they came in here looking for me."

"Good morning, Tom."

"Good morning. It's good to see you." Tom said.

"Hi, Father Michael," a sleepy Danny piped in.

Father Michael smiled at Danny. "It is good to see you this beautiful morning."

Danny smiled and asked for his dad. He saw Tom and waved his hand. Tom smiled and took his hand in his and held it. About seven-thirty, someone came in and took Father Michael out of the room and down the hall. Jillian could see he was praying as he walked away. She saw the rosary in his hand and she flashed back to when her mother lay dying in a California hospital. She remembered how she had begged Father Michael to do something to save her mother. Remembering how she had asked him to speak to God. "He'll listen to you," she had said. Father Michael explained that it didn't work that way and that it was in God's hands. Moments later, her mother was gone. The remembrance of this brought her to tears. She turned to look at Danny, who was sleeping again. Tony and Angela got there about eight o'clock. Angela handed Jillian a bag, explaining that Martha made she and Tom breakfast. Jillian looked inside the bag and pulled out three breakfast burritos wrapped in foil, and the burritos were still hot. Jillian smiled as she remembered the first time she had one of Martha's breakfast burritos. She had eaten two of them on that morning. Tom suggested they go down for something hot to drink. They could enjoy their burritos in the cafeteria.

"Tony, Father Mike is here. He's with the doctors right now. I'll save a burrito for him."

"Thanks," Tony responded.

He seemed to be in good spirits. He looked so much better than the night before when he and Angela had left the hospital. Jillian could tell that the trip home had done him wonders.

As they waited for the elevator, Tom kissed his wife. She smiled and held him close. The elevator door opened, and they stepped inside. There stood Lydia, who greeted both with a very cheerful, "Good morning."

It was awkward at first, but Jillian chose to speak up.

"Lydia, I was out of line yesterday. I understand that you were giving Tom good advice, but seeing you sitting there holding his hand was complicated for me. I was looking for my 'rock' and stumbled across him sitting with a beautiful woman, and she had his hand in hers. I know it was innocent. I was in a bad place at that moment. My behavior was inappropriate, and I'm very sorry."

Lydia held open her arms to Jillian and Jillian hugged her. The awkwardness between them faded. This was a touching moment for Jillian, but for Tom, it was another step towards regaining the wife he knew and loved and missed.

"Jillian, it's okay. Tell me how your son is doing? Any luck finding a donor?"

"No, but we're hopeful."

"I was telling Tom yesterday that it takes time. Your son will manage for a while on dialysis, and there is time. I know you feel time is of the essence, but unless the doctors have told you differently, your son does have time. The registry can take a while to find a suitable donor. Don't lose hope."

"Yes, we know this, but I get so frightened for him. A friend of the family is here now getting tested."

The ding of the elevator making an announced stop interrupted them. "This is my floor. It was nice to meet you. Let's talk again. If you have any questions, maybe I can help. I'm not a renal nurse, but I do have some insight on the subject," Lydia offered, stepping out of the elevator just before the door closed.

Jillian looked at Tom, and he smiled at her. She reached up and touched his face. Tom took her hand and kissed it tenderly. Jillian closed her eyes as their lips met and they lingered in the moment. The next ding of the elevator reminded them that they had reached the cafeteria. As they walked up to the counter to order their drinks, Tom took her hand and gave it a squeeze. They were traveling down a rocky path, but together they would endure it.

They ate their breakfast burritos slowly, and for the first time talked about nothing but the baby. Tom shared with her that he was very excited. The timing wasn't exactly the greatest, but he felt this happiness in his heart as they had been given another chance at having a baby. Tom confessed that he was hoping for another boy, but he was just so happy they were pregnant.

"I have had some time to think, and honestly, I am happy. It only seems natural that you want a boy, but for some reason, I'm hoping for a girl. I have no clue why, but like you said, either way, it will be our child."

Jillian reached across the table and took Tom's hand in hers. "I love you," she said. "When we find out what Father Mike is doing maybe we should go back to the hotel for a shower. I don't know about you, but I didn't get much sleep in that chair, and I could really use a nap. Speaking of Father Mike, he just came out of the elevator," she said, waving her hand for Father Michael to see them.

"So, how'd it go?" Tom asked.

"So far, so good. We are a blood type match which is a good start. I just had some tests, including a chest x-ray and more blood work.

Guess they are looking to see if I can survive donating a kidney for such an old man as I."

"I didn't know we were the same blood type? This is a great start. What else did they do? I never got any further than the first blood test before they discovered I was pregnant."

"Morgan told me you were pregnant. This will be a blessing. I am very happy for both of you. As far as more tests, I'm not sure. They said something about tissue typing for proteins or something like that. I know there is a glucose test. I don't know why they need to do that, but I'll be ready. They said to go downstairs and get something to eat; then be back in an hour. I'm just doing whatever they tell me."

"We'll sit with you while you eat then we're going back to the hotel. You can call me on my cell when you're done, and we'll come back to get you. I never meant anything bad when I insinuated that you were too old, you know?"

Father Michael smiled. "I know."

* * *

Alone in their room, they showered together, and Jillian washed Tom's back. One thing led to another and soon they were making love. Jillian thought of nothing other than being with Tom. She turned off the water and took Tom's wet hand and led him to the bed.

Jillian was purring as she gazed into Tom's eyes. "Thank you."

"No. Thank you," he smiled. "I needed to be with you. I love you so much," he said taking her in his arms and kissing her.

After their lovemaking, they slept like babies and several hours went by until their slumber was upset by the ringing of Jillian's cell phone.

"Hello?"

"It's Father Mike, I'm done for the day. I'm visiting with Tony and Angela, and Danny is sleeping. It's looking excellent. I don't mean to get your hopes up, but it really is looking good."

"What fantastic news. I love you so much for wanting to help Danny. Thank you with all my heart. We're on our way."

"What is that huge smile on your face for? What did Father Michael tell you?"

"He said it's looking good. Can you believe it? Maybe this will be the miracle we have been asking for."

"Sweetheart, we have to wait until all the tests are done. Even after that; remember Morgan said the results take a few days to a week. One day at a time is what we have right now."

"I know, but I can't help feeling excited about this. Come on, let's go over to the hospital and see Danny."

They dressed and drove over to the hospital. They rushed up to Danny's room. Jillian was still wearing her huge smile as they entered the room.

Tony was wearing the same smile. He looked hopeful for the first time in days. "Hi, guys."

"Hi," Jillian said smiling. "How's Danny?" she asked walking over to the bed.

Jillian bent down and kissed him on his forehead. Danny opened his eyes and smiled up at her.

"I'm hungry," Danny said.

"I'll bet you are, sleepyhead. Every time I come to see you guess what? You're sleeping. So, I wonder what's for lunch."

"I'm sure it's nothing that tastes good. They give me stuff I don't like. I want to go home and eat real food," Danny grunted.

Tony came over to the bed and stood by Jillian. He looked at his son and gently touched his nose with his finger. "You'll be home soon, and then Martha will make you anything you want. Just a little while longer and we'll take you home."

They visited for a while then took Father Michael to the hotel to check in. He said he wasn't tired, but Jillian knew the minute he got to his room he would feel differently about that. They had dinner at the hotel then Jillian decided she would talk to Father Michael about her suspicions of being adopted. She knew that whatever the story was with her mother, Father Mike would certainly know about it. They had been that close.

Jillian watched him as he finished his meal then took her chance. "Father Mike, I need to ask you something. For some reason, Morgan and I are not the same blood type and..."

"Siblings aren't always the same blood type. It doesn't mean anything."

"You didn't even let me finish. Our parents have the same blood type so Morgan and I should have the same blood type, but we don't. I have B positive which is impossible unless we don't have the same parents," she said. "Am I adopted? If I am, I know that you would know about it."

"You aren't adopted. There were pictures of Mary when she was expecting you. Those pictures were in the living room photo album. I saw her pregnant with you every Sunday in church. Why in the world would you think you were adopted?"

"I told you. Morgan and I don't have the same blood type. If Mom and Dad have the same, then we would too, but we don't," she said, feeling oddly insecure.

Father Michael looked at Jillian then raised a brow. He frowned a little and shook his head. "Well, there has to be a mistake. Don't worry about it. Just let it go. Someone has made a mistake. It's just that simple. Maybe one of your parent's had a different type, and you have just always thought they were the same. Honestly, Jillian, you shouldn't let your imagination run wild like this. If you had been adopted, Mary would have told you. I would have known."

Jillian didn't want to make a big deal about it, but something wasn't feeling right here. She remembered what Morgan had said, and she believed her brother was right.

"No, I can't let this go. You're wrong about this. Morgan told me that he knew for sure that both Mom and Dad had A positive blood, just like him. I have B positive, and I don't have any idea where that came from. Danny has B positive like me, and I passed that on to him. Something just isn't right here. Morgan said it was impossible for me to have any other type but A positive."

Father Michael grinned at her. "We may never know the answer to this question. Both your parents are gone, and this might end with them. Honestly, if you ask me, I would have to say that either your mother or your father had B positive, and that is where you get it from. Don't bring a mystery into this when there is, most likely, a very simple explanation."

Jillian looked at Tom and then back to Father Michael. She shook her head with bewilderment. She wasn't letting it go, but just for tonight, she would drop the subject. She looked at Tom, and he raised an eyebrow. She just smiled.

Chapter Twenty-One

Father Michael had been in Denver for five days. The testing was over, and the results were in. He was a suitable match, and the procedures were scheduled. After the surgery, Father Michael would stay at the hospital for several days then he would go to Tony's home to rest for a week or so before flying home to Colorado. Jillian, along with everyone else, was ecstatic with the results. The doctors felt Danny would be able to lead a full and healthy life, and be back to his old self within a short period of time. The procedure took over three hours, and Jillian and Tom were there for Father Michael after he was taken out of recovery. Jillian felt the risk was greater for Father Michael and she wanted to be near him until she knew he was out of any danger. Martha was pacing the floor at home with Bella in her arms while Tony and Angela sat quietly waiting for the doctor to come out of surgery and let them know how it all went.

Danny's surgery went well, and everyone was very relieved. Father Michael was the first to be brought into a room where he could have visitors. They knew Danny would still be in surgery, and recovery would take quite a bit longer. Jillian wanted to be there when Father Michael opened his eyes, and so she sat beside his bed and waited.

"You're awake? How do you feel? Are you in pain?"

Jillian was full of questions and Tom patted her arm letting Father Michael get a word in edgewise.

"I assume I'm just fine. I'm more concerned about Danny. Is he okay? How is he doing?"

"He's still in recovery, but the doctor told us that he did very well. You look very exhausted for a hero."

"Even heroes have to rest," he smiled. "I don't consider myself a hero. I love you and Danny is a part of you. However, if he should need another kidney, it's on you. I only have one left."

Father Michael was trying not to laugh at his own joke. The pain was a little sharp. He winced a few times, and Jillian could see he needed quiet so he could rest. She asked the nurse to give him something. The nurse assured her that he was fully medicated and that he needed to sleep. She suggested they get some coffee or something from the cafeteria. Besides, the walk would do them good after their long sit in the waiting room. Tom reminded Jillian that she should rest a little as well.

Jillian kissed Father Michael on the cheek. "Tom's right. We'll let you rest, and we'll be back later. If you need us, I left my cell number with the nurse's station. I love you so much. And yes, you are a hero. You are now at this moment, and looking back, you have always been my hero."

Jillian needed to call Morgan. She knew he would be pacing the floors until he heard anything. She looked at Tom and took his hand. Together they left hand in hand and headed for the cafeteria. Jillian spotted Angela standing at the counter waiting for coffee. Jillian briskly, half walked, half ran, in that direction. The clicking of Jillian's heels caused Angela to turn around.

"Any word on Danny?"

"Danny is doing great. They'll keep him in intensive care for forty-eight hours, and then he will go to the transplant care unit on the third floor. He did so well. You can see him in a while. Tony is with him right now. Give it about an hour, and then I'm sure they will let you in. We didn't explain the situation, and they will only permit the parents in for now, but we'll figure it out. Please, how is Father Michael?"

"That's fantastic news. I knew Danny was a real trooper. Father Michael is in a little bit of pain. They have him resting right now. The nurse kind of kicked us out, gently," Jillian said, smiling. "We'll go back later, but I'm sure he will sleep for hours. I would love to peek in on Danny and then we will probably go to the hotel. Will you call us on my cell when I can see him, please?"

"Sure, or just come to intensive care in an hour. I'll meet you in the waiting room."

"Thanks, Angela; I'm so worried about him."

"Try to relax. The worst is over. Danny will do just fine. He's so brave, and the doctors said he is doing very well. We are so grateful for Father Michael. I want to really spoil him when he comes to the house. You and Tom will have to come for dinner before you go back to New York."

"Well, actually we were planning on staying for a while," Jillian said with a confused expression on her face.

"Jillian, you and Tom have your own life together, and I believe it is time for us all to get back to our normal routines as soon as possible. I assumed that Tom would be needed back in his office before too long."

Tom agreed. "I think that would be best for all of us. As soon as we know both Danny and Father Michael are out of the woods, we really should be getting back to New York."

Jillian didn't know what to say. She wanted to stay until Danny was running and jumping and feeling as good as new. She glanced at Tom, who was looking back at her. He smiled and gave her a look that only she would understand. He was right. Jillian was running on emotions, and they both needed to get back to their lives in New York.

"You're right as usual. We'll go home in a few days. Just as soon as they both are released," Jillian said.

"Father Michael should be released in a few days, but Danny will be here at least a week, maybe longer. Jillian, if we thought there was any reason for you to stay; honestly, we would tell you. I know how much Danny appreciates you being here. He will be okay and up for a visit real soon. You are always welcome to come to Denver any time you would like."

Tom nodded and took Jillian's hand. "Coffee! I need coffee," he joked. "We'll see you in about an hour. Let Tony know that Jillian wants to see Danny as soon as possible."

Jillian looked surprised at his boldness, but Angela smiled and walked away with her tray, and walked toward the elevator.

"Sweetheart, Angela gets a little threatened by you every once in a while. We need to learn not to intrude on their lives. We need to be careful not to overstep our boundaries. I have a feeling that if we go along with what they both want we will be further ahead."

Jillian stood there looking at him. "I don't understand."

"I think you do, Sweetie. Just think about it for a minute. They are newlyweds and trying to sort out this step parenting thing. It isn't easy. The kids are now calling her mommy, and she is going to protect that relationship. Angela is a wonderful person, but she has to feel just a bit insecure when it comes to you. She really is very kind to you, but I can hear it in her voice from time to time. You need to play by her rules, which will be fair, from what I can tell. One word from her to Tony and you could lose what little you have with Danny."

"Tony would never keep Danny from me."

"Maybe, or maybe not, but do you want to take that risk? All I'm saying is you only have a small part in Danny's life. Let the stepmother have what now belongs to her. I made you a promise back in Atlanta that I will never allow Tony to forbid you to see Danny. As a lawyer, I can hold Tony to the agreement in a heartbeat, but let's not get into any trouble here. Tony allows you to see Danny far more than what the agreement calls for. This really is a great arrangement. I think the relationship between you, Tony, and Angela is stable. We don't need to be here when he goes home. That will be their happy family reunion. We are not a part of that."

"I know. I'm not trying to make things difficult for her."

"I'm sure you're not, but when Angela said it was time for us to go home, well…"

Tom seemed to be struggling with his explanation and Jillian wasn't exactly making it an easy on him. He stood there looking at her for a moment, and then that tender smile came over his face.

"We're not getting anywhere with this right now. We're both tired, and I'm hungry. Let's just get something to eat. Are you as hungry as I am?"

"I am. I'm starving."

Tom laughed. "Oh, no, my pregnant wife is hungry. Nothing could make me happier."

Jillian and Tom waited an hour then went to the intensive care unit. Danny was awake but groggy. He wasn't in a very good mood, and it seemed no one was able to make him smile. Danny was in pain, and he wanted to go home. He said that he missed Sydney and was worried that no one was playing with him.

"Hey Little Prince, I can go to your house and play with Sydney if you'd like," Jillian said. "I miss him, too, and it would be really nice to see him. I'll tell him you will be home real soon."

"You will?" Danny moaned.

"Yes, of course, I will. Tom got to see Julie Ann, but I haven't seen her since we came to Denver, so that will give me a chance to see her too."

"Then, you and Tom should go to the house tomorrow afternoon. Julie Ann will be back from Betty's," Angela said. "You haven't met Bella either."

Jillian didn't want to see their new baby, but it was inescapable. "I would love to see your new daughter. That would be great. We'll drop by your house before we leave tomorrow for New York. We'll have to take a rain check on that dinner."

Tom looked at her with astonishment. The nurse came in and said there were too many visitors in Danny's room. Tom thanked the nurse for allowing the gathering and told her they would leave right away.

Jillian looked over at Tony. "We're going to look in on Father Michael then we'll be going back to the hotel."

They said goodbye and went to see if Father Michael was awake. He wasn't, and there was no point in sitting there watching him sleep. They walked to the parking lot and drove over to the hotel. Back in their room, Tom called his secretary, Donna, and asked her to work her magic and get them a flight home the next evening. If there were a way, Donna would find it.

"I'll call Morgan again and let him know we are coming home. I guess they are ready to go back to California. I think he said they were leaving in a couple of days. We sure didn't get to visit much. Promise me we will go see them in a few months."

"Sure, of course, we will. That'll be fun."

Jillian gave Tom that special look that he knew all too well, and he smiled. "You look as if you need a nap?"

Jillian returned the smile. "As a matter of fact..."

Jillian reached for him and kissed him tenderly. "Take a shower while I call Morgan. Then I'll help you fall to sleep."

"Promise?" he begged.

"Yes," she purred.

* * *

The next morning, Jillian and Tom went to see the two patients. Father Mike was sitting in a chair in his room, and Jillian was delighted.

"Father Mike, you're up."

"I am," he concurred with a smile. "Honestly, there isn't much pain or the medicine works very well."

"That's wonderful. I'm so happy you are doing better. I was so worried because of your..."

"My what? Were you going to say, my age?"

"Oh, no, I wasn't," she fibbed. "Okay, yes I was. You're not that old, but you're almost sixty, you know."

"Sixty is the new forty, haven't you heard? If I were too old, they would have never taken my ancient kidney. Actually, I'm over sixty. You lost count somewhere."

Tom was laughing at the both of them. Things were starting to get back to normal again. He patted Father Michael on the shoulder and Jillian gave him a hug.

"You are the next best thing to having a dad, and I can worry about you if I want. I love you more than you know, and now that you are my hero, I love you even more."

"I thought you said I have always been your hero?"

"You have. You most definitely, truly have."

"Sweetheart, I'll stay here and chat with Father Michael, while you go see Danny. Give him my love and tell him I'll see him before we leave."

Father Michael looked surprised. "Jillian, you're leaving? How soon?"

"We're going back to New York this evening. Morgan is still there, and they are leaving tomorrow afternoon to go home. It's time we got back, and Tom really needs to get back to the office."

"This sounds like the right thing to do. As long as Danny is out of the woods, then you and Tom should go home. Besides, who would take care of Lucy?"

"We're not really worried about Lucy. We have some great neighbors now, and Tom's mother could come get her, but, well, it's time to go home. Tom and I discussed it, and we both agree that it would be confusing for Danny to wonder why we are hanging around. He will never know I am his mother, and why would a friend of the family spend all this time here? No, we need to go home. Tom and I are concerned that Angela will take my presence here the wrong way. We don't want to interfere in their lives any more than we have already. Danny is going to be just fine thanks to your love and sacrifice. I will definitely rest better at home in my own bed, and I need to see my doctor as soon as possible. After all, we need to start planning for a baby again."

Jillian looked over at Tom. Realizing what she had just said, and seeing the look in his eyes, she began to cry. Tom put his arms around her, and she surrendered to his comfort. He truly was the calm she sought. He knew her heart, and he knew her pain.

Jillian, trying to regain her composure, smiled. "Okay you two, behave. I'm off to see Danny. I'll be back in a bit."

Jillian turned to leave then rushed back to give her two favorite men a kiss. Back out in the hallway, she hurried to the elevator that would take her to Danny. She walked down the hall to the waiting room and looked around for Angela or Tony, but neither one was there. She wasn't sure what to say to the nurse as she picked up the phone to call the nurse's station.

"ICU. This is Colleen. May I help you?"

"Yes, this is Jillian Bentley; may I come in to see Danny Martelli?"

"Just one minute please," Colleen responded, hanging up the phone.

A few moments later, a nurse that Jillian suspected was Colleen, came to the door and called out her name. This tickled Jillian as she was the only one in the waiting room. She followed the nurse to Danny's room where he was all alone. He looked so tiny in this room.

"Hi," Danny said with more strength than he had the day before.

"Hi Little Prince," Jillian said, finding a lump in her throat. She wanted to hold him so much. She wanted to scoop him up in her arms and run away with him. She hadn't had much time alone with him since this all began, and she wasn't sure what to say.

"Where's Tom? Is he home playing with Sydney?"

"No, Kiddo. He is waiting downstairs having a cup of coffee."

She wasn't sure what they had told him about Father Michael, if anything, and didn't want to tell him something that might upset him.

"He'll come to see you later. We are going back to New York this evening, and we are going to really miss you. We are so happy that you are doing so well. You are such a strong young man."

"I am very strong. Daddy said I have great arm muscles."

Jillian couldn't help but laugh. What a blessing he was to her. "Oh, Danny, you are too much."

Jillian took a chair and pulled it closer to the bed. She took his hand and held it tenderly. She looked at her son, who had been through so much, and for as much as she wanted to cry; she knew she couldn't. She smiled, and they talked about Sydney.

"I forgot to bring the pictures, but I will mail them to you. Just wait until you see how cute Sydney was when he was a baby. His hair was so long you could hardly see his eyes. He was very rambunctious, too. He ran around my house like he was on fire."

Their conversation was disrupted by the abrasive intercom in the hall.

"Code Blue, ICU. Code Blue, ICU."

It made Jillian's heart skip a beat. She felt panic well up inside her. All she could think about was how she had heard this just before her mother had died. She had hoped to never hear it again. Nurses were running through the hall and someone pushing a cart with medical equipment on it. She tried not to look, but Danny was fascinated. He bolted up in bed, and for a brief moment, he was feeling no pain.

"What are they doing?"

"It's okay, Kiddo. One of the patients must need help. They call that a Code Blue, and it makes all the nurses run to the room."

"Can we have one?" he inquired, his curiosity mounting as he watched the commotion outside his room. "Can we have a Code Blue?"

"Can we have what? Oh, no. Don't even say that. No, young man, we certainly cannot have a Code Blue. Things are fine just the way they are. Oh, Danny, we are just fine."

Danny put his head back down on his pillow and winced just a little.

"Are you in pain?"

"It's okay, honest. Don't tell Daddy. I'm not supposed to be moving around until one of the nurses says it's okay. Please don't tell."

"I won't tell, I promise. Now, no more moving around until they tell you it's okay."

"I promise."

Jillian had another twenty minutes with Danny before one of the nurses came in and gently ushered her out to the waiting room where Tony and Angela were sitting sipping on coffee.

"Good morning," Jillian said with a huge smile. "How are you both doing today?"

Angela smiled. "The nurse told us you were with Danny, and we wanted to give you some time alone."

"Thank you. I enjoyed being with him very much. Danny asked me where Tom was. I wasn't sure if I should tell him he was with Father Michael or not. What have you told him about the donor?"

Tony smiled and shrugged his shoulders. "We haven't said anything about where the kidney came from. He hasn't asked. For all we know he thinks it was made. He has no idea it came from a living person."

"Are you going to tell him what Father Michael did for him?"

"I don't know. We'll cross that bridge when we get to it. I'm sure it will come up at some point, and I'll deal with it then. We are scheduled to see a therapist in a few weeks, so I'll ask about how we are supposed to handle it."

"I just wanted to know. Anyway, I told him Tom was downstairs having a cup of coffee. I said we would come back one more time before we left to say goodbye. If it's alright with you, Tom and I are going over to the house later to see Julie Ann, Bella, and Sydney."

"That'll be fine," Tony responded. "Angela, would you call Martha and make sure she feeds them lunch?"

Angela reached into her purse for her cell phone. "Sure, Honey, I'll call her right now."

Jillian excused herself and went to Father Michael's room. She noticed that there were many potted plants along the halls, and the main lobby was full of plants. She thought it odd that she hadn't noticed any of it before. She looked around as she walked, and she noticed all the colors mixed in between the plants and the pictures on the walls. How odd she hadn't noticed there was music coming from intercoms all throughout the hospital. People were sitting in small waiting rooms that she never noticed before. She was astounded at what she had missed. She took the elevator to Father Michael's room. As she was going down the hall, she saw Father Michael coming towards her with Tom on one side and a nurse on the other. It was odd for her to see him in a gown and slipper socks. He seemed so different from the way she had always remembered him. He had always looked so big to her. Seeing him now, needing help to walk, broke her heart. She knew that by the end of the day he would be running circles around them, but for this moment, he needed help. He looked small and somehow frail to her. She smiled as she thought about what he had said about sixty being the new forty.

She waved her hands in the air to get their attention. "Hi, guys!"

They looked up and smiled at her. As she got closer, she could see how pale Father Michael was, but he would be alright... Of this she was certain.

* * *

164

It was close to noon when they got to Tony's house. Martha and Julie Ann greeted them at the door, right along with Sydney. In true form, he leaped into Jillian's arms.

"You're such a good little boy, Syd. I miss you so much," she whispered. Julie Ann stood there next to her with arms stretched high.

Tom scooped her up and quietly told her a secret.

Julie Ann looked up at Jillian. "Oh? No more picking me up until you have your baby? Sydney had better stop jumping on you, too."

Jillian looked at Tom, and he shrugged his shoulders. She loved him for being so protective of her.

"Come with me," Julie Ann commanded. "I want you to see my baby sister, Bella. She is very tiny. Mommy couldn't pick me up either. We had to wait until Bella got born."

"Are you expecting?" Martha asked, offering Jillian a hug.

"Yes, we are. I haven't seen my doctor yet, but I am definitely pregnant. It was hard to be excited considering all that has happened, but, yes we are very happy, now that it is actually sinking in."

Julie Ann was tugging on her hand, and Jillian went with her to meet little Bella. Jillian was taken aback when she saw this baby. Her dark hair and olive skin were breathtaking. She looked so much like her mother, but then she looked like Tony as well. Her eyes were dark brown like her parents. She was beautiful. She had such a sweet round face and huge eyes. She smiled at her big sister as they approached her crib.

"Do you want to pick her up?" Julie Ann inquired.

"Absolutely! But in a little while, okay? I'll have to put Sydney down first."

Martha was right behind them.

Jillian smiled. "She's beautiful."

Martha was beaming with pride. "Bella truly is a beauty. It's a shame Angela has to be away from her so much, but she insists on being with Danny. She loves the children very much."

"I know she does. I can see that in the way she is with Danny. I am very happy for Danny and Julie Ann. They have a mommy now. This is as it should be."

Martha hugged her and gave her a gentle squeeze. Jillian walked into the living room and put Sydney down. He followed her all throughout the house. Jillian knew he was missing Danny and was confused by Danny not being there. She bent down and patted him on the head.

"Sydney, you need to be a good boy. Danny will be home soon. He misses you very much."

Sydney looked at her and cocked his head, first to one side and then to the other.

"I miss you terribly, too, but you're Danny's now."

Martha had prepared lunch, and Julie Ann came running to find them both. She took a hand from each of them and brought them to the kitchen.

"If you would rather eat in the dining room, I can set it up for you, but I thought I'd make you a more casual lunch if that's alright?"

"This is perfect. It will be wonderful eating in the kitchen. Just like old times," Jillian announced, wishing now that she hadn't by the look on Tom's face.

"I'm sorry, Tom. That was thoughtless of me. I didn't mean it to sound like it did. You know that, right?"

"It's fine, really. I know you had some very good times in this house when you lived here."

Martha made an attempt to change the subject, and it worked. She put the food on the table and asked what they would like to drink. Jillian was amazed at how wonderful everything looked for such short notice.

"Martha, you sure know how to spoil a girl. I love your taco salad. Before we leave, I want the recipe if you don't mind?"

"Certainly, you may have it. I'll have Julie Ann make a copy for you."

"Julie Ann can operate the copy machine? Wow! Pretty soon we will be going to her wedding."

"Martha, thank you so much for lunch. It's been nice to visit with you, but we need to get back to the hospital to say goodbye. Our flight leaves in four hours, and so we better get going," Tom said taking Jillian's hand and helping her up from the kitchen table.

Jillian took Martha's hand. "Yes, thank you. Lunch was delicious. Take care, Martha. It was so nice to see you. Father Mike is anxious to have some of your cooking."

Jillian gave Martha a hug, and they both wiped their eyes.

"You two have a safe trip home, and we'll see you both real soon, I'm sure."

"Thanks again," Jillian said, as they walked towards the door with Julie Ann tugging on her arm.

"What is it, Princess?"

"Don't you want to say goodbye to Bella?"

"She's sleeping right now, but you can tell her that they said goodbye," Martha said, giving her a gentle swat on the behind.

Tom picked Julie Ann up so she could give Jillian a hug and then Jillian thought of Sydney. After kissing Julie Ann, she bent down to pet Sydney. As her hand caressed his silky coat, Jillian could not contain herself any longer. The tears began, and she fell completely apart. Martha took Julie Ann to the kitchen, and Tom tried to comfort his wife.

"I'm sorry, I just can't help it. So much has happened and..."

"It's okay, Sweetheart. I know how you feel about Sydney. He was your little 'rock', and he offered you comfort when it was just the two of you. Of course, I know how hard this has been on you and now; here you are, and you have to say goodbye to Sydney one more time."

"I'm okay. It's just a little harder with all that has happened. I'm okay."

Jillian got a tissue out of her pocket and blew her nose. Tom opened the door, and they walked out leaving Sydney to watch them as they shut the door behind them and walked to the car.

They arrived at the hospital and went to Danny's room. Tom left her in the waiting room saying he would like to say goodbye to Lydia while she went in to see Danny. It was still parents only so Tom wouldn't be able to see him. Jillian told herself she didn't mind, but deep down there was a little twinge of jealousy.

Jillian picked up the phone to call a nurse and was soon ushered in to see Danny. Tony and Angela offered to step out in the hall, but Jillian told them that it wasn't a problem. Danny was sleeping, so Jillian bent down and kissed his forehead. It didn't wake him as she had hoped, so she turned to Tony and thanked him for everything. She handed him the keys to the car and said they would be taking a cab to the airport.

"I'll go find Tom then we will say goodbye to Father Michael. Tony, please call if..."

"Danny will be okay, but I promise to call you if any problems should arise."

"Angela, thank you for your kindness; I can see why Tony and the kids adore you."

Tony gave her a hug and whispered in her ear, "Jilly, it will all be okay. I wish the best for both of you and promise me you'll take care of that baby. We'll see you soon. Say goodbye to Tom for us."

Tony released her from his hug and sent her on her way. Jillian turned for one more look at her son then left to find Tom. She looked downstairs in the cafeteria but didn't see him. She checked in the main lobby and still no Tom. She took the elevator to Father Michael's floor and went in to see him. Tom and Father Michael were both sitting in chairs discussing golf. This made Jillian smile as she walked in.

"There you are," she said, looking at Tom. "Did you find Lydia?"

"I did. It was a short goodbye then I came here. I figured the best place to find you was right here, and I was right."

Jillian looked at Father Michael. "How are you feeling?"

"I'm anxious to have some of Martha's cooking. The food here is the pits," he laughed.

"How funny, I know you so well. I told Martha you were looking forward to some of her cooking. She is going to spoil you."

"I'm being released in the morning. Tony and Angela will pick me up and take me to their home. I wanted to go by to see Danny, but he can only have parents with him right now. Oh, I could play the priest card, but I'll see him soon enough. Tom told me you were saying goodbye to Danny. I know that was hard on you."

"It was okay, really. When are you going home to Sweetwater?"

"I'm not sure. I have to check in with Dr. Turner as soon as I get home. What is that look on your face for?"

Jillian began to cry again. This tickled Tom, and he put his head down so Jillian couldn't see his smile, but she did.

"What? Why are you giggling over there?"

"Sweetheart, I'm just touched by your emotions right now. There is no doubt in my mind. You're pregnant."

Chapter Twenty-Two

Father Michael flew back to Sweetwater two weeks after the kidney transplant. Danny was home and recovering nicely. He was anxious to get back to school and to Cub Scouts. His troop came over and spent time with him; which made him even more eager to get back. Sydney never left his side the moment Danny came home. Life was getting back to normal for everyone, except Jillian, who still wanted answers about who her real father was. She kept it to herself, not even discussing her concerns with Morgan. She shared her thoughts with Tom, but not with anyone else.

"I'd like to go to Sweetwater soon. Do you think you could get away and go with me?"

"Sweetheart, I have so much to do. If you can wait a month, then we can make a nice trip out of it. We can go see Morgan afterward. How does that sound?"

"Actually, I'll go by myself if you don't mind. I'll just stay a few days then later we can go to Morgan's. I have a box of Mom's things that she kept in her bedroom closet. The box was locked and so much was going on at that time I didn't bother with it, but I want to see what's in it now. I didn't bring it with me when I was there so it must be in my house somewhere. There may be a clue as to whom my father might be. I'm not saying that I'm convinced Morgan and I have different dads, but it kind of looks that way. Unless Morgan was wrong about our parent's blood types, but he seemed so adamant about it."

"Sweetheart, your brother was probably wrong. He took your mother's word for it, and she could have made a mistake."

"I know, but something tells me there might be some answers in that beautiful, old, wooden box. I'm not telling Father Mike about the box. He has a key to the house and who knows; maybe he wants to protect that information or my mother's reputation. I know that he has to be aware of something. He and Mom were very close. Getting him to disclose that information is another thing. Anyway, if he should call, just tell him I'm coming to visit him. I still think that maybe after Morgan was born Mom couldn't get pregnant again, so they adopted me. I know there are some answers, somewhere."

"I don't have a problem with you going to Sweetwater without me. Just promise me you will get your rest. Don't start thinking Father Mike is hiding something from you. I believe he is on your side. You have always trusted him in the past."

"I know, but this is different. I'm sure that if something was going on back then, Mom swore him to secrecy. Anyway, I could be all wrong about this. I'll talk with Dr. Turner. He was our family doctor, and he took care of all of us. If I can get this blood type thing straightened out then maybe all my curiosity is for nothing. He'll know for sure what Mom and Dad's blood types were. I'm surprised Dr. Turner is still practicing. He should have been ready to retire years ago."

"Why don't you take Lucy with you? She sulks when you aren't home, and I'll be working late."

"Okay, but that will cost you extra for the flight, you know."

"Yes, my darling, I know. It will be worth the extra expense to know you have a companion."

Tom took her in his arms and kissed her tenderly. She melted into his warm embrace.

"Tom? Where do you think we were when we conceived this baby?"

"Probably right here or maybe in Dallas? That would be about the right time. We could have been at the ranch under our tree. Can the doctor pinpoint the date of conception? How soon can we find out what we're having?"

"I'll ask her tomorrow when we go. As far as the sex... I'm still not far enough along. Do you still want a boy?"

"Honestly, I don't think it matters. I've been thinking about a girl lately. Twins would be great," he laughed.

"Don't laugh. They do run in the family. On my dad's side, there are... What am I saying? I don't know who my dad is. I think it just hit me. I have no idea who my dad is. Maybe Mom wasn't my biological mother either."

* * *

Jillian arrived at the Mountain City, Colorado Airport, Wednesday morning. Father Michael picked her up and drove her to Sweetwater. This was Jillian's favorite time of the year. Fall colors were all about. The temperature was a little chilly at night, but the days were still warm. She and Sydney had taken hundreds of walks here in the fall.

"Lucy, look! There's your Uncle Sydney's park. We used to go there all the time," she said, pointing out the window. "Over there is where Ernie, the baker, makes the most delicious croissants in the world. This is where I grew up. We're home, Lucy."

"You don't think she understands you, do you?"

"Of course, she does. She's every bit as smart as Sydney. It just took her awhile to show it. Watch her cock her head," she boasted.

"You're such a good little girl, Lucy."

Lucy looked at her and cocked her head to one side and then to the other.

"Well, I'll be. She is a little smarty after all," Father Michael chuckled. "I never would have believed it if I hadn't seen it with my own two eyes."

"Stop it, you're not funny. Honestly, don't quit your day job. Oh, that's right! You can't quit," she howled. "You're a priest."

They parked on the street in front of Jillian's house, and Jillian used her garage door opener to get into the garage where her car was parked.

"Father Mike, did you check the battery in my car and all that stuff?"

"Yes, all that stuff is taken care of. Aren't you glad you didn't sell your car now?"

"That was a good move on my part. I think I want to keep the house, too. I mean, you can still use it as your man cave, and if Morgan and the family come, they will have a place to stay. I hope that this Christmas we can all get together here like we had planned last year."

"Sounds like a great idea. Did Morgan say he wanted to come this year?"

"I haven't asked him yet. It isn't easy for them to travel with all those kids."

"Let me help you with your bags then I have to run. I'll see you tomorrow for lunch. Let's go to the deli on Main Street then I'll take you to Ernie's for a chocolate croissant afterward."

"That's a deal. Thanks, Mike."

"Do you have enough wood or will you just use the gas?"

"How would I know if I have enough wood? Did you bring me any?"

"No, sorry, I didn't think about it, but look in your refrigerator and you'll see I thought of a few other things."

He went around to the side of the garage to check on the wood supply.

"You have plenty of wood, and if I remember correctly, there is a big stack in the house so I think you're all set."

"Thanks, Father Mike. I'll see you tomorrow. I'll meet you at the deli at noon. I want to drive because I have some errands to run afterward."

"See you tomorrow, Honey, rest well."

Jillian plopped down on the sofa. This had been her home most of her adult life after she had divorced Peter. She always loved coming home after a long job. There were parts of her life she missed in a way. She loved Tom with all her heart and wouldn't trade her life now for the life she had, but this house held special moments for her, and she was content that she hadn't sold it.

Lucy was running around the house, and came around the corner with one of Sydney's toys in her mouth, catching Jillian off guard.

"No, Lucy! Drop it! That isn't yours. Put it down."

Lucy dropped the toy and looked up at Jillian with uncertainty in her eyes. Jillian felt terrible for snapping at her. She scooped her up, and gently stroked her head.

"Of course, you can play with that toy, Lucy. It belongs to you now. Come on, I know there is a ball around here somewhere."

Jillian found a ball and she and Lucy played fetch. When Lucy got tired of the game, she cautiously walked over to Sydney's doggie bed. She shuffled around a bit until the bed felt comfortable and then plopped down on it, keeping one eye open and focused on Jillian.

"That's fine, Lucy. You're such a good little girl. Do you like your new bed?"

It was at this very moment that Jillian finally accepted Lucy as her new companion and was able to let Sydney go.

* * *

Later that evening, Jillian got the wooden box out of her hall closet. She tried a set of keys she had found in her mother's bedside table. Luckily, one fit the lock on the box. She held her breath and then opened the box. It was filled with pictures and papers. Jillian sorted through the photos and reminisced about the many holidays her mother captured with her camera and had put away in this box of memories. There were a few old drivers' licenses that her mother had saved belonging to her and Daniel. His social security card was also in the box, along with, of all the things, an expired credit card. How odd, Jillian thought as she sorted through the box. At the very bottom of the box was a piece of paper that was folded in quarters. As she opened it up, she could see it was a death certificate. It was her dad's death certificate and, for a moment, a feeling of sadness came over Jillian. Then something on the page caught her eye and her curiosity.

"What? How can this be? Oh, there must be some mistake. This is dated ten months before I was born. What in the world? I was three when Dad died. I was three, and Morgan was seven."

Jillian set the death certificate down and walked over to the window. The street lights illuminated the neighborhood, but there wasn't a soul around. Not a single car passing by. What she had read had confused her. She walked back to the couch and sat down, reaching for the certificate again. This time, she read it more carefully. It wasn't a mistake. Daniel Connors had died ten months before she was born. Jillian's mind swirled in so many different directions, it was hard to catch her breath.

No wonder our blood type didn't match. Why did Mom lead me to believe Morgan and I shared the same father? Why the mystery? Why? So who is my father? Whoever it is, one thing I know for sure is he has B positive blood. No wonder Morgan doesn't remember him as well as he should for seven years old. He was only three. Oh Mom, why didn't you tell me? I would have understood, she wondered.

She reached for the phone to call Tom.

* * *

Jillian was on her way to the deli. She had planned out her entire day the night before, but after going through the box, there was no need to see either the doctor or the county clerk. She had the date of death and that about summed it all up. She hoped Father Michael was up for the third degree. Tom had said to go easy on him, and she agreed, knowing that he was abiding by her mother's wishes.

Whatever the secret was, she wanted to know. Jillian felt she had a right to know. She pulled in the parking lot and looked around. She found his car parked over by the side door. She pulled up beside it and then went inside the deli. Father Michael was sitting by the window, and he was sipping on an iced tea. He gave her a wave, and she smiled back at him.

"Hi, been waiting long?" She asked.

"I just got here a few minutes ago. I ordered you water with lemon."

"Thanks, I'm off caffeine again," she smiled. "I'm so fortunate with this pregnancy. I can eat just about anything I want, and no, I haven't had any morning sickness. Actually, I feel very good."

"That's great, Honey. So what do you have planned for this afternoon?"

"Not much, other than getting a chocolate croissant with you after lunch."

Unexpectedly, her attention was distracted by a woman at another table.

"Excuse me for just a minute. I think I see an old friend."

Jillian couldn't believe her eyes. She hadn't seen Kari since high school. Kari had married right after graduation, and Jillian went on to college after giving birth to Danny. They had completely lost touch.

"Kari?"

"Jillian, is that you?"

Kari stood up, and the two women embraced while patting each other on the back.

"I never thought I would ever see you again. It's incredible," Jillian said. "Just incredible. Where have you been?"

"You know I moved to California after I got married, right?"

"Yes, but what happened to your parents?"

"They moved with us, but they kept the farm here. Now they want to sell it, so I was elected to come and get it on the market. What about you? I heard you travel all over the country with, is it, interior design?"

"Yes, that's right. I got married, and my husband and I live in New York. I still have my house here. How long will you be in town?"

"Not long, but long enough for us to have a few drinks and catch up. How about if we get together later this afternoon or would this evening be better?"

Jillian smiled. "I'm here by myself so whatever is best for you. Why don't you come over to the house for dinner? I'll write down my address. Come over around five-thirty. It's so great to see you," she said, hugging her again. "Wait, why don't you join us? Are you alone?"

"Thanks, Jillian, but I'm meeting the realtor. I look forward to seeing you later."

Jillian went back to the table, and Father Michael was pondering the menu.

"Who was that?" he asked.

"Kari Williamson. Well, I don't recall her married name, but we were great friends in high school. I'm sure you remember her. We lost touch right after graduation. She was married and moved away. Imagine, after all this time, I run into her."

"I'm not sure if I remember her or not. What would you like for lunch?"

"Give me a second to look at the menu. What are you having?"

Father Michael smiled. "I'm having a pastrami on rye, it's one of my favorite sandwiches."

A big grin sprouted on Jillian's face. "Well, how about that? Me, too!"

Jillian waited until after they had eaten to discuss the subject of who her father was. She had no idea how to begin, but she knew for certain that Father Michael knew all the details. He hadn't told her because he was her mother's best friend, and obviously, she had sworn him to secrecy. She wondered if he would tell her now since her mother had passed. She folded her napkin and placed it on her plate. She asked for more water and waited until he took his last bite.

"Father Mike, I know."

He looked up at her with such a peculiar look on his face. It wasn't panic or alarm. It wasn't surprising either. This puzzled her.

"Did you hear me? I said, I know what Mom did. I know about Dad dying before I was born. In fact, he died before I was even conceived."

She waited for him to speak, but he just gazed at her. She shrugged her shoulders and lowered her eyebrows. He didn't budge.

"Mike, I know that you know, so save me the time of interrogating the truth out of you, and just tell me. I deserve to know, right? Do you know who my father is?"

"Let's go back to your house. I'll tell you everything you want to know."

Her heart was beating so fast, it was pounding in her chest. She stood up then sat back down. She knew she needed to calm down, for the baby's sake. She just never thought it would be this easy to get him to tell her the truth. Did she really want to know? She was nervous, and Father Michael asked her if she was alright.

Jillian folded her arms and put her head on the table. "Father Mike," her face becoming pale, "I don't feel so well. I need some cold water."

"You're as white as a ghost. This has really upset you. I'm so sorry, Honey. I wanted to tell you in Denver when you asked me, but you were under so much stress. I couldn't risk this upsetting you even more. Let me drive you home, and we'll come back later for your car."

Father Michael motioned for the waiter and asked for a glass of ice water.

"Jillian?"

"I'm okay. Let's just sit here for a few minutes. Really, I'm okay. I just thought it was going to be like pulling teeth getting the information out of you. Now I'm not sure if I really want to know. I mean, I do, but... Did Mom ask you not to ever tell me?"

"Actually, Mary said that if you should find out, and want to know the truth, I was to tell you. So, in a way, I am honoring her by telling you now. If she were alive today maybe things would be different, but I'm all you have for your answers. Do you feel you can you drive now?"

"Sure, but I need to get Kari's phone number. She is coming over for dinner this evening. Will I feel like entertaining her?"

"I don't know. Maybe you should cancel. I just don't know."

Jillian went over and excused herself for interrupting the meeting with Kari and the Realtor. She explained that she may have to cancel and needed her number. Then, she and Father Michael walked out to the parking lot and drove off in separate cars.

As she drove to her house, she called Tom. "You'll never guess what just happened?"

"Sweetheart, are you alright?"

"Yes, but I'm really nervous. I asked Father Michael, and he just stared at me for the longest time. Then he said we needed to go to my house to talk. He said he would tell me everything. He said that my mom wanted him to tell me if I ever asked. Tom, I'm at the house, so I'll call you later. I love you."

Jillian parked in the garage and hurried inside. Father Michael was right behind her.

They both sat down on the sofa then Jillian got back up to let Lucy out. After making sure she did her thing, she came in and sat down again. She looked at Father Michael, and he smiled at her.

"Oaky Jillian, what would you like to know?"

"Well, for starters, is the death certificate correct?"

"Yes. Daniel had died before you were conceived. I want you to know that your mother didn't run right out and find someone. It wasn't like that at all. She was terribly distraught that she had lost her husband. It was tough for her. Morgan was only three years old, and he was more than a handful. There was some insurance money, but Mary wanted to save it for his education. She put it away to draw interest, and she took a job at the parsonage."

"So, do you know who my father is? Can you tell me where or how she met him? How long were they together, and what happened to him? Is he still alive?"

"Which question should I start with?"

"Who is he?" she sighed. "All I know is that he has B positive blood. If I would have known about him, maybe he could have given Danny a Kidney, and saved you from doing it."

Father Michael looked deep into her eyes. "He did."

"What? He did what? What do you mean? You gave Danny one of your kidneys because we are the same blood type. I meant, what? No, that can't be. You're a priest. Mike, what are you trying to tell me? You and Mom?"

"I know it is too much to take in, but we loved each other. She came to me for comfort, and before we knew it we were making..."

"Stop! Stop right there," she uttered, cutting him off. "This isn't funny. What in the world has gotten into you?"

Jillian got up and walked over to the window. Children were playing outside, but the window was closed, so she couldn't hear them. She went to the door and opened it. She took a deep breath and walked out into the front yard. She sat down on the small white wrought iron bench near the walkway and watched the kids at play. She felt a hand on her shoulder, and she looked up at her very dear friend that was now, somehow, her father.

"All these years? I can't believe it. All these years? Do you know how much I wanted you to be my dad when I was small? You played the part so well. Who would have known you weren't acting. Why didn't Mom tell me? Why?"

"Honey, your mom loved you so much. She didn't want to hurt you. When you were struggling with Danny, she longed to tell you then. She would have, but she got sick. She made me promise to tell you the whole story one day. Did you know she kept a diary from when she was in high school?"

"No, but what does that have to do with..."

"Everything! It has to do with everything. I have volumes in a box in my room. They are yours now, but you must promise not to destroy them. If you don't want them, I do. There is not a day that goes by that I miss her any less. I would have left the priesthood for her, and you. She wouldn't hear of it. Before we knew she was pregnant with you, we stopped being alone together, and we made a promise to one another and to God that we would never be alone like that again. I wanted to marry her, but she refused to discuss it."

"Mike, this is all too much for me right now. I want to call Tom, and I need you to go. I won't ever stop loving you, but I am so confused right now. I want you to go, please." Jillian was struggling to keep the tears at bay and needed to hear Tom's voice.

Jillian stood up from the little white wrought iron bench and hugged him. She wasn't mad at him, but she really didn't like the uneasiness she was feeling either. She was upset with the situation and for as much as she loved Father Michael, she felt oddly compromised. She didn't trust her feelings, and she was afraid she would do or say something that would drive a wedge between them. She needed her rock. She needed Tom. She needed the calmness of his voice and his arms around her.

She watched as Father Michael drove away, then she hurried back into the house. First to call Kari to cancel for the evening, and then she sat down to call Tom.

Chapter Twenty-Three

Jillian needed time to digest the news that Father Michael was her biological father. She hadn't called him or tried to reach him for two days, and it was obvious he was giving her some space. Tom advised her to take some time, and that if she needed him; he would be on the next flight. She was doing okay, and she told him so. Jillian needed time, and it felt good to be alone and to try to sort through what she had just learned.

It made no sense at first, but the more she thought about it, the more the pieces came together. She thought about how as a child, Father Michael was always there for her. He taught her how to say her prayers at night, and he would sit for hours at the endless tea parties Jillian would have. It was Father Michael who taught her how to ride a bike. He had helped her mother make decisions concerning both of the children. He accompanied her mother to all the parent-teacher meetings, and it was he that grilled all her boyfriends, making sure they brought her home at the chosen hour set by him. He was there for her at both of her weddings dancing the father-daughter dance. He was very interested in Danny, which was always curious. But now, knowing Danny was his grandson, it all made sense. If she had told him once, she had said a hundred times that he was the next best thing to having a dad. Morgan loved him, but they never had the close relationship she shared with him. If she had only known the truth, it could have been even more special.

Jillian wondered how they were able to hide the truth from the town. How did they explain the pregnancy? There were so many questions. Should she call Morgan? She didn't know how to approach it. What would she say? Would her brother be angry? Why wasn't she angry? There were so many unanswered questions.

Jillian sat on the back porch swing, with Lucy by her side. She stroked her silky fur, and Lucy was soaking up all of the attention.

"Well, Miss Lucy. What should I do? If I had half a brain, I would just go home where we belong. Please tell me, what should I do?"

Lucy looked up at her and cocked her head. Jillian smiled and ran her hand down Lucy's back and through the hair on her tail.

"You're such a good little girl, Lucy."

It was the phone ringing that drew Jillian from her musing.

"Hi. It's me, Sarah. Can we talk?"

"Sarah, I'm sorry I was so upset with you. I really am, but this isn't a good time for me right now."

"It's okay, but if you could just hear me out, it will only take a few minutes. I want you to know that I took your advice, and I told Phillip. We started counseling, and we are working through it. Please forgive me for involving you in my madness and for my distrust. I was just so scared, and I didn't want to lose my marriage after all. We have two kids. That would be a terrible thing to put them through. I know I wasn't thinking about them or Phillip when this first started. I was so selfish, but I think things will be okay for us now. I really do love Phillip and the kids very much. I can't believe I was caught up in this insanity. If it weren't for you and Tom…"

"I'm very happy for you and your family, really. This could have had such a devastating outcome. I'm glad you decided to tell Phillip."

"Thanks. Do you forgive me? Please say you do. I want us to be friends forever."

"We're good, but as I said, you caught be at a bad time. I have an appointment in a few minutes, and I'm not ready to leave the house yet," she lied. "I'll call you next week, and we can talk then. I really am happy for you. I hope you know that."

"Okay, next week then. I'll hold you to it. I love you, my friend."

"I love you, too."

Jillian put Lucy down on the patio and went into the house to take a shower. She was hungry and decided it was time for her to go out and face the world. After she had showered, she got Lucy's leash and took her out for a walk. The little cafe on Main Street had outside dining, and she knew Lucy would be just fine there while she ate. As she approached the café, she saw the sign on the wrought iron fence around the tables that read, "No animals other than service animals allowed inside the patio area." She had no choice but to take Lucy back to the house. Lucy wasn't so excited about the idea of more walking, so Jillian picked her up and carried her most of the way back. She was so tiny, compared to Sydney. Sydney was, at least, twice her size.

"Come on little girl, we're going home."

Father Michael was parked out in front of the house sitting in his car. Jillian walked up to the window and invited him in. She let Lucy down for a potty break, and then they all went inside. There was uneasiness between them. She had always given him a hug, but this morning, it felt quite out of her comfort zone.

"I was just bringing Lucy back to the house, so I can get my car to go get something to eat. Want to join me?"

Father Michael looked pleased. He reached for her hand. Jillian took his hand and then, without warning, she began to cry. The tears became intense, as she broke into an uncontrollable sobbing. Father Michael opened his arms, and she stepped into them as he closed them around her, surrounding her with genuine love. By now, he was crying as well. He gently patted her on the back, and she wailed even louder. It took her several minutes to calm down. Finally, she stepped back and looked at him.

"Now what?" she asked, sniffing back tears. "What do we do now?"

"Let's go get something to eat. We can talk afterward. I have so much to tell you."

"Okay, but let's go to Brady's Cafe. We can sit outside on the patio. We can walk if you are up to walking the four blocks?"

"I'm fine now. It's been a month since the surgery. I can manage a few blocks."

Jillian put Lucy on her bed and told her to stay. Father Michael chuckled as Lucy proceeded to follow them to the front door.

"She is a smart one, that Lucy."

Jillian smiled at her dog. "She hates getting left behind. She really is smart," she said looking up at Father Michael.

As they started their walk to the café, neither said much at first. Finally, Father Michael broke the ice.

"How is Danny? Is he back in school?"

"We spoke last week, and he wasn't back in school yet, but soon. Tony said he is doing very well, much better than anyone expected. I'm so proud of him. I don't know if I will see him for Thanksgiving this year, but I am gradually accepting these changes, and in my heart, I know this is best for Danny."

"What do you mean?"

"In the beginning, after Tom and I got married, I thought I would be Danny's only mother figure. That was selfish of me, but it was what I wanted. I wasn't thinking of what was best for Danny. Getting pregnant, and then losing the baby brought so much into perspective for me. Now that I am pregnant again, I see things even more clearly. It is the right thing to do to let Danny have a close family relationship with his parents. He will never know I am his mother, and now I understand why Tony felt that it was in Danny's best interest never to tell him."

Father Michael looked at her tenderly. "I know this is hard on you."

"No, it isn't, not really. I love Danny. I want the very best for him. Tony is a wise man, and he was looking ahead at a much bigger picture than I could see. Now that Angela is his wife, and the kids adore her, it really is in Danny's best interest to have a full-time mommy. Danny doesn't really remember Tony's first wife, Tracy. Oh, he might have some recollection, but it will get very blurry, and he will begin to think of Angela as his real mom. I only have a small part in his life. I'm more like the aunt he gets to see every few months. I am grateful for what I have, and I am content now."

They arrived at the café and took a seat nearest the sidewalk. A cheerful waiter came to their table.

"I'll have iced tea, and my daughter will have water with lemon."

The waiter looked at them and smiled.

"Father Mike, why did you say I was your daughter?"

"I was just trying in on for size. Besides, the server probably thinks we priests say that all the time. I'm sure he thought nothing of it."

"You're right. He didn't have a clue."

"Jillian, remember last year when I told you I was thinking of retiring?"

"Yes, I remember."

"Well, I am in a sense. I'm leaving the priesthood."

"No, Mike, you can't do that. Mom would roll over in her grave. That is the last thing she would ever have wanted. No, please don't do it."

"Honey, I have been thinking about this for a very long time. Mary and I had discussed it before she died. Actually, it was literally just before she died. She understood why I needed to do it. I'm living a lie, and I have been since before you were born. I believe God has forgiven me, but nonetheless, I am living a lie. I counseled a young couple about six months ago. I gave them advice about something I know nothing about. They were having problems in their marriage.

She had stepped outside their marriage and had an affair that led to pregnancy. Her husband forgave her, but it left their marriage with problems. They came to me for help, and I knew at that moment that I needed to step aside. I was just as guilty as that woman, but there didn't seem to be any consequence for my actions."

"You're wrong, Father Mike. The consequence was not a broken marriage, but the inability to have one. You and Mom did what you had to do, and neither of you were given the joys of marriage together. So, yes, there was a consequence to both your actions," she sighed aloud. "You saw one another almost daily, and you couldn't put your arms around her and hold her. You couldn't walk down the street holding her hand, and your daughter was never able to call you daddy. I'd say you paid a very high price for loving my mother."

The waiter returned to take their orders and, shortly after that, was back with their sandwiches and fries. Jillian patted her tummy and smiled.

"Mike, I can't see into the future, but for now, we need to take this one step at a time. If you are seriously considering leaving, then you can have my house."

Father Michael shook his head. "I won't be staying in Sweetwater. There will be talk, there always is, and it would be too hard. I have lived here most of my life, but I would rather be closer to you if that's alright."

"Let's take it a day at a time. I haven't had a chance to process all of this quite yet. Have you told the Bishop?"

"Yes, he knows the whole story. I told him that I would be leaving, and he explained to me that it takes time. I will be leaving St. Luke's in a month, and I am free to go wherever I choose, but it does take time. If you'd rather I didn't move to New York, I'll understand."

Jillian didn't answer. She wasn't sure what to say. This was still very awkward, and she understood how difficult it had to be for Father Michael. She felt compassion for him. He had been dear to her all her life. Things had changed, but it didn't have to be for the worst.

"Mike, it would be good for you to be closer to us. Remember, I am used to seeing you all the time, and it has been a hard adjustment for me not seeing you so much. I'll be giving birth to your grandchild in six months. Can you find a place by then?"

* * *

Jillian spent the evening at home with her friend, Kari, and learned she was divorcing her husband. Kari shared that she wanted to return to Sweetwater to live and would be looking for a house to buy. She didn't want to live on her parent's farm. Otherwise, she could have moved there. She wanted something small and easy to care for. They agreed to have breakfast at Brady's Cafe the next morning.

Jillian called Tom after Kari left.

"Hi Sweetheart, it's good to hear your voice."

"Tom, I've been thinking about something. If Father Mike, boy it's going to be hard to stop calling him that, huh? Anyway, if he moves to New York or somewhere close I won't have any reason to come back to Sweetwater. I might as well sell the house. I just spent a few hours with Kari, and she told me that she is looking for a house to buy. What do you think?"

"Divine intervention?"

Jillian laughed. "Be serious."

"Okay, I think that if you are ready to sell the house, then do it. You're right, after Mike leaves, there won't be any reason for you to go to Sweetwater anymore."

"How much should I ask? I have no idea."

"Sweetheart, ask Kari what her price range is first. Then if she says something like one hundred fifty to two hundred thousand, meet her in the middle with one seventy-five. That would be a fair way to do it unless you feel whatever her range is would be too low. Call me when you find out what she is willing to offer, and I'll make a few calls. Are you calling a realtor? They will know how to price it. Do you know what she is looking for?"

"Yes, I do. She said she wanted something small and easy to take care of. She likes this house very much. It's close to town, and she loves the backyard. I think she will jump at the chance to buy it."

"You sound excited, Sweetie. How are you feeling?"

"Physically, I feel great," she said, touching her tummy. "Emotionally, well, better than I thought I would be feeling a few days ago. It is so strange to know that Mike is my dad. What's even stranger... I'm not mad at anyone or upset about it. I have always wanted him to be my dad. I must have told him a hundred times he was the next best thing to having a dad. You know how emotional I can get, but I'm feeling very calm except for the fact that I miss you madly. I'd love to reminisce with you tonight. How about I go get a bath and get ready for bed, and you call me back. We haven't had phone sex for a very long time."

"Whatever you say, my darling. Your every wish is my command."

Chapter Twenty-Four

Jillian took a cab to Tom's office and waited for him to finish a call. Tom was taking her to dinner. Things had gone well with the sale of the house in Sweetwater, and it would be closing in forty-five days. Father Mike agreed to pack up the items Jillian had said she wanted, and would bring them when he came to New York. Kari wanted to buy all the furniture and household items since her husband wanted the house in California. They had agreed on a fair price, and both women were happy. Jillian gave Father Michael her car, since his was an older model, and had so many miles on it. She figured his car probably wouldn't last much longer, and her car was practically new.

While she was waiting for Tom, her phone rang. She looked at her phone to see who was calling.

"Tony?"

"Hi, Jillian, I just wanted to let you know that Danny starts back to school on Monday. He looks awesome, and he's doing great. I thought you would like to know. How are you?"

"I'm feeling good. I just got back from Sweetwater a little while ago. I sold my house."

"Really? I thought you would keep it, but hey, that's great. I won't keep you, but I wanted to fill you in on Danny. Say hello to Tom and Angela sends her best."

"Thanks. Tell everyone we said Hi."

Jillian hung up her phone and smiled. She was happy Tony called to fill her in. She was happy they were able to stay friends. Tom was still busy in his inner office, but the door was open, and he waved.

Donna was shutting down her computer, and cleaning off her desk.

"Have a good evening, Mrs. Bentley. I'll be going home now."

"Thanks, Donna, it was nice to see you. You have a good evening as well."

Tom came out of his office and gave his wife a kiss. "I missed you, Sweetheart. Are you two okay?"

Jillian put her hand on her tummy and smiled. "Yes, we're both fine, but hungry."

* * *

Jillian had been home for six weeks. Now that she had sold the house in Sweetwater, the family wouldn't be getting together unless they all met at Morgan's for Christmas. Their house had just closed escrow, and they were moving into the house of their dreams right after Thanksgiving. Melissa wanted everyone to come and share the first Christmas in their new home with them. They had plenty of room and wanted to show off their new house. After discussing it, Jillian and Tom thought it would be a perfect idea and Father Michael was coming, too. Jillian thought it might be the best time to tell Morgan about Father Mike. Jillian was already showing. She was only four and a half months, but to her delight, looked much further along. She was scheduled for her sonogram in a few days. Her lower back hurt and Tom wanted her to take it easy.

"Tom, I can't take it any easier than I am now unless I stay in bed. Then you'd have to wait on me hand and foot."

"I see your point, but still, if your back hurts it could mean you are overdoing it a bit."

"I think we miscalculated a little," she said, removing her blouse. She stood before Tom showing him her tummy.

"It's a lot bigger than the last time, but I'm sure it is always different with each pregnancy," he said, "I think you look kind of sexy."

"Kind of?"

"You look a lot sexy."

"I don't know, but I don't remember showing at all. Maybe we're going to have a football player or a Sumo wrestler. How much did you weigh when you were born?"

"My mother told me, but I really can't recall what she had said. It was a long time ago. What about you?"

Jillian thought for a moment then proudly announced, "I was seven pounds, two ounces. Not too big and not too small," she smiled, "just right."

"Very true, you are just right. So, I think either you should put on your blouse or suffer the consequences."

"I love it when you talk to me like that," she said, removing the rest of her clothing.

* * *

The waiting room was packed. Tom leaned over and whispered in Jillian's ear. "It looks like we weren't the only ones that were busy last summer."

Jillian felt the warmth fill her face. She looked around hoping no one heard what he said.

"Tom, I'm really excited, but I'm a little nervous."

Jillian couldn't help but think about last year as she and Tom waited in the very same waiting room to have the sonogram with the first pregnancy. They had been so happy to find out they were having a boy. She closed her eyes and tried to think of something else. Finally, the nurse called them in, and Jillian climbed onto the table and lay back on the pillow. The nurse came back in and helped her unbutton her blouse. She pulled her slacks down a little then covered her up with a paper sheet. The doctor came in, and the nurse busied herself with the equipment.

"Good morning. How are you feeling?"

"Good. I'm feeling really great, except my low back has been hurting, but, honestly, I haven't been overdoing it."

Dr. Aldridge looked over at Tom. "And how are you?"

Tom nodded and said that he had been busy. He told her that they were anxious and excited about this baby. The doctor did some measuring and took a few notes. Leafing through her chart again, she asked about her weight.

"Are you ready?"

Jillian's face was beaming. "We are more than ready."

"Okay, Jillian. One more minute and we should know."

The nurse put a dab of warm gel on Jillian's stomach and began the sonogram as the doctor looked on. The nurse turned to look at the doctor then abruptly stopped moving the wand over Jillian's stomach.

"Go on," the doctor motioned to the nurse.

Dr. Aldridge seemed to be smiling a lot, and Jillian couldn't help but find it curious. She looked at the monitor, and although it seemed to make sense to the doctor and the nurse, it resembled more of a blurry mess to her. She looked at Tom, and she could tell by the look on his face, he was getting the same feedback. He looked fascinated but confused.

The nurse continued, and Dr. Aldridge came closer to the monitor. A look of seriousness came over her face.

"It's tough to see from this angle, but I think there is a little boy somewhere in there, and it looks to me like he might have a brother or a sister."

"What? A brother or a sister? What is that supposed to mean? Oh, my! Are we having twins?" Jillian gasped. "Twins?"

"It looks that way to me," Dr. Aldridge said.

Tom quickly sat down. "Are you sure?"

"I can't be positive about the sex of the other one, but you are certainly having twins. We'll do another sonogram in six weeks. That should be conclusive, but I'd say shop in duplicates."

"Tom? Does the nursery have enough room for two cribs?"

Tom didn't answer. All he could manage was a stare at the monitor.

Jillian was delighted. She looked at Tom and was amused by the look on his face. He looked a little pale.

"Honey? Are you alright? You don't look so good. Do you need a glass of water? Tom? Say something."

"I'm okay, I think. I'm just so surprised. I can't believe you have two babies in there, that's all. No wonder you are getting so big."

This brought a bit of laughter to the exam room. The nurse handed them a picture of their babies. It was definitely two babies.

* * *

With Christmas just a week away, Jillian and Tom decided to wait to share the news of the twins until they got to California. Jillian was scheduled to have the second sonogram after the first of the year. She had hoped she would have been able to tell the family what sex both the babies were, but that would have to wait.

Jillian had been shopping for Morgan's kids and had already mailed gifts to Danny, Julie Ann, Bella, Martha, and Sydney. She found a designer bag on sale for Martha. It was similar to one Jillian had and Martha had admired it. Jillian hoped she would love it. She couldn't wait to see the look on Morgan and Melissa's face when she announced she was having twins.

"Did you ask your mother if there were twins in the family? We know it isn't on my side now that my dad isn't my dad. That sounds funny, doesn't it? I told you his grandfather was a twin, right?"

"I think you did. Well, Mom said to her knowledge there aren't any twins that she knows of. I guess we will be setting a precedent."

Jillian chuckled, as she stood before the mirror looking at her body.

"Just think. It starts with us. Tom, come here and look at this belly, would you?"

Jillian opened up her bathrobe exposing her tummy. It had grown quite a bit since their last examination. Tom came up behind her and put his arms around her waist, resting his hands on her tummy. Jillian looked in the mirror, and tears of joy streamed down her face. It was actually happening this time. Her babies were growing safely inside her.

"You never looked more beautiful, Sweetheart."

Jillian turned to face him and let her robe fall to the floor. He kissed her, and she felt his love all around her. His touch was gentle and tender. She wanted him and, by the look on his face, the feeling was mutual. Tom took her hand, and they walked over to the bed. The past year had been very hard on both of them, and now; here they were, together, making love and happier than they could possibly have anticipated. Jillian smiled as Tom got undressed. She felt a chuckle coming on and tried to hide her face.

"What? What's so funny?"

Breaking into laughter, Jillian mumbled, "Nothing."

"Something?" he said. "Are you laughing at me?"

"Tom, your tummy is growing just like mine."

"You are hilarious!" Tom took her in his arms. After their lovemaking, they took a nap then later went downstairs to finish wrapping presents. After lunch, they relaxed by the fire.

"I'm so happy we're going to California. It'll be great to see Morgan under better circumstances. It wasn't so ideal the last time. We have been through so much this year. I for one, am looking forward to the new year."

The phone rang, and Tom reached for it.

"It's Dr. Aldridge's office. They had a cancellation, and they can do your sonogram at three o'clock today. Do you want the appointment?"

Jillian was about to jump at the chance, then she thought about the weather. It was snowing. There was bound to be some ice.

"No! Tell them I'll wait for my regular appointment."

Tom looked confused, but he told them what she had said and hung up the phone. "I would have thought you wanted to go just so you could tell the family what sex both the babies are."

"I can wait. I don't want to be out in weather like this."

"I'm sorry, of course, we can wait. I did check the weather report this morning, and we should have great weather for our flight to California. Did Mike say what time he is arriving?"

"Will you call him? Give him our itinerary, and then you guys can compare."

Jillian finished her gift wrapping, and put the extra wrap and ribbon in a plastic box and took it out to the garage. She thought about how this was their second Christmas at this house, and she hadn't decorated either year. Of course, next year would be a different story. They would have their children. Jillian couldn't help but think that by having twins, she was getting her first baby back. She understood it didn't work that way, but the thought kept going through her mind. The garage was freezing, so it only took her a few seconds to put the plastic box on the shelf and hurry back inside the warm house.

Chapter Twenty-Five

Jillian thought Morgan and Melissa's new home was spectacular. Melissa was so proud of the gourmet kitchen with the granite countertops and custom cabinets. The huge window above the sink overlooked the backyard where Melissa would have an excellent view of the play area. Jillian remarked on the tiled floors, and she thought the colors were lovely.

"I love your house. You did an excellent job on the entire thing. Melissa, maybe we should go into business together. I could do the commercial, and you could do the residential."

"Thanks, but with four kids, I'll be busy for the next twenty years or so. We'll talk after that, okay? What about you? This will be the first of many from what you have said."

Jillian smiled. Soon she would tell them about her babies. "I was only kidding. I think my working days are over; at least for now."

"You sure are big for five months. I was hardly showing when I was that far along."

Jillian wanted to wait until everyone was together before she announced they were having twins. She tried to change the subject by asking about the window coverings. Melissa was eager to discuss all the details of her decorating experiences with the house. After the tours had been over, Melissa and Jillian made lunch while the men discussed the storage cabinets for the three car garage. It had an extension on it that would accommodate a boat or small RV. Morgan was thinking about getting a small motorhome for vacations. He said that with four kids, it would be easier than hotels. Melissa was fond of the idea as long as they shared the cooking. She also thought a large motorhome would be a much better idea, reminding Morgan of the size of their family.

Jillian and Melissa brought lunch into the dining room, and the family sat down. The kids took their place at the table, and Morgan put little Mary in the high chair. Jillian was overwhelmed with all that was necessary just to get all the kids at the table at one time.

Morgan and Melissa seemed to have it down pat, but it seemed more like watching a circus at times to Jillian. She thought that at least they had one at a time, whereas she would be starting with two.

"So, Sis, I can't believe Kari Williamson bought your house. Why didn't she just move on to her parent's farm?"

"She said that she wanted a smaller home in town. My house was perfect for her, actually."

"How did she look?"

Jillian looked at Melissa, who was busy with the kids, and then looked back at Morgan, and shrugged her shoulders.

"It's okay if you tell me," he laughed. "We only dated a few times. So, what did she look like? Has she changed much?"

"She looked great. She and her husband got a divorce, and he wanted to keep their house here in California and all the furnishings. That worked out good for me because she wanted to buy everything, right down to the silverware."

"Father Mike, what will you do now that Jillian sold the house. I heard you were using it as your man cave?"

"The sisters won't let me park my motorcycle in the rectory, so I don't know what I'll do."

"Okay, family. Tom and I have an announcement."

"You're moving to California to be near us, right?"

"No Morgan. But it is a biggie. We're having twins."

"No way?"

"Yes, way! Didn't you think I was a little big for five months? Can you believe it? We're having twins."

By now Melissa was hugging her, and Morgan and Father Michael were slapping Tom on the back. Father Michael looked as if he was holding back the tears and Amanda and Rachael were squealing for joy; although they had no idea what having twins meant.

"So you got the twins. How cool. Mom would have been so delighted."

Jillian looked a bit puzzled. "What do you mean?"

"Well, you know that Dad's grandfather was a twin, right? Mom always thought Melissa and I would have twins, but you got them. That is so awesome."

Father Michael spoke up saying he was the son of twins. "They usually skip a generation, don't they?"

"In this case, they skipped two. But who cares. Jillian gets to pass down the Connor twin gene in our family."

Jillian cleared her throat and took a deep breath. "Actually, this is as good a time as any to break the news to you."

"What news? There's more?"

"Yes, it all started with the blood typing…"

"Oh, come on, Sis. You aren't going to start that stuff again. This just proves I was right. Don't you see? Dad passed the twin gene down to you. He was your dad, and there was obviously something wrong with the paperwork I was given from Mom about them having the same blood type. You should be so happy the mystery is over."

"Yes. I know the mystery is over, but…"

Jillian stopped mid-sentence. She saw the look on Morgan's face. Suddenly she was afraid to continue.

"Why did you stop? Awe, come on; this can't continue. There is no 'but'. Dad was your dad."

"No, Morgan, he wasn't."

"I'll take the kids upstairs for their naps. Morgan, come help me."

Melissa stood up and looked at Morgan. He wasn't budging.

"Morgan, please come help me with the kids."

Morgan looked at Melissa and shook his head. Then he turned to Jillian. "Okay, what's this all about?"

Jillian struggled with her words. "Why are you so defensive? You don't even know what I'm about to say."

"I think I do. It's about our parents having the same blood type, right?"

"Yes. That is exactly what I am trying to tell you. Just listen to me for a minute. It is a fact. I am B positive. So you know that I am not a real Connor."

"Sis, I'm telling you right now that one of our parents must have been B positive. Mom got it mixed up."

Mom was right about that. I have the odd blood type. I wasn't adopted as I suspected and Mom didn't run off and have an affair either. It just happened."

"What just happened?"

Jillian swallowed hard. "Mom and Father Mike…"

"What? Oh, I see. This is some kind of a joke. Well, it isn't funny. Gee, Sis. What in the world…"

"Morgan, it's true. I really am Jillian's father. May I explain please?"

"What the hell?" Morgan stood up and started to walk over to where Father Michael was sitting.

"Morgan!" Melissa said loudly. "No! Just sit down!"

It was too late. Morgan had already grabbed Father Michael by his shirt and pulled him up to his feet. Tom stood up and got between them. Father Michael remained very passive, but Morgan was outraged. He told Tom to step aside. Tom refused, and Morgan was screaming for Tom to get out of the way. Morgan was livid and outraged. Jillian had never seen him like this before. Melissa was begging him to stop, and the girls started to cry.

"You slept with my mother? That is impossible. Where was Dad? Mom would never betray him like that. This is sick. This is so sick! Jillian, why would you believe this crap? Father Mike, what is wrong with you? Why would you tell Jillian this lie?"

Jillian was crying. "Dad was dead when this happened. Morgan, he had been dead before I was conceived. You were only three years old, not seven. That's why you can't remember him very well."

Morgan looked at his wife, and she motioned for him to sit down; which he finally did.

"Please, you have to calm down. I'm not supposed to be stressed out. I should have waited until later to tell you. I'm so sorry."

"You're sorry? What did you do? You have nothing to be sorry about. It was this perverted priest. He's the one. It's on him, not you. Okay, I'll calm down, but only because I don't want to put any further strain on my sister. Everyone needs to just stay out of my way for a while. I mean it."

Jillian looked at Tom, who was still standing and she watched as Father Michael sat back down at the table. Melissa was getting the baby out of the highchair, and asking the girls to take Morgan Junior upstairs. Morgan went to the garage, and they heard a car engine rev up.

"Please, he'll come back in a while. Just let him go. I've never seen him this upset, ever." Melissa was crying, and Jillian sat there in shock. Tom came around behind her and put his arms around her. She looked up and began to cry again. Father Michael remained in his chair. It was as if he had no idea what to do or say at this point. Melissa took the children upstairs leaving the three alone in the dining room.

It was several hours before Morgan came back, and he found them outside on the patio. It was cool outside, but not cold. Melissa had fixed both the men a drink, and Jillian was having a cup of herbal tea. Morgan sat down next to his sister. Jillian could smell whiskey on his breath. He was calm and even smiled.

"Okay, who wants to explain to me what is going on? I will sit here and listen. I won't say a word."

"I think I should be the one to tell you. You won't like some of it, but then it was hurtful to me, too. Mom lied to us…"

"No, she didn't…"

"You said you would be quiet. Now just listen to me. Mom did lie. She said that Dad died when I was three years old, and you were seven. I brought his death certificate," she said, handing the piece of folded paper over to Morgan. "Dad died leaving only one child, you. Mom was heartbroken. She loved Dad. She sought out comfort from her only true friend. One thing led to another, and it just happened. You know, Morgan, I can relate to this more than you know. Mom and Father Mike were in love in high school. You knew that, right?"

"No. I didn't know they had been in love. I knew they went out together, but love?"

Father Michael remained quiet as did Tom. Tom actually appeared to be holding his breath.

Jillian continued. "Father Mike made a commitment and went off to the seminary and Mom went off to college where she met Dad. This part doesn't matter. That's their story. Everybody in Sweetwater knew that Mom and Mike were best friends. She turned to him for reassurance and that love rekindled. Morgan, please have some compassion. Mom kept a journal from the time she was a child until after I was born. Mike has given the journals to me, and after I read them, perhaps you would like to read them as well."

Morgan looked at Father Michael. "I don't know what to say to you right now. I get it, but I don't know what to say."

"Morgan, what we did was wrong. We both suffered for what we had done. We never wanted to hurt anyone, but the truth was bound to come out someday. Mary was always worried that if you found out, you would not be as forgiving as Jillian. She was right, but you have to know she loved you very much. She loved your father and when he died she was frightened and alone with a small boy to raise. When she came to work at the parsonage, it was only weeks after your father had died. We were together every day. It was hard on both of us. When we found out she was pregnant, I wanted to leave the priesthood and marry her. Your mother felt that we had sinned enough, and refused to ever discuss marriage or my leaving, ever again. I am so sorry."

Morgan didn't look as outraged as before. He looked hurt, but his face softened. Melissa came out to the patio and handed him a drink. He practically grabbed the glass from her, tilting it upwards, and downed his beverage. It was as if she knew he would do that as she handed him another, and went back in the house to chase the kids.

"I need to digest some of this. Father Mike, I am very sorry for the way I acted. You know that I care for you as a family member. I didn't mean what I said. Please forgive me. I'm not saying I will accept this, but it isn't about me, is it? We are all so thankful that you were able to help Danny."

Father Michael stood up and offered his hand. Morgan shook his hand and then excused himself, expressing that he should help his wife with the kids. He bent down and kissed his sister and then went inside the house.

Jillian looked out from the patio and smiled. "Isn't it interesting that the weather here is so pleasant this time of year compared to New York?"

Neither Tom nor Father Michael replied. They sat quietly looking out at the lovely view from the porch. Lucy was sitting next to Jillian, and she began to lick her hand. Jillian looked down and smiled.

"You're such a good little girl, Lucy. Come sit on my lap."

* * *

Rachael and Amanda got up early and went in to wake up their parents. It was Christmas morning, and they wanted to go downstairs. Rachael disappeared and returned quickly with a rather sleepy Morgan Junior. He began to cry, and Melissa picked up her son.

"It's okay, Sweetheart, your sisters want you awake so we can all go downstairs and see what is under the tree."

"Yippee," Amanda squealed. "Come on, Daddy, get up."

Morgan smiled at his children's excitement. He jumped out of bed, scooped up Amanda, and grabbed Rachael. Mary slept through all the ruckus, and Melissa carried little Morgan Junior down the stairs, followed by her husband and daughters. The lights on the tree were exceptionally bright in the early morning. Morgan asked if the girls would go gather Auntie Jillian and Uncle Tom.

Melissa looked at her husband and sighed. "What about Father Michael?"

"Oh, don't look so sad. I was planning to wake him myself. Honey, would you put some coffee on, and I'll help gather our family."

Chapter Twenty-Six

As Jillian lay anxiously on the exam table, Tom paced the floor.

"Honey, come sit down. You look like a worried old hen. We know there are two babies and in a few minutes, we will know for sure what we are having. Come here and hold my hand."

The nurse came in and began with a few vitals. When Dr. Aldridge came in, she asked the nurse to start the sonogram. All the while, Jillian, and Tom watched the doctor's expression looking for clues. When she smiled, Jillian took a deep breath, and before she could utter the words, Tom beat her to it.

"What are they? Please? I can't stand the suspense any longer."

"It appears you have fraternal twins; a boy and a girl. Congratulations."

Tom sat down, while Jillian closed her eyes, trying to imagine the four of them together. Jillian smiled then opened her eyes and asked to see the pictures. She looked at Tom, and he reached for her and held her hand.

"Go tell Mike while I get dressed. I'll meet you out in the waiting room."

Tom kissed her and went out the door.

"Dr. Aldridge," Jillian murmured. "Are my babies okay?"

"Why Jillian, why would you ask that? They are very healthy from what I can see. Their heartbeats are strong, and they have grown."

"Thank you, Doctor. This is a miracle, you know?"

"Yes, I do know. I am quite privileged to witness these miracles every day. Now, I'll see you next month. Just relax and enjoy your pregnancy. Enjoy the peace and quiet, while you have it. If you need anything, please, call the office."

"I will. Thank you, Doctor."

* * *

Jillian had less than a month to go, and she was as big as a house. Her lower back hurt most of the time, and she was tired. Tony was bringing Danny and Julie Ann for a weekend visit, and Jillian was having a hard time getting things ready. Tom hired some help, and soon the house was immaculate. Now Jillian could relax as she waited for Danny and Julie Ann. Mike was staying in the guest house and had been doing a lot of the cooking. Jillian was happy to have him close by. He was available to take her to the hospital, should Tom be stuck in court when the time of arrival came.

Jillian had begun reading her mother's journals. She thought it was so remarkable that she could now visualize her mother through her mother's eyes. Her thoughts and memories had been written down on paper, and Jillian was amazed to read the words inscribed by her mom, especially as a teenage girl. The journals began when Mary was a child. Jillian was so captivated by her mother's words; she could barely put them down.

Tom picked Tony and the kids up at the airport and filled them in on Jillian's progress.

"She's feeling tired. Danny, when you see her, you will be so surprised how big her tummy is. She is so excited to get to see you."

"What about me?"

"Oh, Julie Ann, Jillian is very excited to see you, too. Wait until you see the presents she has for you and Danny. She has both your favorite foods in the refrigerator, and Lucy is waiting to play with you."

"Tom, is she doing okay with the pregnancy? Twins are tough on the body."

"She's doing great. Her due date is less than a month away, but the doctor said they will probably come early. She never looked more beautiful. She is just radiant."

Jillian was waiting in the kitchen, as they pulled into the garage. Danny came running in and hugged her tightly as best he could. He looked at her stomach, and his mouth flew open wide. Julie Ann came in with Tom and Tony. She gave Jillian a hug and asked about her presents. Jillian smiled.

"Some things never change I guess."

The kids were delighted with their gifts. Julie Ann was holding Lucy, and playing with her quite a bit. Jillian was surprised as she had not shown much interest with Sydney. Lucy seemed to be enjoying the extra attention.

"I see you are making friends with Lucy. That's good. I can't pick her up right now because I can't see her over this big tummy of mine. Thanks for playing with her."

"I like her. She is so cute. She wants to be my friend."

"Tony, how are Angela and Bella?"

"It's hard to believe that Bella is a year old. She is getting so big. She'll be walking soon. Angela would have come, but well, I guess I'll tell you now, she has morning sickness."

"What? Oh, Tony, what fantastic news. Do the kids know?"

"Yes, Julie Ann isn't too thrilled. She'll get over it just the way she got over Bella once she was born. She loves her little sister very much."

"Life goes on, doesn't it? We are all so blessed. We still want a house full, but we think we had better slow down a little. With twins, I think I'm going to be one busy mom. Father, I mean, Mike, is here to help out. I have no idea how he is with diapers, but he said he is willing to learn. We love having him close by. Everything is as it should be. We're hoping he will want to live in the guest house forever."

"I'm so happy for you and Tom. Okay, I promised to make lasagna, so I better get busy in the kitchen."

Jillian went to the family room and sat down in her favorite chair. She watched as Danny played with his new train set, and laughed as she watched Julie Ann try to get Lucy to join her tea party.

The weekend went by quickly, and Tony and the kids would be leaving in a few hours. Tony was packing up for the kids when he noticed something in Julie Ann's bag. He looked for her and found her in the kitchen with Jillian. Lucy was tucked under her arm as she held her gently.

"Jilly, did you put Lucy's leash in your bag?"

"Yes, Daddy. I'm taking her to Denver. She wants to go home with me."

Julie Ann looked over at Jillian and asked if she could have Lucy. She explained that since she gave Danny a dog, she should give one to her. Julie Ann explained that Lucy would do just fine.

"Honest, Daddy. I asked Lucy to be my dog, and her head went up and down. She said she has been waiting for a little girl to take her home, and that's me."

Jillian looked at Tony just as Tom came in. She didn't know what to do. She expected Tony to do something. Tony looked dumbfounded. Danny came running in and asked what was going on. Julie Ann told him of her plans to bring Lucy home with them, and Danny said she couldn't do that. Julie Ann started to cry, and it seemed that everyone was at a loss about what to do. Tom had the look of an attorney written all over his face.

"Julie Ann, I have a proposition for you."

"What's a proposition?"

"Let me put it another way. I have an idea."

Julie Ann laughed. "I know what that means."

"Good, my idea is this. Since Lucy is a girl, then we will see to it that she has puppies, and then you can have your pick of the puppies. That way, the puppy will think you are its mommy."

"No! I want Lucy. It isn't fair. She wants to be my dog. Watch this."

"Lucy, do you want to be my dog forever?"

Lucy cocked her head from one side to the other. "See? She really does."

Jillian threw her hands up in the air. "Tony, can Julie Ann have a dog?"

"Well, sure. But I can get her one. I am as surprised at this as you are. She has never shown any interest in Sydney, so I just figured it didn't matter one way or the other to her."

"Daddy, I don't want some other dog, I want Lucy. She loves me, watch."

She bent down, and Lucy licked her face. "See, I told you she loves me."

"Princess, I'll go get Lucy's travel bag. She can go right under your seat on the plane. Daddy will have to pay extra for her to ride home with you. You have to promise me you will love her always. I mean it. You have to always love her and take good care of her."

Jillian looked at Tom. "Here we go again."

"Are you okay with this Sweetheart?"

"Tom, we have two babies on the way. I think Lucy will be happier with a little girl all of her own. Yes, I am okay with it."

"Thanks, Jillian, I love you so much."

"I love you, too, Princess."

Jillian gave Lucy a pat on the head and told her to be a good little girl. Tom told her he would get her another dog and Jillian laughed.

"Let's wait a few years, okay?"

Tom took Tony and the kids to the airport. Jillian relaxed and chatted with Mike. Tom got home a few hours later, and Jillian was sitting in her favorite chair with an overnight bag, an angelic smile on her face. Tom looked surprised and asked where she was going.

"We are going to the hospital. I already called Dr. Aldridge, and she will meet us there. Our babies seem to be in a bit of a hurry, but a few weeks early is no biggie for twins. Look out world, the Bentley kids are on the way."

More from Susan Vance

In her first novel, ***Eyes like Mine,*** Susan takes you on a heartwarming journey wherein many lives are held in the balance. Susan tugs at the rawest emotions one can feel with the heart. Loving someone, and being in love, and knowing the difference. She brings this all to life in, ***"Eyes like Mine."***

"Danny" is the sequel to Eyes *like Mine*

Through my Mother's Eyes is the third book in the Eyes series
Jillian is given a look back at her mother's life through a series of journals. After discovering the answers to many questions in ***"Danny,"*** Jillian finds out what really happened as she reads the journals. Finding out her mother was only human and made mistakes like everyone else. She fell in love and experienced a broken heart.

"Emma's Deliverance" is a touching journey through the life of a frightened child. She watched, as her entire family was murdered. This small child was found several days later, hiding in her parent's closet. She was terrified, alone, and in shock. It would take many years and the love of her foster family to bring her back. Finally, she meets the love of her life only to find she is having nightmares again. Her imagination is driving her to the brink of insanity. Does she tell Jason and drag him into her madness or try to hide what is happening?

"A Change of Heart" is a heartwarming story of love, betrayal, and heartache. Jennifer must make some hard choices to find happiness. Caring for her adult, drug addicted sister causes more pain than she could have imagined. Finally, she has a chance at real love with, Fred. But who will care for her sister?

"A Tangled Web of Deception" touches on the subject of internet romance fraud. Olivia's best friend, Julia, is happily married or so Olivia thought until she discovers Julia is involved with a man she has never met. When Julia is willing to give up all she has to be with her internet lover, Olivia begs her to reconsider. Meanwhile, Olivia is rebuilding her own life after the death of her husband of seventeen years. With three teenagers to raise, she must put them first but what about her feelings. Finding that she is attracted to three men in her life, she must make a choice between them.

"Forever My Sister" is the story of, Hilary, and her sister, Hannah. At thirty-seven, Hilary hadn't had a serious or meaningful relationship, unlike her sister who had been married, divorced with three daughters, and in and out of many relationships. Finally, Hilary meets Kirby and falls in love. Meanwhile, Hannah is in an abusive relationship, and Hilary doesn't know how to help her. As her relationship with Kirby turns into marriage, she is forced to watch Hannah suffer the beatings and belittlement of Jesse.

In **"Leaving Savannah"** we meet Chelsea Devereaux. Stuck in an emotionally abusive marriage, she finally gains the courage to leave. Afraid he will find her, she runs away and tells no one but her father where she is. Desperate to be free of Matthew, but she is afraid to file for divorce fearing he may find out where she is. Never expecting to trust another man, she meets and falls in love with Ethan, who is nothing like her husband. When her father is injured in an accident, Chelsea must come home to Savannah to be with her dad. Matthew finds and stalks her. Can Ethan protect her?

Follow Susan on Facebook
www.facebook.com/susanvanceauthor

Danny

Susan Vance

www.ingramcontent.com/pod-product-compliance
Lightning Source LLC
Chambersburg PA
CBHW050930120626
46552CB00001B/127